W9-AUC-045

"Skillful plotting, an intriguing legend, a compelling mountain lion . . . all wrapped around a wonderful tender love story. Romance at its best!"
—Sandra Hill, bestselling author of *Love Me Tender*

SCARS FROM THE PAST

Jonah's kisses were incredible. His mouth molded against Dawn's. He used his lips, his tongue, to torment, to taunt, to stimulate. His hands were magnificent, stroking and kneading as though he were a master chef and she were unformed dough. One hand cupped her breast. She arched into it. The sweet sensation concentrated in a single sensitive area, surged liquid heat through her entire body.

"Jonah," she moaned, holding him close, wanting him closer still.

It was unfair. She wanted to feel his skin against her. She pushed him away to unbutton his shirt. She felt her pants drawn down her legs even as she pulled his shirt from his chest.

She gasped. Stopped moving. Stared.

Jonah's strong, hard chest had a long, puckered scar from his clavicle down to the end of his ribcage.

"Oh, Jonah, I'm so sorry," she whispered. "No one should have to suffer like that." Sorrow welled within her for this man and what he had gone through.

"Not even convicts, you mean?" Suddenly, his chilly tone sent a shiver down her back. "Not even convicts like me?"

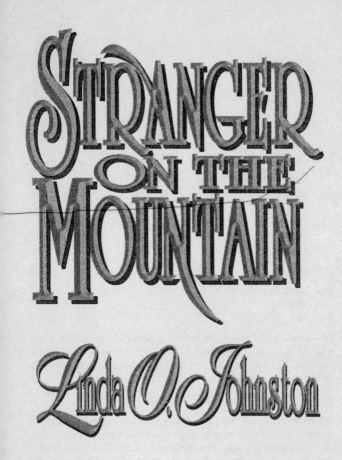

STRANGER ON THE MOUNTAIN

Linda O. Johnston

LOVE SPELL BOOKS NEW YORK CITY

LOVE SPELL®

March 1999

Published by

Dorchester Publishing Co., Inc.
276 Fifth Avenue
New York, NY 10001

ISBN 0-505-52301-9

The name "Love Spell" and its logo are trademarks of Dorchester Publishing Co., Inc.

Printed in the United States of America.

To mountain lions . . . and courage.
To Estelle and Don Zangwill . . . and courage.
To my son Eric and changes in lifestyle . . . and courage.
To my son Keith, on the road . . . and *my* courage.

To fellow writers and critiquers Marilyn, Janie and
       Larimee, Karen, Hermine, Betty and Sally,
       and Jann . . . and dauntlessness.
To Penn State University and the Nittany
       Lions . . . and success.
To endangered species and their advocates . . .
       and perseverance.
And, as always, to my husband Fred . . . and love.

AUTHOR'S NOTE

I would like to thank Joe Kosack of the Pennsylvania Game Commission and Mike McCarthy of the United States Fish and Wildlife Service for unstintingly taking the time to answer my questions, no matter how hypothetical or picayune, about what would happen if a mountain lion actually were to appear today in the mountains of Central Pennsylvania. However, I have to admit to interpreting a bit here and there and exercising poetic license to make the story flow.

Thanks also to Mark Martello, D.V.M., for the veterinary advice, and to my editor, Christopher Keeslar, for taking a chance on an unusual story.

Prologue

She stalked slowly through the woods, a tawny stranger to these weathered mountains.

Her strides were long and graceful, her senses alert to sounds, to movements . . . to prey. She was hungry.

She sensed that her kind had long been absent here. Once, large cats had been plentiful in the central Pennsylvania highlands. Mountains had been named for them. People had fled their fierceness.

But no longer. Not here. Men had faced their fears and hunted the cougars as the cougars hunted their quarry. Men had caused the lions of the mountains to disappear.

This lone and wary stalker was the first to return. Why, she did not know. Nor did she comprehend how she had arrived. She was conscious of none of such matters. She simply was here.

This was now her territory.

There was a rustle at her side. A deer, perhaps? Or

11

maybe a rabbit or wild turkey? She stopped, remaining still as she listened. The sound came again.

Quickly, she sprang into action.

And killed.

Chapter One

"What do you mean, he's missing?" Dawn Perry leaned forward in her desk chair, barely aware of its irritating squeal. Her hand trembled as it clutched the phone receiver tightly to her ear. "Susie, are you sure my grandfather didn't just go out for an early morning walk?"

"Of course I'm sure." The familiar shrill voice on the other end of the line sounded worried. Susie Frost was Amos Wilton's live-in helper at the Haven, his wildlife sanctuary. She hadn't always been the most reliable employee, but to Dawn, people who loved wildlife enough to feed animals several times a day—and clean their enclosures—could be forgiven nearly anything.

Except playing practical jokes that weren't at all funny.

But Dawn knew Susie was not joking. Staring around her cluttered law office in the hope that its

13

familiarity would calm her, she swallowed her trepidation. It would not do anyone any good for her to panic, least of all her wonderful, generous—and sometimes capricious—grandfather.

"Tell me what happened," she said slowly into the phone, twisting several strands of her long black hair between her fingers.

She could picture big-boned Susie in her usual blue jeans. She was probably standing by the wall phone at Amos's house, which doubled, when necessary, as the Haven's nursery, storage structure, and even an extra animal enclosure. Dawn heard animal noises in the background, not an unfamiliar occurrence.

"Well, yesterday afternoon," Susie said, "Amos got a phone call. He asked if I could handle the evening feeding, and I said yes. Then he left."

"Did he say where he was going?"

"No, but . . ." Susie paused.

"But what?" prompted Dawn, trying to keep her voice calm.

"Well, there was a look on his face that I just didn't understand. It was as if he had seen a stairway coming down from heaven."

"What?" Dawn closed her eyes and rubbed their lids as her head began to ache. A part-time student at nearby Penn State, Susie was studying poetry these days, and her favorite works were those that included metaphysical metaphors. But Dawn wasn't in the mood today to put up with her whimsy. "Susie, please just tell me—"

"I *am* telling you," she insisted. "Your grandfather looked to me as though he was thinking about something . . . well, extraordinary."

Dawn shook her head, again commanding herself to remain patient. Slowly, she said, "And you didn't ask what it was?"

14

"Well, no. He just said he'd heard a rumor about something showing up on Eskaway Mountain, and he had to find out about it."

Dawn felt an icy chill creep up her back. Was her grandfather lost on the mountain? Or hurt? That was more likely, since he knew Eskaway as well as he knew his way around the Haven.

At least it was springtime. During the day, the outside temperature was well above freezing. But at night . . .

"You're certain he didn't come back and then go out again?"

"I'm sure," Susie said. "I went to bed at my normal time. I usually hear him when he comes in late, or even when he's puttering around in the kitchen. But not last night." Susie's room was on the ground floor of Amos's house.

"But maybe this time—"

Susie didn't let her finish. "I admit I was pooped. I've been studying hard for exams. But even if I missed Amos last night, I should have seen him this morning. He always wakes me to help feed the beasts. But I just woke, thanks to the complaints of a lot of hungry animals."

Dawn glanced at the small brass clock surrounded by papers on her cluttered desk. It was nine o'clock. Amos always started feeding the animals at seven.

But . . . he knew the mountain. He knew the dangers of exposure if he were out all night.

What if something had happened to him?

Unwillingly, Dawn's mind turned toward the latest source of gossip in the small town of Eskmont. Lettie Green, the irascible old woman who owned the auto-repair shop, had hired an ex-con on parole. What if he was dangerous? Another local man had gone missing a couple of weeks earlier. What if—

Linda O. Johnston

"Dawn, I'm really worried." Susie's words echoed Dawn's thoughts. "I have a ten o'clock class, and I've called Tom Carter to come over and stay with the animals. But Amos—will you look for him?"

Would she ever, Dawn thought.

"He's not really a missing person, Dawn," said Clemson Biggs, the captain of the three-person police force of Eskmont, Pennsylvania. His prominent nose and teeth gave him the appearance of a beaver. The counter in the small police station's reception area reached to his barrel chest, but despite his shortness and the paunch at his gut, he emitted an air of control. And he was a good friend of Amos's. "At least I can't file a missing-persons report till he's been gone twenty-four hours. But I know your grandfather. He's careful, and he knows Eskaway as well as anyone. If he was out there all night, then something could be wrong."

"That's what I'm afraid of," Dawn murmured, hearing the catch in her own voice.

"Now, don't worry," Clemson commanded. "At least not yet." He wore a gray uniform that matched the walls in the small police station, which doubled as the town's post office. Through the door to the hallway, Dawn saw the curious expressions on the faces of people waiting to buy stamps.

"But this isn't like Amos. And I knew that if I came here, I could rely on you to help." She had thought about just dashing off and looking for her grandfather by herself, but realized how fruitless that might be.

Clemson's lips parted in a pleased grin that revealed his large teeth. "You did the right thing."

"Clemson . . ." Dawn spoke hesitantly, knowing she might be out of line. "That stranger Lettie hired. Could he—"

16

"His name is Jonah Campion," Clemson interrupted. "I helped Lettie check him out. Yes, he was in prison, but he's on parole now. And no, I don't think he harmed Amos. Or Sherm Patterson, for that matter."

Sherm was the local man who, two weeks earlier, had disappeared without a trace. Dawn had heard whispered rumors about this Jonah Campion's possible involvement, but no one could say for certain.

Still, Clemson did not seem concerned about him. And Clemson was head of the Eskmont police. "All right," Dawn said. "But I'm still worried. Isn't there anything we can do?"

"Even if it's too soon to worry officially"—the policeman lifted the receiver of the phone on the counter—"this sounds like a good time for another practice session of the Eskmont Volunteer Rescue League."

In just over half an hour, about thirty people in outdoor gear were crammed into the police station lobby.

Clemson had called out the volunteers, explaining that he hoped this was just a false alarm, but that they could always use another practice run.

"What about our 'practice' a couple weeks ago, when we were out looking for Sherm Patterson?" grumbled Ray Koslowski.

"Another false alarm," Clemson agreed. "Or at least we think so. Sherm's still missing, but the likelihood, according to his daughter, is that he's . . . well, off ill somewhere out of town."

"Drunk, you mean," said Ray with a smirk.

Ray was the town plumber, large and beefy, with hands that seemed too big to get into tight areas between pipes. Still, he was a good plumber. And he had shown up to help.

17

The fact that Dawn disliked him because of his abrasive personality, and because he enjoyed hunting wild animals, was irrelevant.

"Maybe Amos is off on a toot, too." Ray laughed out loud.

Dawn took a step toward him, but Clemson held her back. "We all know Amos better than that," Clemson said. "He's a straight shooter and hardly ever drinks. And I doubt anything's happened to him." He shot a soothing look toward Dawn. Cut it out, Clemson, she thought. His kind attempts to calm her only deepened her concern. "But you all know and like Amos," he went on, "so just in case . . ."

"That's right, Clemson," said Ray, clearly wanting to be in charge. "We're the first ones who'll want to help if Amos is in trouble. A man who spends all his time talking to birds and squirrels, well, you just can't tell what he's gotten into." Dawn bit her tongue as Ray winked at Lettie Green.

Lettie was in her sixties, like Ray. Dawn had heard rumors that Ray was wooing Lettie, though they seemed an unlikely couple. Lettie had a mop of dyed red curls and a pinched mouth that managed to give only a half-smile back in exchange for Ray's less than humorous jokes.

This time, though, she scowled. "Put a zipper on it, Ray," she ordered. "Spending the night on that mountain isn't funny. Not unless Amos intended to camp out." She shot a questioning glance toward Dawn, who could only shrug. She did not know what gear, if any, Amos might have brought along.

With Lettie stood a much younger man, tall and craggy. A stranger. He had to be *the* stranger. The ex-con. Jonah Campion.

Dawn studiously avoided looking at him, but she

could feel his eyes on her, and it made her uncomfortable.

Well, of course people were looking at her, she told herself. The ex-convict wasn't the only one. She was the center of attention, since she had gotten Clemson to call everyone together to hunt for Amos. It was embarrassing, particularly if nothing had happened to him.

But if something had . . .

Ignoring the tears in her eyes, Dawn turned back to the counter, using the phone on it to call the Haven once more. She had done so several times since arriving at the police station. Each time, Tom Carter had confirmed that Amos had not returned, or called.

Darn him, Dawn thought. *Grandpa, you had just better be all right.* But she was shaking with worry. This wasn't at all like Amos. She had never, in her entire life, known him to be unreliable. He had been both mother and father to her as long as she could remember—had taken over the job of raising her when her mother had married for the third time. Or was it the fourth?

It was now nearly eleven o'clock. She had changed into the jeans and hiking boots she kept in her car, and had a backpack slung over her arm. She was ready to hunt.

Clemson used a bullhorn. "Thanks for coming, everyone," he said. "I'll follow procedure, put you into two-person teams and assign areas. Soon as you find Amos, call in right away. Everyone check with me often, and I'll give the word when we've got him here safe and sound, and red-faced for causing such a ruckus."

At the affirmative rumblings of the crowd, Dawn smiled despite her concern. She loved this small town and its people; they cared about one another. She listened to Clemson's further instructions about sticking to the rules, staying with their partners and checking in often. As Clemson began to pair them up, he got a phone call. "For you," he said to Dawn.

It was Tom Carter. "Just thought you'd want to hear about the call Amos just got. It was Slim Evans." Slim was one of Amos's fishing buddies. They had known each other forever. "He wanted to know if Amos was ready to go on their outing to Eskaway Mountain," Tom continued. "When I told him he'd gone last night and might be missing, Slim got all upset, said he should never have said anything."

"About what?"

"He wouldn't tell me," Tom replied. He promised Dawn that he would let Clemson know the moment he heard anything from Amos.

Dawn tried calling Slim but got no answer. What had he told her grandfather? Was it the answer to where Amos had gone?

When she got off the phone, she noticed that everyone was gone but Clemson, Lettie, Fisk—Lettie's other employee—and Jonah Campion. But Fisk had not been there earlier, and he was talking to Lettie in earnest. Finally, she turned Fisk around, gave him a small shove toward the door in apparent exasperation, and looked at Clemson. "Drat and quadruple drat," she said. "Sorry, Clemson, but there's an emergency at the shop that Fisk here can't handle on his own. I won't be able to join the search." With no further explanation, she turned and left with her employee.

So just that quickly, there were only three people left in the police station: Clemson, Dawn and the stranger. And she knew Clemson couldn't participate in the search. He had to stay here, where he was on duty, to take calls when people looking for Amos checked in.

There was no expression in Jonah Campion's gaze as he met her eye—but he still managed to send a shudder up her spine. Somehow, his blank look conveyed distance. Aloofness. Detachment.

But he was a damned good-looking man despite wearing such a discomfiting expression.

And he was the only one left with whom Dawn could search. Her? Go with an ex-con? Not likely.

She knew the mountain nearly as well as Amos. She didn't need accompaniment.

"I want to tell you about Tom's call," she said, taking Clemson aside to let him know her plan. She related what Tom had said, then whispered, "I'll be searching on my own, Clemson. I—I don't want to go with . . . a stranger."

"A parolee, you mean?" Clemson's voice was low, too. "I understand, Dawn. But you know I can't let you search alone. Too dangerous."

"But I know the mountain, and—"

"No," Clemson said firmly. "This is different. It's procedure. You wait till I find someone to go with you or you don't go at all."

She bit back a retort, knowing he couldn't stop her—but he could delay her further by arguing. "What crime did he commit?" she asked, turning her eyes briefly toward the stranger, who stood alone near the far end of the counter in the police station lobby, thumbing through the familiar brochure containing the protocol of the Eskmont Volunteer League.

"Embezzlement."

Just then another call came in. "It's one of the search parties," Clemson reported in a minute. "Amos's truck is in the paved lot at the bottom of the east slope of Eskaway."

Even more frantic now to leave, Dawn drew in her breath. What was she going to do?

If it took going with this Jonah Campion—convicted of a white-collar crime, nothing violent—to get Clemson to stop arguing and let her proceed to the mountain to look for Amos . . .

"All right," she finally agreed, turning back toward the man who stood alone.

He took a couple of steps toward her on the scuffed linoleum floor, and she stood her ground with effort. "So we know now where to begin our search," he said. His voice was gruff, but his tone matched the total lack of interest shown in his demeanor.

He had a long face with a thick jaw and a slight cleft in his chin. There were deep lines beside his nose and mouth and on his forehead, as though he frowned a lot. His hair was tawny brown in color, long enough on the top to fall over his thick brows. He could have used a shave.

He was gorgeously masculine. But Dawn wanted nothing to do with him.

Plus, with his apathetic attitude, why the heck was he going on this search?

No matter. Right now, she needed him. Pretending to turn her attention to adjusting the backpack straps on her shoulders, she stole another glance at him, further sizing him up. He was a large man. He wore a blue plaid shirt that seemed stretched across his broad shoulders, tight jeans that hugged strong, thick leg muscles, and hiking boots similar to her own—but much larger.

He looked too rough to be merely an embezzler. But Clemson would have known if there was more. She would be cautious. And, if necessary, she could take care of herself.

Nothing would keep her from this search.

"Come on, Mr. Campion," Dawn said, gesturing toward the door. "Let's go find my grandfather."

*   *   *

Jonah knew what she was thinking, the beautiful woman who walked beside him, with deep, exotically shaped brown eyes as cold as the compressed center of an iceberg. He was lower than the microbes on the soles of her well-worn boots. He was as depraved as Jack the Ripper, the Unabomber and Dracula, combined.

He was an ex-con.

Well, he didn't want to be there any more than she wanted him around. But his employer, Lettie, had insisted on it. Joining the Eskmont Volunteer Rescue League was part of the job, she had told him.

Once he was outside in the parking lot with Dawn Perry, her long, shining black hair blew in the breeze. She walked with a sway to her slender hips, making him recall that, once, he'd had a sex drive.

What she thought of him didn't matter. Nevertheless, he wanted to plant himself in front of her and take her slight shoulders, in her beige windbreaker, and shake her until she admitted that he was a human being. Just like her.

Yeah, right. All that touching her would accomplish would be to get him accused of assault and battery. After all, once a criminal, always a criminal. Wasn't that how it went?

So instead he merely said gruffly, "Would you like me to drive?"

That seemed to startle her. She stopped on the pavement, which had nearly emptied of vehicles. She had taken a key from her pocket and extended it toward a plain-looking green Ford, a two-year-old compact that probably had an automatic transmission, air-conditioning and the standard radio. She seemed the type who would have had it serviced regularly, in accordance with the owner's manual.

23

He was making himself begin to think like a mechanic.

"Well," she said, probably to fill the silence. He could imagine her thoughts: Would it be better to be in control, driving her own car? Or in his, with his hands busy on the wheel so he couldn't do . . . whatever ex-cons did. He didn't help her. He just waited. "Sure," she finally finished. "I'm so concerned about my grandfather I imagine I'll be a better navigator than driver anyway." She attempted a smile, but it didn't get very far before it faded, leaving her full, pink lips slightly apart, her expression again sour, as though she worked to keep all emotion from her lovely face but failed to hide her disgust.

He had an urge now to do something brash to get her to appear anything but revolted. Maybe he could pull her into his arms, kiss her until she screamed. Or responded. Maybe she liked rough ex-cons.

He doubted it. And despite it all, he was still too civilized to do such a thing. Instead, he acted like a perfect gentleman, showing her to the ten-year-old Toyota he had managed to buy despite having a minimum-wage job. He opened the door for her and put out his hand to help her in.

To her credit, she hesitated only a moment before taking his proffered hand. He closed his eyes briefly as he felt her warm, gentle fingers in his.

It had been a long time since he had felt the smoothness of a woman's skin, even for such innocent contact.

Oh, lord! For a moment, all he could think about was how beautiful this woman was. Never mind that she considered him contemptible. She was pretty, and vulnerable in her fear for her grandfather. That, in itself, was appealing. Familial love and loyalty. If only—

The touch was over in an instant, leaving his fingers empty and tingling. She was in his car, and it was time to drive her to find her missing relation. He got in beside her and started the engine. "So, how do we get to the east slope?" he asked briskly, all business.

"I'll direct you as we get closer," Dawn replied. He liked the sound of her voice, deep and throaty yet totally feminine.

"Fine," he said, heading the car toward the highway leading to the nearby weathered peak he had learned was called Eskaway. "It's a big mountain, even the eastern slope. Any ideas where your grandfather would have gone?"

"Nothing definite." She sounded so worried that he glanced over at her. She caught his gaze and squared her shoulders, apparently not wanting to look weak to him. "But maybe something will come to me once we get there."

"You know," he said after a long moment, "it might be he just wanted to be alone for a while." Jonah could understand a man's need for privacy, and for solitude.

He could understand that—even if he had a relative as pretty, and as concerned, as Dawn Perry appeared to be.

"Amos wouldn't just run off overnight," she said haughtily. "He has to be home to keep an eye on the animals."

"Animals?"

"He runs a shelter for wild animals: those who are injured or orphaned, or just need a place to stay to protect them."

"I see." And Jonah did see. It was a prison for wild animals.

While his mind whirled about that vile concept, he realized he had nothing more to say. No longer did he want to make conversation. And so he drove on in silence.

25

Chapter Two

He was right, Dawn thought. It *was* a big mountain. She stood beside Jonah's car in the recreation area's sole paved parking lot, looking up at the vast, tree-covered slopes.

Her grandfather might be lost somewhere up on those hills. Or injured. Or . . . She squared her chin. Now was not the time to think of all the horrible things that could have happened. But whoever had called Clemson was right; Amos's battered blue truck was there, along with a bunch of other parked vehicles—some of which she recognized as belonging to fellow search-team members.

He would never abandon his truck.

He had to be up there, but if he were . . .

She shook her head vehemently, ignoring the way her hair whipped about her shoulders. He was fine. He was probably just on an impromptu camping trip that he had simply forgotten to tell her about. When he got back, he would laugh affectionately at her and make a pun about her having made the proverbial mountain out of the molehill of his perfectly explainable disappearance.

Of course he would.

In the meantime, she would look for him.

It would be better, though, if she were alone. She glanced toward the driver's-side door, where Jonah was just exiting. He had done nothing to make her feel nervous, and yet the silence in the car for the last few minutes had seemed . . . well, more than disquieting. It was as though his efforts at being civil, since they had met at the police station, had taxed him unbearably, and he no longer wanted to participate in such nonsense.

But what had triggered his muteness? Had it been something she had said? They would have to talk while they were searching together, wouldn't they?

"That's Amos's truck," she said to make conversation, and pointed.

He glanced toward it, then up at the slopes. "He's probably up there, then," he said, his voice still gruff. At least he was speaking again. But his unsympathetic tone made her fear for Amos all the keener.

"Do you want to stay here while I look?" she demanded icily.

Surely that wasn't contrition in the look he gave her, was it? "No," he said. "I want to help."

Sure he did. But this time his tone held sincerity that she could only believe was feigned.

Dawn had borrowed a cellular phone from Clemson, and she called him now, hoping that Amos had appeared. He could, after all, have gotten a ride into town, though she could not imagine him leaving his truck.

"Sorry." Clemson's voice crackled with static over

the phone. "And no one who's checked in yet has seen Amos, either."

So the search was necessary. Dawn turned toward Jonah. The sun was nearly straight up in the sky, and he squinted into it, shading his eyes with his hands. She wondered for a moment what color his eyes were. She hadn't noticed before.

Once they got onto the thickly wooded hillside they saw no signs of other people. Dawn realized with discomfort that she truly was alone with this Jonah Campion. Well, just because he had been to prison did not mean he would act in an inappropriate manner toward her. He had been there for embezzlement, for heaven's sake. And why should he bother her? When he had looked at her at all, it was as though she weren't present. He had no interest in her.

And there was certainly no reason that his lack of interest should depress her. Not in the slightest.

But Amos . . . they had to find her grandfather. They had to find him alive and well. They simply had to.

Soon they were tramping through the carpet of damp fallen leaves, snapping twigs as they walked uphill along a tree-lined path that had probably been there since the days of the Senecas and other Indians who had once dwelled in the center of Pennsylvania.

"Do you have any idea where on the mountain to look?" Jonah asked again. The path was wide enough that he walked beside her. Though she was nearly five foot eight, he was a lot taller. More substantial, too, with the muscles she could imagine rippling beneath his woolen shirt. Like her, he carried a backpack.

She supposed she should have felt intimidated by his much larger size. She wasn't, though. "Let's just follow Clemson's rules," she suggested. "Once we get halfway up, we should start going in circles, small at first and growing larger to make sure we don't miss Amos if he's there."

"Fine," he agreed. He stepped up his pace, and she hurried to keep up with him.

"Amos!" she yelled into the forest. "Amos!"

In a moment, a voice beside her echoed hers. "Amos," called Jonah Campion. Here in the open, calling into the wilderness, his was a commanding voice, deep and resonant. Dawn wondered suddenly what it would feel like to hear her name on his lips.

Foolishness, she told herself, and kept walking.

She felt chilly at first, in the cool dampness of the forest's shadows, but the exercise of walking soon warmed her. The air carried the pungent aroma of the decomposing leaves on which they trod and the spring freshness of the maples and other trees that rose above them. They called out often for Amos, but there was no response. Not that there were no sounds. Birds sang in the trees, and the skitterings of startled small animals often followed her footsteps and Jonah's in the soggy underbrush.

The path meandered between tall, straight trunks of the few evergreens and the more twisted, irregular shapes of deciduous trees. Now and then, fallen branches blocked their way, and they had to go around. Occasionally they walked through clearings, and the brightness of the sudden sunlight made Dawn blink.

"This is nice," Jonah said after a while. He sounded reverent. Awed.

Surprised, Dawn asked, "What's nice?"

"This mountain. These woods. Everything seems fresh. Nearly untouched by human hands. It's as though we've gone back in time, before civilization."

His pronunciation of the last word was full of mockery. Obviously he did not think much of civilization.

Or its rules. If he had, he probably would not have wound up in prison.

Dawn found herself wondering more about his crime. Not that she could ask him.

Not directly.

"Where are you from, Mr. Campion?" she asked. She was slightly out of breath, since their pace had not slowed.

"Jonah," he said. "That's my name."

He did not answer her question, so she tried again. "I take it, Jonah, that wherever you came from, there weren't mountains like this, or forests."

"Not too far away," he said. "I grew up outside Philadelphia."

"Philly is a wonderful city for tourists," she said. "I've been there several times." Who were his parents? she wondered. How had they wound up with a son who had been to prison? Did they still care about him?

Amos would love her even if she had done something terribly wrong. Amos . . . *Oh, lord, Amos, where are you?* She nearly cried aloud, but instead she made herself continue her inquisition. "Were you born there?"

Her voice shook, and she noticed Jonah glance at her before he answered. "Yes."

"Did you go to school there?"

He made a noise that, again, sounded affirmative, but it did not seem to invite further questions.

Nevertheless, Dawn asked, "And how long did you live there?"

"Until I was thrown in prison. Is that what you want to hear—all the particulars of my unsavory life?"

There was anger in his voice now, and Dawn was struck again by their isolation from other people.

"Not especially," she said frostily, embarrassed, since that was exactly what she had been probing for.

He stopped and looked down at her. His eyes studied her face. Now she was able to discern their color. They were an unusual grayish shade of green. And the way he examined her with them—if she felt cool in the mountains again, all she would need to do was plant herself under Jonah Campion's intense gaze.

In fact, she felt too warm. Much too warm. And uncomfortable. "Well, maybe I did want to learn more about you," she finally admitted, skirting by him to continue walking along the path. She hoped he would stay behind her. But no, he was once more close at her side. And so she continued her explanation. "Eskmont is a small town, and people there talk. I knew, even before Clemson said so, that you were . . ." She hesitated, looking for a polite way to say he was a criminal.

"Incarcerated. An ex-con. Yes, I am." He touched her arm, stopping her once more. His face was shadowed by more than the branches hanging overhead when he said, "Look, Dawn."

He had done it. He had said her name. But she could not dwell now on the sound, on the intimacy of it, as he continued, "My past is . . . past. It's nobody's business but mine, and Lettie Green's, since she was nice enough to hire me when no one else would. And, to some extent, Clemson's, since I'm sure he feels compelled to keep an eye on me. If you're afraid of me, then tell me so and I'll take you back down the mountain. Otherwise, let's just go look for your grandfather. Okay?"

"Okay. But—" As ashamed as she felt, Dawn needed to explain herself. "You may not know it, Jonah, but I'm an attorney. It's my job to be curious about people and their relationship to the law. If I was getting too personal, I'm sorry, but—"

"A lawyer? You? It figures." He laughed bitterly.

31

Linda O. Johnston

Puzzled by his odd reaction, Dawn asked, "What do you mean?"

He shook his head, brushing back the long lock of light brown hair that had fallen into his eyes. His smile this time was self-mocking. "I found you attractive, that's all. I should have known that my taste in women shouldn't be trusted."

A dozen angry retorts sprang to Dawn's lips. In the end, though, she said nothing.

In a way, he had paid her a backhanded compliment. He found her attractive.

Until she had told him she was a lawyer.

Well, she found him attractive, too—physically. But that was all. The last thing she wanted was any involvement with a criminal, even one who had supposedly paid his debt to society.

Maybe she was being unfair to him, she admonished herself. Embezzlement wasn't exactly the most heinous of crimes. Maybe—

But he didn't want to talk about it. And *any* felony was significant.

She, of all people, knew that the judicial system worked. Not perfectly, perhaps. But she trusted it. She had to.

But what woman, she couldn't help wondering, had made Jonah Campion mistrust his taste in the entire sex? And how?

She continued up the path without another word— at first. But the silence, other than the normal mountain noises, soon became uncomfortable. Worse, her mind kept dwelling on Amos. Where was he? Was he all right? She called out to him a few times, but felt like crying when she got no answer.

"Look! Up there!" she finally said to Jonah, pointing toward a bird soaring above a break between tree branches.

"What is it?"

She shaded her eyes against the sunlight and watched for a moment. "Yes, I'm certain: it's a peregrine falcon. They're endangered, you know."

"Does your grandfather have any at his Haven?"

Dawn replayed the sentence before answering, expecting she had missed the sarcasm that was frequently in Jonah's voice. But there had been none.

"Not now," she said. "He and I tended a couple of injured ones when I was a kid, and he nursed one back to health about a year ago, too. But he releases them back into the wild as soon as possible."

"Nice man, your grandfather," said Jonah, again with no irony in his tone.

"Yes," Dawn replied, "he is."

At least that had broken the ice. Dawn proceeded to tell Jonah some of the natural history of the mountains, explaining the most common plants and animals generally found there: deer and squirrels, bears, bobcats and foxes, raccoons and skunks; the birds, including the many kinds of raptors; the trees, such as hemlocks and pines, maples and beeches.

A short while later, she thought she heard something and stopped along the path. It was narrow here, and the undergrowth and littering of leaves practically hid the trail.

"What's wrong?" Jonah asked. He halted beside her, and somehow his presence was comforting, for she had an eerie sensation of being watched.

"Sssh," she said softly. She turned her head, listening for the noise again. But the woods beside them held no sounds other than the usual distant birdcalls and the whisper of the wind.

"Did you hear something?" He kept his voice low, as she had requested.

She continued to scan the thick, darkening cover of

the forest. "I think—" On a slope beside them, she saw a flash of something light in color, tan perhaps, like a deer. She hurried off the path, into a thick stand of beeches, toward it. But she must have been mistaken; she found nothing there, heard no sounds. Nothing moved.

She turned to go back down to the path and gasped, startled to find Jonah right behind her. He steadied her by grabbing her shoulders.

"Are you all right?" he asked.

"Fine." But she wasn't. She knew she had heard something. Seen something. But nothing was there.

And the odd feeling that had come over her . . . it was as though she had been examined from a distance. Studied by someone who had been looking for her.

She shook her head and forced herself to smile. "Guess I was just hearing things," she managed to say. Jonah did not look convinced, but he allowed her to maneuver around him back toward the path.

The trees were close together here, and to pass by him Dawn could not avoid touching him with her body. She was aware of the way her breasts brushed against his unyielding chest, and she nearly gasped aloud at the sweet sensations that spread from the points of contact throughout her body, until they settled way below in a pooling warmth.

She moved away quickly. Idiot! she told herself. Just because she had not been near a man for so long did not mean she should allow herself to become aroused at the merest contact with this one.

She started walking again, as quickly as she could. "Amos," she called. She did not want Jonah even to imagine how his body had affected hers.

Soon they had made it halfway up the mountain, as planned. Dawn neither saw nor heard anything out of the ordinary. She had no further sensation of being watched. A couple of times they ran into other search teams.

But no one had seen Amos. Dawn was distraught. She had received no calls from Clemson to let her know her grandfather had been located by someone else. By then, the sun had passed its peak in the sky and had started down, beginning to create deeper shadows. They still had plenty of search time until dark, but . . .

Dawn called the police department. Clemson had gone out for a few minutes, but the officer who answered the phone had no good news. "Sorry, but no one has found Amos yet," he said.

Dawn felt like crying, but she didn't. There wasn't time. They needed to complete their search, and quickly.

"Do you want to start looking in circles off the path now?" Jonah asked. "That was the plan Clemson suggested."

Dawn shook her head. "There's another trail near here that I've hiked with Amos. I'd rather try there first."

Jonah agreed, and after getting her bearings by finding a stream that gurgled nearby, Dawn led him toward the other path.

The terrain was different here; there were more clearings, strewn with boulders and interspersed with bushes and other low-growing plants. A few yellow and white spring flowers had already begun to blossom. Dawn drew closer to try to determine what they were, kneeling over them and touching their fragile petals. Bloodworts, perhaps?

When she turned around, Jonah was nowhere to be seen. "Hey!" she cried out, standing once more. Not that she was worried; she knew the way back down better than he. But still, they were supposed to stick together. And what if he got lost? He was her partner for this search. He was her responsibility. "Jonah? Where are you?"

Nothing.

Maybe he had found Amos, though that seemed a stretch. And why wouldn't he have told her before taking off?

"Jonah?" she called. "Amos?"

In a few moments, some thick, green-leafed branches of a sizable bush beside the clearing started to shake. Dawn's heart began to pound, and she took a step backward. Not that there were many dangerous wild animals left on this mountain, but there were occasional sightings of bears and bobcats. And even a deer, if frightened, could hurt a human.

"Jonah?" she called again, but more softly.

He emerged from among the quivering branches. "You forgot something important in your nature lecture," he said. He looked serious as he approached her.

"What's that?" she asked, suddenly frightened. Had he spotted some sign that an animal had injured Amos?

"Mountain lions."

She stared at him. And then she laughed. "What makes you think there are any mountain lions here?"

"I saw one."

She shook her head. "That's impossible. The last mountain lion in this area was killed about a hundred and fifty years ago."

Jonah was close to her once more on the narrow trail. He put one large hand gently onto her shoulder, as if his touch might convince her. Maybe it could about some things, she thought, acutely aware of the light, soothing weight upon her arm. But it could not make her agree with something that simply could not be.

"Dawn, I tell you I saw a mountain lion. I think it was as startled as I was, but just at first. It stared at me for nearly a minute, and then it ran away into the woods."

"You probably just saw a deer. Their coats are light brown, too." She thought of the tawny flash she had seen a while earlier. The noise she had heard. The sensation of being watched. Surely it hadn't been—

"Think what you want." He pulled away. She immediately missed the contact between them, and she knew he was irritated at her lack of belief. But how could she credit what she knew was impossible?

Quite impossible. And yet . . . she could not help recalling vividly a tall tale told to her by her grandfather over and over when she was a child. A family legend that Amos had probably made up, after his own two marriages had ended sadly, after he'd watched Dawn's mother flit from one husband to the next.

A story that had to do with the loss of cougars from the mountains of Central Pennsylvania, and what would happen on their return . . .

She realized she was staring at Jonah. "What are you thinking, Dawn?" he asked. "There was a look on your face, as though you were a million miles away."

"Just a couple of decades," she replied with a laugh. "We'd better get going, but—well, I don't know what you saw. I just doubt it was a mountain lion."

"Right," he said. "Then you won't want to hear the rest." He turned his back on her and headed not down the path, but back in the direction from which he had come, without looking to see if she was following.

"What do you mean?" she called. He certainly was sensitive, she thought, hurrying to catch up. But then, she had practically called him a liar. She hadn't meant to, but he simply had to have been mistaken.

There were no mountain lions on Eskaway Mountain.

"I mean," he said over his shoulder, "that the non-existent mountain lion showed me the way to go."

Dawn stopped dead, gripping the rough bark of a nearby pine to steady herself. Was the man crazy? Maybe that was the reason he had committed a crime.

He must have expected her to halt, for he turned back. "Are you coming?"

"Would you care to explain what you said?" she countered.

The most unexpected look came over his craggy features: sheepish, yet defiant. "Not really," he mumbled. He shoved an errant lock of hair away from his face. "But when that mountain lion leaped off into the woods, I had the strangest feeling it wanted me to follow."

Dawn recalled again the sensation of being watched, and a shiver slithered down her legs. She had never felt uneasy up here on the mountain, not even when she had come alone. Not until today.

She took a deep breath, inhaling the cool, moist air. "Well, by all means," she said brightly. "Let's follow that phantom cougar."

Jonah scowled and opened his mouth as though readying a nasty retort, then closed it again. "Yeah," he said, then headed back in the direction in which he had been going.

She didn't think he knew the mountain slopes, but he did not seem to hesitate as he plowed forward, turning this way and that as though following directions. She wouldn't aggrandize the way he went by calling it a trail; it was too narrow and twisty. But Dawn noticed that the leaves on the ground seemed to have been tamped down—by footsteps? And some branches hanging low over the area were broken.

Someone had been by. Had it been recently?

"Amos," she whispered, afraid to call aloud—afraid of how she would feel when he didn't answer.

But Jonah apparently had no such compunction. "Amos! Amos Wilton, are you out there?"

And then he stopped. "Just a minute," he said. "I hear something."

In a moment, Dawn heard it, too: a man's voice in the distance.

"It could just be one of the other search parties," Dawn whispered, not wanting to get too hopeful. Still, she called out hoarsely again, "Grandpa?"

"Over here!" came the muffled reply.

Dawn hurried in the direction from which the sound seemed to have come, skirting the trees and other obstacles in her way. She heard Jonah following close behind. "Grandpa, keep talking," she called. He did. In a few moments, she was staring into a steep, elongated pit that had to be fifteen feet deep. Its floor was strewn with mounds of leaves—and her grandfather stood at the bottom, looking up at them. He was smiling. There were a backpack and a bundle of rags beside him, and he held a dark tarp about his shoulders.

"It's about time you got here, Granddaughter," he said good-naturedly. "Now, get me out of here, and I'll tell you all about it." He looked over at Jonah, who stood beside Dawn, his hands on his hips and an amused expression on his face. "Thanks for helping her, son."

"You'll tell me about what?" Dawn asked distractedly. "Grandpa, are you all right? You aren't hurt, are you?"

There was a look on his face that she had never seen before. His eyes were practically glowing, and his smile was huge. He didn't look hurt, but—"Dawn, you'll never believe it."

"Believe what?"

"What I saw. The rumors were true. I saw a mountain lion. A cougar has come back to Eskaway Mountain."

Chapter Three

Jonah should have felt vindicated that the old man had seen the animal, too. Instead, he felt inexplicably hurt; Dawn's refusal to believe him had pierced him like a sharpened tree branch through the gut.

What did he expect? She was, after all, a lawyer.

But he had seen the mountain lion. It was unmistakable: a large, tawny creature poised with its forefeet on a boulder, hunched over and staring right at Jonah as though ready to spring. Its paws were large, its neck stretched. Its face was feline, but nothing like any house cat's Jonah had ever seen. No, it was broad faced, with a large, pink nose outlined in black, long whiskers, and a feral expression in its gold-green eyes. But Jonah saw intelligence there, too. And courage. Although it had appeared startled at first, it seemed to relax, warily, as it stared at Jonah. It showed no fear.

And why should it? It was in its own element here, wild and unrestrained. If it wanted to, it could pounce on Jonah and injure him badly. Even kill him.

But it had spared Jonah. And Jonah had envied it, for the cougar was ruler here in its home. It had nothing to fear. It could do as it pleased.

It was free.

And when it had leaped off into the woods, Jonah had had an inexplicable urge to follow. He felt as though the animal had soundlessly called to him, communicated with him.

That part, he knew, was ridiculous. But they had found Amos. And whether or not Dawn had believed him before about seeing the large feline, she believed him now.

Amos was waiting for help inside that pit. He looked healthy enough, fortunately, though Jonah figured the older man should be checked by a doctor after spending the night exposed to the elements.

He would have been a doctor, if . . .

This wasn't the time for lamentations. First things first. Jonah studied the pit. There was a cleared, charred area toward one side; Amos, fortunately, had apparently been able to light a fire the night before. But there was no easy way to climb in and out, not with the edges as steep and as covered with loose, uncompacted dirt as they seemed. There was a faint, odd smell about the place, too, as though something had died nearby, though Jonah saw nothing unusual.

He tore the backpack from his shoulders and laid it on the ground, reaching inside for the rope that Clemson had trained his volunteer rescuers to carry and use. He noted that Dawn did the same. "Here," he said, knotting both coils around a nearby tree. Then he fastened the other end of his own about his waist and rappelled down the slope, causing some of the dirt along the side to tumble to the bottom each time his feet made contact. Fortunately, Amos had moved aside.

When Jonah was on the leaf-strewn earth beside the older man, he rolled up the tarp, then tried stuffing it, along with the heap of clothing on the ground, into Amos's backpack. It overflowed. "How did you get all this in here in the first place?" he asked.

Amos shrugged. "I didn't." He offered no further explanation.

No matter. Jonah hefted the pack onto his own back, then tied Dawn's rope around her grandfather. "Stand back again," he told Amos. Then, with Dawn's help in steadying him, he used his rope to walk up the side of the pit, again trying to ignore the mini-landslide each footstep caused. In a few minutes, he reached the top. Then, with Dawn assisting, he pulled Amos up.

She hugged her grandfather. When she looked up, she had tears in her eyes.

"Thank you," she whispered to Jonah, with a wide, happy smile.

They had found her grandfather. He was all right.

And Jonah would have done this every day for a year, just to see that smile again.

Quickly, he busied himself with untying the ropes and winding them back up to be put again into Dawn's backpack and his. He must be light-headed to the point of dementia, here in the thin mountain air. Why else was he feeling such an attraction to this ill-tempered woman? And her a lawyer, no less.

And there had to be a logical explanation for his illogical urge to follow that cougar as it had run away.

With a shake of his head, Jonah stepped over to the place where grandfather and granddaughter were having their reunion and stuck out his hand. "How do you do, sir?" he said. "I'm Jonah Campion. I work for

Lettie Green. I'm glad we found you. Were you aware of the search parties out here looking for you?"

Amos Wilton took his hand and shook it with fervor. "Hi, son." His broad-featured face was leathery and tanned, with deep lines running every which way, like a road map. But there was a lot of character on that face. There was kindness in his eyes, though Jonah knew better than to judge people by appearances.

Amos turned then toward Dawn. "Did you cause a fuss over me, young lady? You should have known not to worry."

"Oh, no. I didn't worry when Susie said you were out overnight and hadn't even gotten back to feed the animals."

"Sarcasm is not becoming," Amos chided. "And I'm sure you made certain that Susie or one of the others took care of the Haven in my absence." He looked at her as though waiting for confirmation. She nodded. "I'm sorry I got caught up here," the old man continued, "but there was a reason."

"Seeing a mountain lion." Jonah could hear the strain in Dawn's voice as she waged a losing battle not to sound sarcastic again.

"There was that," Amos agreed. "But that wasn't all. I'll tell you about it on the way down." He looked up at the sky through the canopy of trees. "We should get moving. Looks like storm clouds may be rolling in."

Sure enough, the sky was growing darker, though it was just the middle of the afternoon.

Jonah reminded Dawn, "Shouldn't you let the police know you found Amos?"

"Oh, yes. Of course." She looked flustered but made the call. Jonah could hear the excited voice of Clemson Biggs over the phone.

"Let me talk to him, honey," Amos said before she hung up. "Clemson, that you?" He paused. "Yeah,

44

yeah, I know. I'm an old fool. But listen, will you? I found Sherm Patterson." Jonah heard Dawn's gasp. Amos gave an apologetic look to his granddaughter and said softly, "No, I'm sorry to say. He was a goner when I found him. Same pit where I spent the night, as it turns out; I got myself trapped. Fortunately, he'd come up preparing to spend a while; it was his extra clothes I used to keep warm, his tarp I used as shelter, though I'd brought my own matches. Anyway, I've got him well covered with leaves and dirt; I'll show your boys where to find him."

Jonah had lived in Eskmont long enough to have been there when Sherm Patterson, a clerk at the local grocery store, had been reported missing. An extensive search had been conducted for him, but he hadn't been found. Jonah had felt suspicious eyes on him as he walked through town, and he had been impotent to stop them. Some people clearly assumed he was responsible for Sherm's disappearance. He was, after all, the town's only ex-con.

Then came the story told by Sherm's disgusted daughter: that he was probably off on a binge in some bigger town.

But now, it seemed, the original concerns for Patterson had been justified. He was dead.

Amos hung up. "He said we should start back, but he's going to meet us at the bottom with a crew to come up to start investigating what happened to Sherm. He's treating me like a damned baby, doesn't want me to stay here after being out all night."

"He's right, Grandpa," Dawn said.

He glared at her. "Anyhow," he continued, "I told him some landmarks for finding this damned crevice, and we're to leave markers on the way down."

Jonah asked, "What did happen to Patterson? Could you tell?"

"Not really, but—Look, I'd better start at the beginning. Tell you both what brought me out here and all. But first, have you got any of those fluorescent-painted trail markers in your backpacks?"

Jonah dug out the packet of bright orange sticks about a foot long and an inch thick that Clemson had insisted that the volunteer search teams carry. He saw Dawn do the same.

"Great," Amos said. He took several from his granddaughter, walked to the far side of the pit and stuck the sticks into the ground at the top. "Sherm's down there," he muttered.

As they started off on the trail downhill, Amos planted another stick into the ground. The sticks would glow, even in the dark, and lead the investigators to Sherm's body.

Jonah watched Dawn take her grandfather's arm. She appeared to want the reassurance that he was there as much as to help him down the trail.

The shadows were lengthening. The small patches of light visible through the trees were dim. The air was growing crisper beneath the clouds, and a gusty breeze had begun to blow. Jonah wanted to hurry Dawn and her grandfather along. He didn't imagine it was a good idea to get caught in a thunderstorm beneath all these trees. Clemson's crew would have to come up here despite the weather, to deal with Sherm. He didn't envy them.

Jonah also had the feeling that, despite his own warning about impending rain, Amos would not be hurried. Maybe he could not go any faster after his night outdoors.

"Okay, Amos," Jonah said. "Tell us what brought you up here in the first place." He maneuvered his way beside Amos on the path, hoping to help the older man. But they could only walk two abreast. He figured

Dawn would not appreciate bringing up the rear, but he could not help that for now.

"Yesterday afternoon," the old man said, bending over to pick up a long tree limb that he began using as a cane, "I got a call from Slim Evans."

"So I heard," Dawn said.

As he took up a more hurried gait, Amos explained, obviously for Jonah's benefit, that Slim was one of his old fishing cronies who also boasted of a hint of Native American blood. Up in the mountains a lot, Slim always kept an eye out for animals in trouble. Also for unusual sightings.

"This had to be the most unusual ever," Dawn called from behind them. There was still a disbelieving note in her voice. Did she doubt both Jonah and her own grandfather?

"Yep," Amos agreed. "Slim sounded so smug—the old coot! He claimed he'd found tracks that could not belong to any species of wild animal found locally. He suspected a cougar. He asked if I wanted to check it out, and of course I did. He wanted to wait until today, but I didn't. So I went on my own."

"You should have brought someone else, Grandpa," Dawn said. "Like me. At least you could have told me where you were going."

"I would have, if I'd known I was going to trap myself in a damned pit," Amos said. He was starting to sound winded, so Jonah made himself slacken the pace just a little. "I thought I'd just look for a few signs, not find any, then be back down to tell Slim he was dreaming. But first thing, I found the remains of a deer. It had been killed recently, and its vital organs had been eaten away. Now, that was a good indication of something big, like a mountain lion. I began to get excited. But then, I thought I found some signs that Sherm Patterson had been out here too: his old leather

47

vest, a shoe hidden under a bunch of leaves. That's when I started looking for him."

"And you found him," Jonah prompted, slowing at a fork in the trail. He wasn't sure which was the way down.

Amos had no hesitation, though. He pushed ahead of Jonah along the trail to the left, planted a fluorescent stick and called over his shoulder, "It took a while. I called for Sherm, followed some false leads, but then, there he was. Or what was left of him. Down in that pit, where you found me."

Amos stopped. Even in the dimness Jonah could see the sadness on the old man's face. "I had to identify him by his wallet; there wasn't much left of him, I'm sorry to say."

"Oh, Grandpa!" Dawn said. She sounded justifiably upset. Jonah had an urge to drop back and comfort her. But having him put his arms around her would probably be the last thing she would want. And so he kept his stride beside Amos as the older man began again down the path, not briskly but not slowly, either.

"It's all right, honey," Amos said to Dawn. "I've seen worse. It's just that I've known Sherm for a long time. I found some handholds, climbed my way down into that pit to look, but then started a little landslide and my handholds disappeared. That's what trapped me down there with poor Sherm."

"But we didn't see him," Dawn protested.

"Like I told Clemson, I covered him over as best I could. He was under a mound of leaves on the opposite side of the pit."

Jonah would have liked, for Dawn's sake, to have changed the subject, but asked instead, "Could you tell what happened to Sherm?" What if he had been murdered? The townsfolk were certain to blame Jonah.

What would he do then? He could run, but—

"I can't be sure. Not with the condition he was in. The coroner will be able to figure it out."

Jonah fervently hoped so—and that Sherm Patterson had died of natural causes. Otherwise, he was the prime suspect. And he knew darned well he could not rely on the system to protect him, no matter how innocent he was.

On the rest of the way back down the mountain, Dawn remained quiet much of the time. She listened as Amos chattered to Jonah, relating even more detail about local flora and fauna than she could ever hope to learn.

And then he returned to the subject of the mountain lion. "Dawn, honey," he said, turning back to her, a radiant expression on his face. It reminded her of Susie's earlier description, in which she'd said Amos looked as though he had seen a stairway coming down from heaven. He did look that way. "It was the damnedest thing. I was looking for the cougar, and it found me instead. Looked right down into the pit at me. Maybe it was sizing me up for supper, but it probably thought I was too much of a tough old buzzard. Besides, it already had some food waiting—that deer." He paused. "Do you realize what the return of a mountain lion to Eskaway Mountain means?"

"Yes, Grandpa," Dawn said with a sigh. "I know what you think it means."

"What does it mean?" Jonah asked. Dawn wondered if her grandfather would regale this stranger with the folktale she had heard over and over as a child.

Instead, Amos explained how mountain lions had been hunted to extinction through most of the eastern United States more than a century earlier, and how amazing it was that one had reappeared here.

49

But Dawn knew what was really on his mind: the family fable that obviously still meant a lot to Amos.

The Native American part of their family had lived around here forever. There was a legend that centered about this area, and the existence of mountain lions, and how an Indian princess had lost her love. As Dawn had gotten older, she had realized that the story sounded like a confused amalgam of local lore, including the several stories about Nita-nee, the Indian princess who had given nearby Nittany Mountain—and hence the Nittany Lions of Penn State University—their name.

Then there were the legends, not all local, about mountain lions who helped people find their ways out of the woods. They sounded as reliable to Dawn as the family legend.

But the upshot of it all was that Amos believed the return of the mountain lion to the area would bring their family luck.

No, more than luck. Love.

And Dawn—what did she believe?

She was a realist. She had already loved—and lost. Lost terribly, thanks to the murderer who had killed her fiancé, Billy, long ago, and not because of the failure of her relationship, which was the crux of the supposed legend. Without a mountain lion on Eskaway, her grandfather's tale went, no one in her family could ever find his soul mate. But she had had Billy. They had been in love. They would have stayed in love forever, if he hadn't been killed. Amos's story was simply untrue.

But for just a moment, Dawn glanced ahead toward the strong, muscled back of the man who had accompanied her here. Jonah's light brown hair ruffled about his head as he strode forward in the lessening light. He was a man who appreciated the mountain, the forest. He seemed fascinated by all that dwelled up here. His walk was tall and proud, not the gait of a man ashamed of anything he had done. Not the gait of someone who had been in prison.

There was something about him . . . something contradictory: roughness entwined with vulnerability. Elemental stone combined with fire.

Something intriguing.

If he hadn't been a criminal, if she dared to let herself believe in Amos's fable, maybe she would imagine that this man who had just come into her life was destined to be special to her, but as it was, she was being absurd. Fanciful.

No, it was better to focus on reality. Billy had been the love of her life. She needed no one else.

But what if whatever she had seen and heard, whatever she had felt watching her, had actually been the mountain lion? Imagine, a real cougar, returned to the mountains of central Pennsylvania.

She was a lawyer, sure—but she had helped Amos at the Haven for years. She loved and revered wild animals.

Now that she was beginning to believe in its existence, she, too, wanted to see the mountain lion. Even if its presence could not bring love into her lonely life.

"So it kills animals much larger than it is," Jonah said. His tone was speculative, and Dawn wondered what he was thinking. She found out nearly immediately. "Do you think it could have killed Sherm Patterson?" He sounded so hopeful that Dawn glared daggers at his back.

"Unlikely," Amos said, sounding as indignant as Dawn felt. "Why would it? There's plenty of game around here, and like I said, I'm all but certain this one had killed recently."

"That deer you found, Grandpa," Dawn interjected. "Was it out in the open?"

"Nope. It was cached away under some dirt and leaves to protect it till the predator was ready to finish it, and I'll bet it was the cougar."

"Then there's no reason for it to have harmed Sherm," Dawn said, shooting a triumphant look toward Jonah.

"Not unless he riled it," Amos agreed. "And I doubt they'll find any evidence of that. Sherm's reason for going into the woods wasn't likely to bother the wildlife. I'll bet it was just to get away from home long enough to drink in peace."

"I see." Jonah seemed thoughtful for a moment; then he gave a short laugh. "Interesting that I, of all people, would convict the poor beast of murder without having all the facts."

Dawn saw the sympathetic look Amos turned on Jonah. She assumed Jonah was alluding to his own conviction. Was he implying that it had been wrongful?

Right. Just like every other inmate in all the prisons in the country, Jonah hadn't committed the crime for which he had been convicted.

As a lawyer specializing in victims' rights, she could believe that even less than the existence of a cougar here in central Pennsylvania.

"A mountain lion here, Grandpa," said Dawn, finally joining the conversation. "Do you suppose hunters will leave it alone even if it had nothing to do with Sherm's death?"

"Don't know, honey," said her grandfather, a grim note coloring his voice. "But that's why I need to make sure it stays safe."

Amos could not have been more delighted, he decided as he accompanied his granddaughter and that Jonah fellow down the end of the trail. Amos had actually seen the mountain lion's return to Eskaway Mountain.

He felt a little stiff and a lot achy after his unanticipated night outdoors, but mostly he felt exhilarated.

Pausing to lag behind the other two a bit, he watched the unyielding set of Dawn's shoulders as she walked beside Jonah in the growing darkness as the storm rolled in. They didn't say anything to one another. But, hang it all, they sure made a nice-looking couple.

And if seeing a mountain lion now was any indication, Dawn could finally have the right kind of relationship with a person of the opposite sex—unlike anyone else in their family for generations.

Oh, Amos knew that Dawn didn't believe a whit of the family legend. There were days that Amos, too, had had his doubts; how could he keep believing that someday cougars would reappear in these parts, after an absence of a century and a half?

But he had to believe. The legend had been told to him by his own grandfather. And he had known of no one related to him who had been lucky in love. Yet.

Someday he would write it all down, for the story of the ill-fated Indian princess who was allegedly their ancestress, the death of her lover and the involvement of a mountain lion, sometimes got a little muzzy in his mind. But the upshot was that, with the absence of cougars from the area, no one in his family could have a happy ending to a love story.

And now, at last, there was a chance for Dawn.

But not if she was a stick-in-the-mud. She had to practice flirtation sometime. Why not with this Jonah? It didn't need to lead to anything.

"Hey," Amos called to Jonah and Dawn, who had gotten ahead of him. Both stopped and turned. He was immediately aware of the absence of noise without their footfalls.

He caught up with them. "Why don't you tell me how you happened to be looking in this area for me." That should get them talking.

He listened intently for a moment as Jonah explained how Clemson had dictated the search was to be conducted. But then Dawn contradicted him and began her own version. Soon they were speaking directly to one another—each snappishly rebutting the other's story.

Sounded like there was a lot of tension between these two, for total strangers. Amos was uncertain how he felt about that.

Maybe he shouldn't have gotten them speaking after all.

And then Jonah said something about having seen the mountain lion, too. Followed it a ways, or something. That really riled Dawn.

If the way Jonah looked at Amos's granddaughter was any indication, the man was hooked. Not that he was ready to advertise the fact. Far from it.

In fact, Amos suspected the poor fellow didn't know it yet.

And how did Dawn feel? Well . . . Amos would keep an eye on them both, he decided as they reached the last part of the trail. He had heard about Jonah in town, knew he had been to prison. Amos would have to find out more about him from Clemson and from Lettie Green. Lettie wouldn't have taken him on as an employee if his crime had been violent, Amos knew. And the guy had served his time.

Still, Jonah wasn't likely to be the right one for his granddaughter—even though the man was the first one Dawn had even looked at sideways since she'd lost Billy all those years ago.

Because of Billy's murder, and the way his killer was quickly brought to justice and tossed into prison for life, Dawn had taken the road to law school without a thought. She had no doubts that the legal system was the most wonderful institution since Santa Claus. Now, she fought for what she perceived to be justice. She was a straight shooter. Too straight sometimes, to Amos's mind. Followed the letter of the law, kept her car at the speed limit, never fudged the teeniest deduction on her income tax. Never, ever told a lie, as far as he knew.

Even if this guy Jonah had paid for whatever crime he'd committed—no, even if he were innocent—he'd been convicted, and Dawn would have a problem trusting him. Amos knew that.

But even if Jonah wasn't the man for her, at least now she had a good shot at happiness when she did find the right one.

"So tell me, Amos," Jonah said finally, dropping back so he could speak with the older man. "What's the next step when we reach the bottom? I know you said Clemson would be there, ready to go up to where you found Sherm Patterson."

He wasn't that interested in the procedure, but he wanted to include Amos in their conversation. Dawn now seemed determined to find fault with everything Jonah said.

Not that it mattered, for he would never have to talk to her again once they had reached the bottom of the mountain.

She was snobbish, narrow-minded and ill-tempered. She obviously despised him, and she didn't even know him. Not the real him. She knew only where he had been, without understanding his side.

She didn't believe a word he said. Well, the hell with her.

But she was also the most beautiful woman he had ever met. And intelligent. Kind—to her grandfather, at least. And caring toward all the animals and plants on the mountain slopes.

But not to an ex-con.

And somehow her disgust hurt him more than he could recall being hurt by anyone else he had met since he was first arrested.

He laughed derisively at himself. He was developing a crush on a shrew. How was that for loving wild animals?

He drew his attention back to Amos. "Poor old Sherm," the old man was saying. "From what I gather, Clemson will have to go up and secure the area tonight. Or maybe the county coroner will do it."

"Since we're sure the mountain lion didn't get him," Dawn said, her look at Jonah daring him to contradict her, "then was there any sign of foul play?" She maneuvered her way to her grandfather's side, effectively blocking Jonah on the narrow trail so he had to either lag behind or run into a tree trunk. That was all right. Though she might think she was getting the better of him for the moment, her maneuvering along the twisting trail ahead gave him a great perspective on her back—and her curvaceous rear—even in the fading light.

Even if he didn't like her attitude toward him, that didn't mean he couldn't admire the view.

"Ah, my granddaughter, the lawyer," Amos said with a laugh. "Always looking for someone to be liable." But then he grew serious. "But no, honey. I didn't see any sign of foul play, though that had best be left to an expert to analyze. But there were a couple of empty liquor bottles wrapped in his clothes, his favorite brand. My guess is that he went up the mountain to escape for a few hours, fell into the pit and died of exposure. It's wet in these mountains, and though it's spring, it still gets pretty darned chilly at night—like I just experienced. Or maybe his heart just gave out. Who knows?"

"Poor Sherm," Dawn echoed. Jonah could see her shudder, and resisted again the urge to take her into his arms for comfort. Not that she would let him—Amos's granddaughter, the straitlaced lawyer.

Jonah remained behind the others for the rest of the walk. He didn't mind. It was wonderful out here in the woods, with the moist wind beginning to blow. He could almost feel the animals still active during the day brace themselves for the rain that was sure to come, hear the nocturnal creatures begin to stir as it grew ever closer to evening. Jonah felt alive again now, more than he had since he had first been accused of a crime.

The mountain, with its wooded hillsides, meant life. Freedom.

He would have to come back on his own someday to explore further. Maybe he'd get to know that mountain lion a little better, here in its own territory.

He smiled to himself at his own whimsy. If he weren't careful, he just might start to feel human again, now that freedom was all around him.

They had reached a small, cleared picnic area complete with tables, a barbecue grill and rusting metal garbage cans. The parking lot was finally visible on the trail below them, and none too soon; a light mist had begun to fall.

The lot was crowded now with vehicles and milling people waiting to hear Amos's story—and to go up after what was left of Sherm Patterson.

Jonah realized he would soon be separated from

57

Amos and his granddaughter. Though they were likely to run into one another in the small town and be forced, by courtesy, to be pleasant to one another, Jonah would probably never have to have a conversation with the judgmental Dawn Perry again.

Why didn't that thought make him feel better?

Dawn touched Amos's arm, halting him near a picnic table. "Before we get down there, we'd better talk about how you want to handle the lion."

The clearing was much lighter than the trail had been with its thick overhang of trees, and Jonah took in the sight of Dawn's rosy, windburned cheeks and tousled hair. Her large, exotic eyes were narrowed slightly in the breeze, and her generous lips were parted. She was a damned lovely woman, all right.

Get your mind back in line, he ordered himself, looking down at the hands he had to scrub so hard each day to keep them from becoming grease stained. He had an engine to rebuild the next day. That was his reality now, not Dawn Perry, the lawyer.

She was still talking to her grandfather, whose white hair was quickly becoming matted down in the dampness. "You'll probably have to mention the cougar. Clemson will want all the details. And someone else is liable to spot it, too. Plus, anyone going up on the mountain will need to be warned, in case it's dangerous."

"Yes, I'll have to report it." Amos sounded unhappy about the idea. "What a shame, but there's no choice. I'll want to start right away to get a permit."

Permit? What was he talking about? Jonah stood absolutely still in the mist, listening to grandfather and granddaughter discuss the mountain lion with which Jonah had come face-to-face. The *free* mountain lion.

"We'll have to find out if a permit is needed," Dawn

said. "With animals that are known to be around here, it's clear which require permits and which don't. I think there are some subspecies of mountain lions that are considered endangered species under federal law, but we'd have to get close to determine if this is one of them. We'll have to make some phone calls to figure out the legalities. The sooner you capture it, the less chance there'll be for someone to kill it first."

"Capture it?" Jonah had been reaching down to pick up some trash an inconsiderate picnicker had left on the ground, but he stopped, his sudden, overwhelming rage threatening to detonate inside him like a bomb. He could not believe he had heard right. Surely they didn't mean what they were saying.

He slammed his hands hard against the nearest trash can, sending it rolling. The explosive sound echoed up the mountain. "Do you think you're going to try to cage that poor wild animal in your damned sanctuary, rather than letting it rove free, where it belongs?"

He could barely make out Dawn's shocked expression in the dim light, but she stared at him as though he were crazy. "We're going to try," she said softly, in contrast to his own shout. "For its own good. Otherwise—"

"You leave that creature free," Jonah said through gritted teeth. "Or you'll answer to me."

59

Chapter Four

Dawn stared at Jonah Campion. Diamond-hard determination shone in his narrowed eyes as he glared right back at her.

She thought she saw something else there, too—an emotion she could not name, since she hardly knew the man. Fury, possibly. But why should he seem so outraged on behalf of an animal?

Maybe, though, it wasn't anger. Maybe it was . . . pain.

He had mentioned freedom. Perhaps he identified with the cougar, equating the Haven with prison. But they were not the same. Not at all.

"I don't think you understand, Jonah," she said gently, pushing damp strands of dark hair away from her face. This wasn't the time or place to argue, not with the rain falling and a thunderstorm pending. "It's for the mountain lion's own good. I'll explain more later. Right now I want to get my grandfather out of here."

Jonah nodded. "Clemson had better let us take Amos to the nearest hospital right away, have him checked over. It's no joke for someone his age to spend a night outside in the elements."

Starting off down the final leg of the trail, Amos snorted. "No hospital. I've spent more nights 'in the elements,' as you call it, than most men half my age. I'm fine. I just want to give my report to Clemson, send his investigators on their way, then get home to my animals."

"But, Grandpa—" Dawn began, catching up with him. This was one thing upon which she could agree with Jonah. "You should at least have Doc Marsden check you over, make sure you aren't suffering any ill effects from exposure, and—"

"The only ill effects I'm suffering are a result of standing around arguing with you two."

Dawn threw an apologetic look at Jonah. Despite how matted down his water-darkened hair was, how the shadows caused by the storm clouds emphasized the crevices of his face, he was still one handsome hunk. And despite his unsavory background, he had behaved like a perfect gentleman with her on the mountain. Well, not perfect. He'd been irritable, contentious—and she had enjoyed being with him, damn it! He had somehow kept her mind from total devastation at her grandfather's disappearance. And then he had found Amos.

"Hey!" came a cry from below. "There they are!"

Dawn had to edge her way into the crowd. Her grandfather and Jonah were right behind her. Well-meaning people had thrust umbrellas into their hands, but they hadn't opened them yet. Fortunately, the rain remained light.

"I knew I deserved a welcoming committee," Amos

61

said, "but this one's bigger than I expected."

Jonah stood alone at the end of the trail looking uncomfortable and every bit the outsider that he was. Dawn, surprised she felt sorry for him, had the impression he wanted to leave quickly. But, to his credit, he stayed. Clemson would want to talk to him, too.

In moments, Amos was surrounded by people clapping him on the shoulder and welcoming him home.

"You old fool," cried Slim Evans, a tall man even older than Amos. He bent down and slapped Amos gently on the back. "You scared me half to death, running off without waiting for me. Did you see anything?"

Amos lifted his eyebrows mischievously without responding, and Slim guffawed. "You did, didn't you? Well, don't that beat all?"

Slim's message had sent Amos to Eskaway, Dawn thought in irritation. He'd meant well, but she could have kicked him for stirring up her grandfather's interest that way. At least no harm had been done.

Dawn was thrilled to see the warm outpouring from Amos's other friends, too. "Hold on," he finally said. "You folks want me to make a speech?"

"Sure," said Ezzie Foreman, a tall man in a baggy black raincoat. "Tell us what happened. On the record." As he pulled out a notebook and a tape recorder, Dawn recalled that Ezzie was a reporter for the *Centre Daily Times*. "Is it true you found Sherm Patterson's body?"

Several other media representatives surged toward them, unfamiliar people with microphones and television cameras.

"I don't think my grandfather is ready to be interviewed for a news story," Dawn protested. The wave of onlookers had pulled her farther into the crowd, away from Amos—and Jonah. "Give Amos time to—"

"To tell his story to me," interrupted Clemson. "This is an official police investigation." In his Eskmont Police Department rain slicker and hat, and carrying his radio in his hand, he looked less like a beaver and more like a trained officer of the law. He bustled away when one of the investigation team called him over.

"You did find my dad?" Carleen Dillinger asked Amos. In her mid-twenties, she was Sherm's daughter. Her husband's family owned the Eskmont Diner. Her small hazel eyes were open wide, and her thick shoulders slumped as though waiting for the blow she knew would come. Beside her stood Lettie Green.

"Well, yes, honey," Amos admitted, maneuvering his way over to take Carleen's hand. "I'm sorry."

"Clemson said—you said—" Carleen's usually outspoken personality seemed suddenly to evaporate.

"I'm sorry," Amos said again, even more gently. Carleen looked as though she had expected his words, but tears welled in her eyes. Lettie put an arm around her.

"How'd he die?" demanded Ray Koslowski. With his hair plastered down by rain, his face appeared even more pudgy than usual. His gaze wandered over the crowd until it lit on Jonah.

Damn him! Dawn thought. There was no reason to believe that Jonah had had anything to do with Sherm Patterson's demise. She neatly thrust aside the fact that she'd had the same concerns earlier that day.

"We don't know," Dawn said. "We'll leave that to the coroner to determine." For Jonah's sake—and the mountain lion's—she wished she could assert her grandfather's opinion that it had been of natural causes. But as a lawyer, she knew it was more prudent to say nothing.

Trying to appear nonchalant, she edged through the mist toward Jonah, dodging through the crowd of on-camera reporters and people pulling lights, tarps and other equipment from police and coroner's vehicles. Jonah's face had taken on the stony indifference that had been there the first time she had seen him. He had moved to stand beside his car.

To Dawn's dismay, Amos followed her. Others joined him, including Slim and Ray. Looking at his granddaughter, Amos shrugged. He appeared tired, and though he now wore a poncho, his face glistened, slick from the light rain. "Well, I want everyone to know right off that it looked to me like natural causes," he said. "I think poor old Sherm succumbed to *the elements.*" He emphasized the words, obviously enjoying his little mockery of Jonah, but without looking at the butt of his joke. Despite her exasperation that he was talking out of turn, Dawn wanted to hug her grandfather. Now was not the time to call the crowd's attention to Jonah Campion.

She at last reached Jonah's side. Although she did not look up, she felt his eyes on her. Was he glad for her unspoken support, or would he rather she would just mind her own business?

"What elements?" Ray persisted. "Carleen said that when her father disappeared, he left his car at home but not his lightweight gear. She thought Sherm had enough equipment with him to camp out for a month. Except that she thought he'd taken all that to fool everyone; she figured he was off somewhere having a *high* old time, if you get what I mean."

Seeing the pain in Carleen's eyes increase, Dawn wished she could kick Ray in the shins. No, that would be battery. Maybe she could file a lawsuit against him for mental anguish.

"We'll let the coroner determine what happened to Sherm," said Clemson firmly. He had left the group of investigators to join the crowd around Amos. "Now it's time for all you folks to leave so I can have a talk with Amos and the people who found him."

Thunder rumbled in the distance, followed by a flash of lightning. The rain came down harder.

"Damn!" Clemson said, looking at Eskaway Mountain. "What a night to have to go back up there."

A few members of the crowd conveyed further well-wishes to Amos, then left. Among them were Carleen Dillinger, who got into someone else's car to be driven away, and Slim Evans. Finally even the media people began packing their gear, except for the couple of them apparently determined to go up the mountain with the investigators.

Ray did not leave, though. He merely raised his umbrella. "Did you see Sherm?" he persisted. "How did he look?"

A sad expression washed over Amos's face. He appeared to Dawn as though he could use some moral support.

Fortunately, he received some from Lettie Green, who patted his shoulder. Then she turned to Ray, hands on her hips. "Dump the dumb questions into one of your favorite old commodes, Ray," she ordered, "and flush it. Like my late, lamented husband and your best hunting pal Arnie would have said, 'Dead ain't pretty.' That's all any of us needs to know. Right, Amos?"

His smile looked tired but grateful. "Right," he agreed.

Ray's voice was mildly chiding. "You know how Arnie would have finished, Lettie."

"Of course I do: 'But we all have to eat.'" She shook her finger at him as though scolding a wayward child instead of a beefy man who towered over her. "That doesn't exactly fit here, Ray. Sherm wasn't one of the helpless creatures you big, brave men hunted and I

65

wound up cleaning—except for the ones you kept to stuff, of course."

Dawn didn't like Ray's odd half-smile. "Maybe he was, Lettie. In a way." He asked Amos again, "How did he look?"

"About as terrible as you'd imagine a man would who'd died more than a week ago in the woods," Amos finally retorted.

"You didn't see any bullet wounds?" Ray obviously had a morbid sense of curiosity, Dawn thought. Why didn't he just give up? "How about animal bites? And not just the usual corpse-chewing rodents. Rumor has it that there's some new wild animal around here. A big one. But I'll bet our beast-loving friend here wouldn't tell the truth about that, even if it were obvious a critter killed Sherm, would he?"

"Animal?" asked Clemson. "What animal?"

So that was what Ray had been hinting at, Dawn thought. Poor Amos. This was certainly not the way he wanted to make the cougar's presence public knowledge.

"There's a mountain lion up there," he muttered to the policeman. "No reason to think it's a danger to people, but you'd better warn the investigators, just in case."

Clemson stared at him. "You kidding? I haven't heard of a mountain lion around these parts for . . . well, I never have. They've been gone for the last hundred years. You going to capture it?"

Dawn felt Jonah stiffen beside her. She purposely bumped into him, hoping he would get the message and not start an argument here. There was too much at stake for the cougar. Jonah's arm was straight and tense at his side, and she felt as though she had touched the unyielding trunk of a sturdy hemlock.

"No, Amos isn't kidding, are you, Amos?" mocked

Ray. "A great big mountain lion—one that just might not be dangerous." He laughed.

Amos's wizened face contorted in anger. "We've no reason to think it would hurt a human."

"And you've no reason to think it wouldn't," snapped Ray. "I need to organize a hunting party. Can't let a damn big cat kill our neighbors like Sherm, now, can we?"

He turned to the few remaining citizens in the parking lot. Several nodded their heads in agreement.

He turned back to Amos and grinned, his smile smug on his pudgy face.

"Just hold on," Amos demanded. "There's no indication that a mountain lion had anything to do with what happened to Sherm. And any cougar up on Eskaway is very likely to be under federal protection as an endangered species, so don't you go off shooting at it, you hear, Ray?"

"I hear you, oh almighty Amos Wilton," said Ray, with a smirk on his face. "You coming, Lettie?" He waved his umbrella at her.

The auto-repair-shop owner had donned a brimmed yellow rain hat. "Guess I'd better, unless you want to walk. Someone as sugar-sweet as you just might melt." The older woman's smile was as serenely innocent as Dawn had ever seen it, and it nearly made Dawn laugh. Then Lettie tossed what appeared to be an apologetic look at Amos. "I'm driving," she explained. She left with Ray.

Now, this was an appropriate time to make her point with Jonah Campion, Dawn thought. She turned to face him. "You understand now," she said softly, "why we have to capture the mountain lion and keep it in the Haven, at least for now, till we can be sure it'll be safe."

His eyebrows were knitted as he glowered down at

her, and she glimpsed again the hint of pain she thought she had seen before. For a moment, she felt tempted to take his hand, for if ever a man seemed to need soothing, Jonah Campion was he.

But though her fingers twitched, she did not touch him. He might only resent her attempt to be kind.

Another clap of thunder sounded in the distance. Dawn had to strain to hear Jonah's whispered reply. "I understand why you think so," he finally said. "But that doesn't mean I will ever agree."

Why was he getting so belligerent about a damned wild animal? Jonah asked himself, continuing to glare at beautiful, argumentative Dawn Perry.

He, who had put all emotions aside for years, now found himself contending with wave after wave of feeling, thanks to this willowy young woman in a dirty windbreaker and blue jeans.

Why should he, who cared about nothing and no one, take a stand against Dawn and her grandfather on this issue? It should be of no consequence to him.

Except that it *was* of consequence. He had traded stares with the cougar on the mountain. He had felt awe at its power, envy at its ability to bound away, into the green depths of the hillside forest.

It was free.

He, too, was free—now. But only partially. He was on parole, but even if he were perfect from now until forever, he was branded with a criminal conviction. No one would ever think of him again without attaching the label at the end, "convicted felon." Least of all himself.

He would not, could not, sanction stealing its freedom from the mountain lion. How could it survive, enclosed and fettered, even if captured "for its own good"?

"Look," he said to Dawn, wanting to squeeze her shoulder, to convince her, somehow, with his touch.

Sure! As though that would persuade her of anything, except that he was a presumptuous fool. Instead, he reached down and picked up a damp twig from the ground beside him. He snapped it in half, then snapped one of the halves in two. "I know you think you're acting in the animal's best interests, but who's to say what those are? Why not ask the lion?" He was being only half-facetious. "I mean, if it were a creature that could talk back, do you think, if you explained the situation, that it would agree to—"

He did not get to finish his question, for Clemson came over. The plastic cover of his police hat was beaded with drops of rain. "I've finished questioning Amos. How about the two of you explaining how you found him."

"It was Jonah who found him," Dawn said. "He had a . . . hunch."

Jonah thanked the lovely woman beside him with a look. She had argued with him, on the mountain, when Amos had asked how they had found him; she was not arguing now. On some level, she must have accepted his story. But not the substance of it.

He hadn't accepted the substance of it, either. Not fully. He did not want to appear crazy on top of everything else—but there had been some kind of interaction with the cougar. And it had led to . . . well, yes, he could call it a hunch. It *was* a feeling. It gave him direction. And it had led him to Amos.

He was glad he had contributed toward saving the older man. Especially since he understood how happy that made Dawn Perry.

Not that she would owe him anything. But under other circumstances, if he hadn't been a convict, maybe she would have seen him as—what? A real man, one she would want to get to know better?

Who knew?

But life was filled with reality. And in reality, he was what he was.

The sky was growing darker, but at least the rain had not increased. With Clemson's coaching, Jonah told his side of the search on the mountain—not leaving out his brief communion with the cougar, but not embellishing it, either. It had simply been a quick confrontation before the animal had vanished into the forest. And as for having an idea where to look for Amos—well, as Dawn had said, he'd had a hunch.

He listened to Dawn's version. "I was so worried up there, Clemson, I can't even tell you. We were searching for so long without a sign—and then Jonah had his idea about where to go, and we called out and Grandpa called back. It was such a relief."

She threw a glance at him. It was a soft look, filled with happiness. And, perhaps, gratitude. It sparked something deep inside. Something human that he thought no longer existed in him.

He waved his hand slightly as though erasing her gratitude and his own feelings. She had no call to be grateful to him. He was just doing his job; hadn't his boss, Lettie, told him he'd had to join the volunteers?

"We were just lucky," he said gruffly. "So was Amos. There wasn't any shelter in that pit; if he'd been out in the storm that's brewing, I'm not sure he'd have fared so well."

"I doubt it. Well, thank you, young man, for your assistance." Clemson held out his hand, and Jonah shook it.

"Yes," Dawn said, "thank you, Jonah. For everything." Her voice sounded hoarse, as though she were full of emotion, and he detected a moist sheen in her dark brown eyes. She, too, held out her hand.

Reluctantly, Jonah took it in his. It was cool and soft, and she clasped his firmly.

"Please don't worry about the mountain lion," she said. "We won't do anything quickly, and even if we get a permit, we don't have to use it."

"I'll just bet that, if you go to the trouble of getting one, you'll simply stick it in a drawer and forget about it." Jonah purposely put a sarcastic note into his voice. He did not want to bait her, but the memory of her hand in his was playing havoc with his psyche. Better that he remember her as angry and spiteful with him. "Once you have that little piece of paper, you'll have all the incentive in the world to decide the animal is better off loose, I'm sure."

"What you can be sure of, Mr. Campion," Dawn said stiffly, "is that we will do whatever is necessary to save that mountain lion."

Dawn had hoped, with that exit line, to leave Jonah's presence. By then, most of the townsfolk had departed from the parking lot, and the investigators and some intrepid reporters had begun their trek up to find Sherm.

That left Amos, Jonah and her together once more.

"Time to go, Grandpa," she said. "Will you give me a lift to the police station? My car's still there."

At his agreement, she climbed into the passenger seat of Amos's truck. It felt cold and smelled as though Amos had recently eaten one of the Eskmont Diner's famous cheese steak sandwiches, smothered in onions.

She watched as Amos turned the key in the ignition. The engine sputtered to life . . . and died.

"Drat it!" her grandfather exclaimed, then tried again. Nothing. "Damned battery isn't more than a year old," he grumbled.

Dawn did not bother to ask if he had left the lights on; he wouldn't tell her if he had. Instead, she looked out the windshield. Jonah's car was beginning to pull out of the parking lot. She hopped out and waved. The rain was coming down harder, and she shielded her eyes with one hand.

Jonah stopped and rolled down the window. "What's wrong?" he called.

She pointed to Amos's truck. Jonah pulled beside them, got out some jumper cables, and used them to try to start the engine. It didn't work. "I think the battery has had it," he confirmed. "Tell you what, Amos. Leave the truck and give me the keys. Fisk and I will get it to Lettie's and fix it."

Dawn hadn't wanted to ask Jonah Campion for a ride back to town from the base of the mountain, so she used Clemson's cellular phone to call her law partner. Marnie Wyze came promptly in her new Acura Legend. Dawn got in, taking only one more glance back at Amos's truck—where Jonah leaned beneath the open hood.

Amos continued to refuse to go to the hospital, but when he admitted that he had eaten only a few berries and some granola since the previous day, Dawn insisted on treating Marnie and him at Sugar's restaurant. Her first choice was usually the town's only other eatery: the diner. But it was owned by Carleen Dillinger's in-laws. Dawn wanted to forget, at least for now, Amos's ordeal on the mountain.

Not to mention that she wanted to leave behind her own sojourn there with the enigmatic Jonah. She had no need to think about him any further.

Then why did her mind seem to focus on nothing else?

Over hearty meat loaf, tempered by a salad, Dawn

gave her partner a brief rundown of the day's events.

"Do you suppose the district attorney will prosecute someone for Sherm's homicide?" Marnie asked as Dawn finished. "After all, we've an ex-con in town."

Dawn began counting to ten. Yes, Sherm was dead, but there was just too much conclusion-jumping about the cause. And her law partner should have known better.

"No persecutions!" Amos exclaimed before Dawn could frame a reply. "Or prosecutions either. Like I've said all along, I don't think anyone's to blame for Sherm's death but Sherm."

"We'll see," said Marnie.

Marnie had once worked in a DA's office. Imagining her partner already framing arguments against Jonah, Dawn wanted to scream. Jonah hadn't even known Sherm—had he?

Dawn had once been the closest of friends with Marnie—until they had gone into partnership together. But tiny, vivacious Marnie, with her shining blond hair and deceptively sweet personality, had proven just a bit too conniving. She specialized in helping her clients by finding legal strategies that were lawful, but sometimes just barely.

Still, the two made a good team, complementing each other's skills and knowledge. Marnie didn't mind defending criminal cases, even when she suspected a client was guilty. Dawn took on only civil matters, preferring to represent plaintiffs against those who had wronged them. And when they brainstormed a case, Marnie opened Dawn's eyes to all sorts of legal possibilities that she might not otherwise have considered in her straight-and-narrow approach. In turn, Dawn helped keep Marnie honest.

The rain had stopped by the time they finished eating. Dawn's car was still parked by the police station, and Marnie dropped Amos and Dawn off there.

"Are you okay for just a few more minutes?" Dawn asked Amos. "I need to make a quick stop at the office."

"You're not going to do any work tonight, are you?" Amos's tone was incredulous.

There was a lot she had not gotten done that day, thanks to searching for him. But she wasn't about to tell him that. "Not really," she lied. She was so keyed up that she doubted she would sleep well anyway. And right now, she wanted to keep her mind active until it conked out on its own. Otherwise, her thoughts would leap off in too many directions, where she did not want them to go. Thoughts of Sherm Patterson, of hiking through the mountains—and of a certain very disquieting man.

"I just need to pick up a file or two for tomorrow morning. I promise I won't be long."

Once again, Jonah stood at the foot of Eskaway Mountain. This time he was with Fisk. They had brought Lettie's big wrecker, to tow Amos's truck, if necessary.

It was later that same evening. The rain had slackened, though it had not stopped. Jonah had picked up a black slicker at the garage, and its hood kept his head dry.

The investigators' vehicles were still in the parking lot. Jonah looked up onto the slopes that he had traversed earlier with Dawn Perry. So many factors had contributed to his having spent that small amount of time with her: Amos's trek onto the mountain. Sherm Patterson's body turning up.

The appearance of the mountain lion.

"Hey, Campion, you ready?" Fisk's voice broke into his thoughts.

Just as well. He was beginning to moon over Dawn

Perry like some hormone-saturated teenager. He might as well dream about a date with Hollywood's top ingenue—whoever that might be these days. He had not gone to a movie since the first week he had gotten out of prison, when he was trying to reexperience everything he had missed. To feel normal again.

It hadn't worked.

"I'm ready," Jonah said emotionlessly. "Let's try this battery again before we hook the truck up for a tow."

Fisk attached jumper cables from the wrecker to the connections under the hood of Amos's truck. He was about twenty years old and had not yet gotten over a severe case of teenage acne. He wore a wispy goatee, and never did a great job of cleaning his hands after a hard day at the garage.

Jonah, sitting in the driver's seat, revved the engine. It caught and turned over, then died. Just to be sure, they tried again. The second time it stayed on, but Jonah still suspected one very sick battery.

"Follow me," Jonah called out the window. "I'll drive this baby to Lettie's—if it makes it."

He wondered, as he steered along the winding mountain roads, if he should not have let Fisk take the wheel of the truck. It was Amos's truck, and Amos was Dawn's grandfather.

And he needed no further reminders of Dawn.

But as he drove into town, Jonah could not help looking up at the second floor of a building across the street from the tiny courthouse—the building that housed Dawn's law office.

Before, on the way to get Amos's truck, Jonah had asked Fisk if he knew of Dawn Perry, and where her office might be. "Sure, I know," Fisk had said. "She works in her own law firm: Wyze and Perry. Miz Perry helped my mother once. Ma owns her duplex and had some trouble with a tenant who was trashing the place. Miz Perry helped kick him out and get Ma the back rent. Her office is on the second floor, there."

He'd pointed to the two-story gray stone building, on the corner of Main Street, that Jonah was passing now. The bottom floor, complete with a plate-glass window, housed a mom-and-pop pharmacy. At the eaves of the roof, along the second floor, a couple of grimacing gargoyles stood watch. Although it was nearly seven o'clock, some lights upstairs were lit. Was Dawn there, hard at work?

As a lawyer, he reminded himself. She apparently believed in the blundering mess that was the legal system. But he didn't. Not now. Not ever again.

He made himself concentrate instead on the town itself. Eskmont, Pennsylvania. A quaint village whose tallest buildings were two stories high, whose downtown still contained lots of small stores side by side, built of pastel-painted wood frame or of carved gray stone. The buildings were surprisingly well maintained for their age, unlike many older towns in the east and midwest.

Though towns like nearby State College had stores from the big chains, they had not moved in here. They probably would not do enough business to make it worthwhile.

He pulled the truck into one of the service bays in the garage, then killed the engine. Fisk was right behind in the wrecker.

Jonah let the truck sit for a minute, then turned the key in the ignition again. This time it did not start.

"That truck has been around nearly as long as that old so-and-so Amos," came a deep, muffled female voice from beside him. He rolled down the window. Lettie Green stood there, her hands on her large hips, staring at him. "I trust you'll find a way to save it."

"I think the battery is dead," Jonah said. "I'll use the tester, though, to make sure."

"Fine," Lettie agreed. "But first, come into my office for a minute, Campion, will you?"

Sure, he would. Her question was not really a request, but a command. Well, that was all right. Despite Lettie's sometimes abrasive personality, he liked her. And he owed her. A lot.

She motioned for him to sit on the pseudoleather straight-backed chair across from her metal desk. The desk was clean, without a single piece of paper on it. To her left was a large file cabinet; he had seen Lettie put customer records into alphabetical order inside it.

"So, Campion, tell me about Amos Wilton's rescue."

Strange question from her, he thought, but he nevertheless recounted how he had been assigned to go with Dawn—without revealing his own pain when he had realized she wished to reject him as a teammate. After all, what intelligent young woman wouldn't object to going into the mountains alone with a former con?

Then he explained their search on the slopes, his brief encounter with the mountain lion, their rescue of Amos.

"I see," said Lettie when he was through. She paused for a moment. "What did you think of Amos?"

Jonah stared at her for a moment. What did she want him to say? "He seems like a nice man," he finally replied. "Kind, both to people and, apparently, to animals. Dawn said he runs a sanctuary for injured animals. She told me how they had saved peregrine falcons and the like."

Lettie nodded, and her bright red curls bounced about her round, powdered cheeks. "Yes, you're right. Amos *is* a nice man. I've known him since we both were kids. And yes, Campion, antique old buzzards

77

like us were fledglings once, too, just like everyone else. But it's strange that only recently . . ." Her voice trailed off, and she seemed to stare at something over Jonah's head.

"Pardon me?" he asked.

She looked at him again. Her dark eyes were set deep among folds of skin as wrinkled as that around her mouth. Yet she had prominent cheekbones and a delicate chin that hinted she had been a beauty when she was young. In her own way, she still was. "Never mind," she grumbled. "Look, Campion, there's something I want you to do for me tomorrow night."

"Sure, Lettie." But catching the contemplative smile on her face, Jonah wondered what it was.

Chapter Five

"Let me help this evening," Dawn said as she drove Amos home. "You should get to bed right away."

"Just drop me off," Amos replied. "Susie will have taken care of the animals already."

Dawn knew there was no use arguing with him. Not now. But she would stay to make sure he was okay.

She maneuvered the car along the country roads outside town till they reached Amos's wildlife sanctuary. The arched sign over the entry read DOUBLE LOCK HAVEN. The shelter's full name was a play on the name of a nearby town: Lock Haven.

The animals' enclosures were always fastened shut. But even the thickest locks had been installed by Amos with love.

As she pulled along the driveway toward Amos's house, Dawn glanced down the path toward the compound beyond the trees, where the animals were kept. She wondered for a moment what Jonah's first impression of this place might be—not that he was likely ever to visit this shelter where animals were caged.

"What are you daydreaming about, Granddaughter?" Amos cut into her thoughts.

She felt herself flush. "You," she said, pulling the car into an empty space. "And what a wonderful job you're doing with the animals here."

He peered at her suspiciously from the passenger seat, but his light brown eyes twinkled. "Would you like to tell me exactly why you're buttering me up?"

"No, but you'll find out," she bantered in response.

She opened the car door. "Amos!" came a shout from the house. In moments, Susie Frost rushed toward them. She was large without being overweight. As usual, she was clad in blue jeans and a T-shirt. "Amos Wilton, where in heaven's name have you been?"

Dawn decided to let her grandfather make explanations to his employee. "Have all the animals been fed?" she asked.

"Of course." Susie sounded indignant. "It's nearly nine o'clock."

"Just wanted to help," Dawn explained. "Now, Grandpa, let's get you into the house. Can I fix you something warm to drink?"

"Stop fussing!" Amos ordered. "I've been getting myself to bed for seventy-four years and don't aim to stop now. Why don't you just visit some of your friends?"

"But—" Dawn objected.

"Stop into the house to say good night before you leave," he finished, and headed into the house with Susie.

Dawn always enjoyed seeing the animals. And she had gotten nowhere with Amos. She headed down the path toward the enclosure area. Overhead lights strung on tall poles illuminated her way. Rainwater, still puddled in cracks and gouges in the worn asphalt walkway, shimmered in the cool breeze. Dawn was glad she'd worn her windbreaker.

The shelter was far from silent after dark, for many of its inhabitants were nocturnal. Chatterings and screechings rent the still air, and an owl called out a quizzical "Whooo."

Dawn went first into Birdland, a large, airy building at the base of the hill that contained cages for all kinds of birds. Her favorite was a red-bellied woodpecker. Its broken wing had not healed well, and the bird would never be able to fly again into the branches of a tree to peck at the trunk for insects—but it still gamely made holes in logs Amos left for it. "Gotten enough grubs lately?" Dawn asked. The bird glared indignantly.

Then there were the sparrows and waxwings, a black-capped chickadee and a few wood thrushes, and even a red-tailed hawk. Amos had saved their lives, and once their injuries were healed he would release them.

"Good night," she called as she doused Birdland's lights. She was exhausted, so she did not spend a lot of time wandering around the outdoor pens. Instead, she entered the second building, which was the size of a substantial barn. It contained mostly small mammals, and despite how clean everything was kept, its odor was quite different from the birds' home.

She looked into one comfortable, sheltered hutch after another, to talk to a litter of adorable cottontail rabbits whose mother had been killed; to murmur encouragement to a listless beaver that remained off its feed; to chatter to a chipmunk; to look at a soft, fuzzy mink. "See you soon," she called as she left.

Then she went to the barn where larger animals were often kept. Its only inhabitant at the moment was a white-tailed deer that had been hit by a car on a country road, though at times Amos had rescued bears, bobcats and coyotes, and had even housed some orangutans from a zoo while a new home was found for them.

Dawn remembered the primates' sad faces as they looked out of their roomy, but still barred, enclosure. And for a moment, she saw a sorrowful Jonah Campion, too, in the recesses of her imagination, staring out from his cell. Toward freedom . . .

Could she, after his fuss about it, stand to see a mountain lion right here, in the Haven? Confined and caged and robbed of its liberty?

Damned right, she could—if it would save the animal's life.

So what if she found Jonah Campion attractive? So what if he had helped Amos? She owed him, but repayment should not consist of endangering the cougar that Amos and he had seen.

That, just maybe, she had glimpsed.

She longed to really view it, too—just to see with her own eyes that a mountain lion *had* returned to this area. It had nothing to do with Amos's silly folktale about the lovelorn of the Wilton/Perry family.

They would have to obtain government clearance, capture the cougar and keep it here. That way, trigger-happy Ray Koslowski and his kind would have no opportunity for target practice on the unexpected visitor to the area.

Where would they put it? She wandered the barn till she reached the side that had once held the orangutans. There was a tall, roomy enclosure there, empty now. A ceiling-high chain-link fence separated it from the rest of the building. It had barred windows that could be opened to the outside, and there was plenty of fresh air. The area was clean, and Amos would read up on what a mountain lion might like in its new habitat to feel at home, to keep it exercised and alert. A small tree, perhaps, for sharpening nails and climbing? Rock ledges to leap onto?

He cared for his animals. All of them. So did Dawn.

She wondered what Jonah would think of this place. Not much, she was sure. For no matter how many amenities Amos might put in here, the mountain lion would still be confined.

She heard a mournful howl from an outdoor enclosure. She had never thought so before, but was the animal protesting its incarceration?

Lives were saved here. She would not allow herself to believe that its inmates did not consider the Haven a sanctuary, but a prison.

When she returned to the house, Amos was on the phone in his homey kitchen, leaning against the wall.

The lines on his face looked deeper than before his disappearance. His white hair was windblown and wispy.

He looked old, her grandfather, and it made her heart ache.

She was about to nag him to go to bed when he said into the receiver, "Ah, here she is." Then, to her, "Granddaughter, a bunch of us are meeting at the diner tomorrow for supper. It's a cheering-up time for Carleen and her in-laws." Though his eyes were red with shadowed bags beneath, they shone with excitement.

"I didn't think her husband's family liked Sherm," Dawn said.

"But he was Carleen's father, and they love her."

"All right," she agreed. People in Eskmont always tried to help their neighbors, after all. It was one of the things she loved about the place.

Amos smiled.

*   *   *

Although the diner was crowded the next night, everyone seemed engrossed in their own conversations. The only thing Dawn saw that anyone did to cheer Carleen's family was to increase their income.

She was dismayed when her grandfather headed for a corner table for four. Two seats were already taken: by Lettie Green . . . and Jonah Campion.

Of course she would run into him in this small town. There was no need for her heart to speed up just because she saw him.

But she had not considered that she might be having dinner with him. "Grandpa!" she exclaimed under her breath. "What's going on?"

He didn't answer. When he reached the table, Lettie and Jonah stood. To Dawn's surprise, Amos gave Lettie a big hug. They had known each other forever but were not close friends.

Were they?

Lettie's carroty curls were pulled away from her face by a silver headband. She had put on makeup that made her shrewd eyes stand out despite the wrinkles around them, and she wore a pretty blue dress. She did not look like an automobile mechanic that night, but like a woman on a date.

Was that it? Had Amos set this up to be a double date? But he wasn't seeing Lettie; Ray Koslowski was. And Dawn certainly wasn't dating Jonah.

Jonah looked ill at ease as he caught her eye. Positive he was as innocent as she, she smiled. "Hi," she said brightly.

"Hi." The expression on Jonah's craggy face remained rueful. He held a chair out for her—next to his. He wore a white knit shirt with short sleeves that bared the lower portion of his substantial biceps. His arms, veined and sinewy, were covered with a smattering of tawny hair. His trousers were tan, and he wore moccasins.

He looked great.

Dawn was glad she had decided on a flowing skirt and peasant blouse. Not that she cared what impression she made on Jonah. But at least she didn't look like a muddy mountain hiker again.

"So how is Amos's truck?" Dawn asked when they were all seated. She had picked up her grandfather at the Haven, and his battered vehicle had not been there.

"Purring like one of his favorite cats," Lettie said. "The battery needed to be replaced, plus a couple of connections were corroded. Jonah spotted the problems right away and fixed them. He's also checking the brakes and transmission, the works. That's why we haven't gotten it back to Amos yet."

Before Dawn could respond, one of the waitresses, Bette—Carleen's sister-in-law—came over, a pad of paper in hand. "Is Carleen okay?" Dawn asked.

Bette had the face of a trucker, but the kind eyes of an angel. She shook her head. "She's taking it hard. Ol' Sherm wasn't much, but Carleen loved her dad."

"And how is everyone else around here?"

"Oh, we're getting along. Poor Sherm, though. Wish we knew what happened to him." Dawn saw her glance furtively and accusingly toward Jonah for an instant before looking away.

Dawn cringed inside. By the way his expression hardened, she knew Jonah had noticed, too. She ached for him, till she reminded herself that people usually didn't go to prison without reason. And when something later went wrong, it should be no surprise when people suspected a former convict.

When Bette had gotten their drink orders and left, Dawn turned to Amos. "I thought we were participating in a cheering-up party for the diner's owners and staff."

He smiled sheepishly. "Looks like they don't need it, so I guess we'll just have ourselves a nice supper."

Dawn glared at him. He looked toward Jonah. "Will the truck be ready tomorrow?"

"Unless I find something else wrong." Jonah reached for his glass of water and took a sip. He looked even more uncomfortable now. Unfair, Dawn thought irritably, for Amos to stick them all into this situation.

What could she do to put them more at ease? She searched for a neutral topic. Mechanics! That would interest Lettie and Jonah. She asked Jonah, "Are there certain kinds of cars you particularly enjoy fixing?"

"Not really," he said. "Although I do like tracking down a problem. It's like solving a puzzle."

He liked puzzles? He *was* a puzzle. She would not have imagined someone so impatient would enjoy complicated problems. Dawn filed away that bit of information, then asked, "How long have you been fixing cars?"

His look turned stony again. "About five years," he said. "It was the trade I learned in prison."

"Oh." Dawn squirmed a little. Her neutral topic had suddenly turned more controversial than any she could purposely have chosen.

"Before that," Lettie said, "Jonah was—"

"Lettie . . ." Jonah's voice was hardly above a whisper, but it got his boss's attention.

She stopped. "I know I promised, but you brought up the subject, young man," she grumbled. "And I still don't know why you don't want me to talk about—"

"Humor me." The two glared at one another.

Dawn's curiosity was piqued. What had Lettie intended to say? Maybe she could just ask Lettie later.

On the other hand, the woman wasn't the kind to

share confidences, or anything else for that matter—
except her own opinion.

Bette arrived with some home-baked white bread,
and everyone focused on passing the basket around,
buttering slices and exclaiming about how tasty it
was.

"Even though the weather was great today, I heard
that another storm is due tomorrow," Dawn said. Now
that was a neutral topic. Unless the sound of thunder
had driven Jonah crazy, caused him to commit embezzlement—

She shook her head at her own inane thoughts. But
it had worked. Through the time their dinners were
served, and long into their eating, the conversation
stayed light: on the weather, the performance of the
Nittany Lions football team the season before and
what was anticipated next fall, television, movies. . . .

Lettie had unbridled opinions on all the topics. She
loved football, but those danged sitcoms—"They just
aren't funny anymore. Not like 'All in the Family,' or
'The Mary Tyler Moore Show.' " And Amos seemed
fascinated by her.

Dawn noticed how her grandfather gave Lettie
tastes from his chicken potpie. She, in turn, let him
sample her meat loaf. They laughed together. Flirted.
Clearly enjoyed themselves.

Lettie and Amos?

"So tell us what it was like up there on the mountain," Lettie said to Amos. Emily Post etiquette be
damned, the older woman had her elbows on the table, and all her attention was on Amos—as if she were
a young girl enthralled with her first date.

Lettie and Amos!

As the conversation progressed, the topic inevitably
turned to the controversial.

"It wasn't so great, being with Sherm down there in

that miserable pit. But then . . . then it came and looked down at me. The mountain lion."

Dawn hazarded a glance at Jonah. His expression was attentive but bland. Well, no one doubted now that Amos and he had seen the animal.

And no one was discussing its fate. Not at this moment, at least. Maybe things would remain calm.

"That must have been a zinger of an exciting experience for an animal-loving man like you," Lettie said to Amos. "But I can't say I'm pleased about the idea of a big cat like that showing up around here. They're dangerous. I've a friend in Montana whose daughter was mauled when she was just a kid." She shook her head. "Much as I'm all for your saving God's helpless little creatures in your shelter, Amos, I'd just as soon that darned cougar go back where it came from before it hurts someone."

"There's plenty for it to eat around here," Amos said, "and as long as it doesn't get hungry, it shouldn't bother anybody. I, for one, am delighted to see it here." He winked at Dawn before turning an affectionate eye on Lettie.

"But how did this mountain lion happen to show up?" Lettie asked. "Last I heard, there weren't any left around here."

"I don't know where it could have come from," Amos admitted. "There are quite a few left out west, and an endangered bunch in Florida, but they're virtually extinct in the eastern United States. Hunted till there were none left, more than a hundred, hundred fifty years ago."

Jonah got into the act. "What's the difference between cougars and mountain lions?" he asked.

"There is none," Amos said. "At least not commonly. There are different subspecies, but they're all generally referred to under either name. Sometimes they're called pumas or even panthers. Then there are the more descriptive names, like ghost cats, devil cats, catamounts, painters and screamers."

"And the one we saw," Jonah said. "What could you tell about it?"

Amos shrugged. "I don't know. At the angle I saw it, I couldn't even tell if it was male or female. It was substantial in size, though. And there was something in its eyes—don't know what you thought of it, Jonah, but it got to me. Yes, that cat definitely got to me."

"What do you mean?" Lettie demanded. Dawn wished she hadn't. She remembered Jonah's story that the mountain lion had somehow communicated with him, told him where to find Amos.

And then there was Amos's foolish belief in the family fairy tale. . . .

"I can't really explain it, Lettie," Amos said. He put his hand on the table on top of hers. "But that cougar . . . Silly, I know, but I felt like it had been looking for me. I was upset about having got myself caught in that pit like some dumb yokel, but after the cat looked down at me, I knew I'd be all right. Now, don't bother telling me I'm ten times a blockhead; I know it. But that's how I felt."

Dawn glanced at Jonah, only to find him watching her. There was a challenge in his gray-green eyes, as though he dared her to contradict her grandfather. To try to make a fool of *him*.

But she had felt eyes on her in the forest. Had seen a flash of something like a tawny coat. If they had been overcome by their imaginations . . . well, she had been, too.

"I only wish I had seen it," she said aloud. Jonah's eyes widened, as though he were surprised at her comment. So was she—even though it was the truth.

"No question but that's one wish that'll come true,"

Lettie stated. "Amos tells me the two of you are going to work on getting the government to let you capture that cat."

Dawn watched Jonah's expression harden. "We'll see," she said noncommittally. She turned back to her own dinner: an excellent piece of trout. It was the same thing Jonah had ordered. They actually had something in common.

But she strongly suspected that their enjoyment of trout was the only thing they shared.

Soon they all had finished eating. The evening was drawing to an end. Dawn was almost sorry when Bette put their cups of coffee beside them, although they still could linger for a while.

A teenage busboy came over, one of Bette's kids. He picked up their dirty dishes, then made a show of counting the flatware. His grin at Jonah was a challenge.

Dawn dared a glance toward Jonah. His nostrils flared, and he appeared as though he were Mount St. Helens about to blow.

And then Lettie said, loud enough for the boy to hear, "I don't know whether you and Dawn know it, Amos, but Jonah was sent to prison for something he didn't do."

"Here I thought I saw him on a rerun of 'America's Most Wanted,'" the boy said, winking at Dawn. She scowled and turned back toward Jonah. If he were a dangerous felon, now would be the time for his rage to show.

Jonah's fists were clenched on the table. "Excuse me," he said through gritted teeth. He rose, flung his napkin onto the table along with some money, then stalked away.

*　　*　　*

Jonah was fuming. Why had he ever allowed Lettie to talk him into this fiasco of an evening? She had told him it would be a business dinner, so he'd had a hard time refusing. In fact, he couldn't refuse.

But he had not known they would be joined by Amos and his pretty but judgmental granddaughter. Dawn probably loved that last bit, with the kid who'd made a show of accusing Jonah of stealing from the diner. It had taken all his will to stifle his urge to throttle the brat. Then there'd been the waitress's veiled accusations about his imagined involvement in Sherm Patterson's death. But worst in some ways was Lettie's attempt to defend him. That had been the most humiliating.

He had reached his old Toyota in the parking lot. He had inserted the key into the door when he felt a touch on his arm.

"Jonah," Dawn said, "wait a minute."

He still wanted to slug something. To shout and rage—but he had learned through ugly experience to control such urges. He pulled his arm away. "Why should I wait?" he said in a hiss. "So you can satisfy your curiosity? Find out if the convict was guilty as charged? If he killed someone, or stole the silverware?"

"Let's take a walk, Jonah. Please."

"Why?"

"You're too upset to drive right now," she said practically. "And it's a pretty night. Please come. You don't have to say a word."

"I don't intend to." But he did accompany her along the sidewalk beside Eskmont's Main Street. Docilely. As though he weren't seething inside.

They did not touch, but he was well aware of her willowy form beside him, the way the gentle swing of her hips swayed her long skirt. *Damn!* Until meeting

Dawn Perry he had not been so aware of a woman since . . . since before his life had blown apart.

He didn't like it. His life was under control now. He needed no disturbances to his peace of mind.

"This is Jim Callahan's hardware store." Dawn looked into the window of the darkened shop. "His grandfather started it. Jim's about six years older than me. What he really wanted was to join the Marines, but then his father had a heart attack, so here he stayed."

"Family loyalty," Jonah said. He tried to make the words sound belittling but instead heard a note of envy in his tone.

Where, tonight, was that hard-won control he so prided himself on?

He felt Dawn's gaze on him. "I suspect," she said, "you've a lot of ghosts inside to exorcise." She hesitated. "I have good ears for listening, if you ever want to talk."

"Why should you listen?" he demanded. "I'm just an ex-con who intends to oppose your attempt to cage a wildcat. I'm an auto mechanic, and you're a lawyer. I'm a stranger, alone here; you grew up here, have a caring grandfather." He wondered why he said anything. He had sworn to himself he wouldn't.

But the rawness inside was nearly too much to take.

"You're right. I have Amos. And friends. But there's only so much I can tell them about how I feel, for fear of making them feel bad, too." There was a simple sadness in her tone. "But when I've been able to talk, it's helped a lot."

He was surprised by her directness about her emotions. And he was even more surprised that he cared. He began to calm, thinking about her and her feelings.

They had reached the next storefront. It, too, was dark. Acting on impulse, he took a step toward her, cupped her chin in his hand. He asked softly, "What has hurt you, Dawn Perry?"

She shrugged. The smile she attempted was wry. "Not a lot." But he was not about to let her get away with that. He looked deep into her marvelous dark eyes, waiting. "Well," she finally said, "my mother did. She's on marriage number six, I think. And her husbands—well, suffice it to say she was never around."

"What about your father?" Jonah asked.

Dawn snorted and pulled away. "He was husband number two. When they split, he wanted nothing to do with either of us."

"That must have been tough." Jonah was glad, after pushing her for an answer, that he sounded sympathetic. He was not good at emotional conversations, but he wanted to be there, at that moment, for Dawn Perry. She had, after all, offered to listen to him. "There's more, isn't there?"

She was still hesitant. "Sure." Her tone was determinedly breezy. "We all have things we'd rather forget. I've told you a couple of mine. It's your turn now." She turned her lovely face up toward his with an expectant look. She appeared as though it mattered that he open up to her, too. As though she cared—and the thought made a huge lump form in his gullet.

He cleared his throat. "You know the big thing I want to forget." He tried to sound as nonchalant as she did.

She nodded. "Prison." She passed. "Lettie says you didn't do it."

She didn't ask the next logical question: *did* he do it? But he knew she expected him to answer.

At that moment, it mattered a great deal to him what Dawn Perry thought. It shouldn't, though. She wasn't his type. Not at all. "You're the lawyer," he finally said. "You of all people know the legal system doesn't always work as it should."

"And it didn't for you." The words were a statement, but she didn't sound as though she truly believed them.

His muscles tensed suddenly. What was he thinking, allowing himself to mellow that way? *Damn!* The night and its emotional roller coaster had gotten to him. He should never have bent even a little, begun to reveal what was inside him. Dawn was still the same woman who had argued with him every moment on the mountain yesterday. So what if she had shared with him some of what troubled her? It wasn't enough.

"No, it didn't work for me." He hoped he sounded unconcerned. "Suffice it to say that someone can be wrongfully convicted on purely circumstantial evidence." He couldn't help it. He had to goad her. "Of course, in your experience I'm sure there has never been anything wrong with the system. That it always works."

"It works when it has to." Her voice was very small, and he looked at her. Her eyes were moist.

No. He would not thaw again this quickly. But what was making her so unhappy? "Tell me what happened." He kept his voice cool.

She shrugged. "Nothing. We need to head back now, to—"

"Tell me." He had a sense that whatever she held back was very important to her—and that made it important to him to find it out.

"It's nothing," she repeated more vehemently.

He, too, could get more insistent. "Tell me," he repeated.

She glared at him with her large, dark eyes, as though weighing whether to continue. "Oh, what the heck." She took a deep, ragged breath and looked away. When she spoke, her voice was cool, offhand. "I was engaged once, my last year of undergraduate school. Billy was his name. He was—" She stopped and swallowed, then continued in a rush, "He—Billy was murdered."

Jonah felt himself stiffen. No wonder she hadn't wanted to talk about it. Murdered. The man she had loved. Perhaps still loved.

Too bad he couldn't change places with this Billy. No one—not even his sister—would grieve over him this way. "I'm sorry," he said gruffly. What else was there to say?

"No need. It was a long time ago." Although she squared her slender shoulders, under the dim light of the street lamp behind her, she looked sorrowful. And beautiful.

And he was melting again despite himself.

"Besides"—she was obviously still trying hard to sound matter-of-fact—"they caught the killer: a kid, crazed on drugs, who needed money for more. He was tried, sentenced and thrown into prison for life. There was plenty of evidence. The trial enthralled me; the entire legal process did. That time, at least, it worked. And so I became a lawyer. Maybe Billy's death was fate, since I'm a damned good lawyer and probably wouldn't have become one otherwise. Who knows?" Her smile looked as brittle as a thin sheet of glass.

"Who knows?" he repeated gently. She had bared her soul to him. Somehow that moved him a great deal. He reached toward her, wanting to take her into his arms.

"There you two are!" called a male voice behind him. Dropping his arms, he turned. Lettie and Amos were coming up the sidewalk, hand in hand. "We have to go to Dean's Dairy for dessert," the old man continued.

"No, thanks."

"We won't take no for an answer." His short-tempered employer stared at him through narrowed eyes. She wouldn't fire him if he didn't go—but she might hold it against him.

"I'm tired, Grandpa," Dawn said from beside him.

"Nothing like a good hot-fudge sundae as a bedtime snack," Amos replied.

As Dawn's eyes met Jonah's, they twinkled in the dim light. Her composure had returned. If she was willing to be coerced into a late-night treat, then why not him, too?

They walked side by side, following the older couple.

Walking down the street with Lettie, Amos swung her hand. He wanted to cackle. His little scheme was working.

Or had it been Lettie's? After all, she had called him first to suggest this evening.

That emotion he had sensed between Dawn and this Jonah Campion—it was still there, so thick he could dip it with an ice-cream scoop.

He hadn't liked it much before—not until he had asked Lettie about Jonah's crime, his past.

She said Jonah didn't say much, but Clemson Biggs and she had done some digging. Jonah's alleged crime had been embezzlement. The evidence against him had been nearly nonexistent, except that he was there at the wrong time and place. He'd denied his guilt over and over. But Jonah had been prosecuted by a lawyer who'd used the case to bootstrap his way from a minor position in the Philadelphia city attorney's office to a great job on the Pennsylvania attorney general's staff. And when the attorney general himself could no longer run for office, there this vulture would be.

Jonah sounded like an innocent man to Amos. And more important, one who could pry his granddaughter out of her shell.

It wasn't surprising, of course. Not now, when the family legend was finally coming true.

And Amos could nudge it along.

They reached the dairy shop. "Here we are!" Amos cried, thrusting open the door. And then he stopped. *Damn and double damn!* Why had Ray Koslowski decided tonight, of all nights, to get a snack at Dean's?

Chapter Six

Dawn saw anger flare in Ray Koslowski's small eyes as he noticed Amos and Lettie walk into the nearly empty dairy store together. She hurried to catch up with the couple. "Maybe we should forget about ice cream tonight," she said.

"It'll be fine," Lettie replied. She strutted toward Ray on the pink-tiled floor as though she were in her own shop, her blue dress fluttering around her short legs. Hands on hips, she peered up at the burly man. He stood beside a refrigerated case full of milk and cheese, holding a paper bag in his hand. "So, Ray, are you on your way home? What a shame." She did not sound at all regretful, and Dawn had to suppress a smile. "It looks like you've finished your business here."

"I thought you were too busy to go out tonight, Lettie." The plumber spoke softly, through gritted teeth.

He was dressed in work overalls with grease stains at the knees.

Jonah walked toward them, as though ready to defend his employer. Dawn hoped it did not come to that, but she liked Jonah's protective response. He was as tall as Ray, but not as beefy. But she had no doubt that he was strong. His muscles were well defined beneath his knit shirt, and she had felt his power as she had helped him pull Amos from the pit on Eskaway.

"Like I told you," Lettie said to Ray, "I had other plans. Important plans." She turned back toward the group she had come in with, but her toothy smile was clearly for Amos. If the atmosphere had not been so tense, Dawn would have smiled when the woman winked at her grandfather.

"What? Spending the evening with a flunky of a mechanic who's an ex-con, and a skunk-lover who'd rather save animals than people?"

Dawn wished she could say something to counteract the verbal attack as Jonah flinched slightly at Ray's comment. She took a step toward the plumber, ready to interrupt if he said anything else.

"Put a lid on it, Ray," Lettie demanded, "and twist it tight." Though she was much smaller than the man, she stood defiantly in front of him, glaring up into his face.

Ray put his hands up in a gesture of retreat, though the expression on his round face was anything but contrite. "What did I do?" he said. Lettie drew her short body up to its fullest height as though preparing to air all her grievances with the man, but he did not let her finish. "Tell you what." He turned toward the teenager behind the counter who had been watching the interplay. "Give my friends here anything they want." He placed a large bill up on the counter.

"Thanks anyway." Amos grabbed for his own wallet.

"My treat," Ray insisted.

Amos pulled out some money and put it on the counter, then picked up Ray's bill and grinned. "I'm paying tonight, but we can consider this a contribution to the Haven."

Ray snatched his money back. "Not from me," he said with a snarl. Then he laughed. "You gonna put the pretend mountain lion into your shelter, Amos? What happened? Did you see a few footprints like everyone else and think you spotted a monster?"

"I know people claim to see mountain lions all the time," Amos said softly. "But I actually did."

"But it didn't attack you? Or Sherm?" Dawn saw Ray catch Lettie's gaze, then raise his own toward the ceiling as he shook his head disbelievingly. "A big wildcat just said howdy to you on the mountain? Much as I'd like to bag one as a trophy, I just gotta believe you were seeing things."

Amos shrugged. "Believe whatever you want, Ray." He didn't sound as though he cared what Ray thought.

Ray didn't seem to like that one bit. He took a step toward Amos, but Lettie moved in front of him. He peered around her at Amos with exaggerated sympathy. "I don't suppose you were drinking like poor ol' Sherm and started having hallucinations, did you?"

"Is it possible, Amos," said Lettie, "that Ray is right? That you were mistaken somehow and there wasn't a cougar?" She sounded hopeful.

"Cut it out, Ray," demanded Jonah suddenly. His hands were balled into fists at his sides. "If Amos says he saw a mountain lion, he saw it."

Ray's scornful gaze landed on Jonah. "Why should I believe him? Because a convict told me to?"

Dawn watched Jonah's eyes glint with steely anger. His strong chin lifted. "Because this *convict* saw it, too. And since you don't believe in it, then you shouldn't believe in bagging it. That animal belongs where it is, free, out on the mountain, without anyone harassing it. *Convicts* don't like anyone who messes with a fellow creature's freedom. I hope you understand what this *convict* means." Jonah did not raise his voice, but the iciness of his tone, the way he stressed the word *convict* made Dawn shudder. If Ray Koslowski had an ounce of sense, he would not doubt Jonah's sincerity. And whatever threat Jonah had implied, it would not be good for Ray.

The silence grew. Ray stared at Jonah, as though deciding whether to pick up the gauntlet that had been tossed. After a moment, he began, "I don't suppose *you* ran into Sherm up there, did you, convict? Before he died?"

Dawn interrupted. "You're right about the mountain lion, Ray. There might not be one at all."

"Really?" asked Lettie.

Not wanting the brewing argument to ignite into a fist fight, Dawn moved the topic back to the original one, ignoring the glares from Jonah and her grandfather. The important thing, after all, was to protect the mountain lion. If Ray thought it didn't exist, he wouldn't hunt it.

"In case it's really there, though," she continued, "we'll keep people informed about everything being done to find and protect it. Since you're concerned, we'll make sure someone lets you know what's going on, along with the police, the media, the Pennsylvania Game Commission, the federal Fish and Wildlife Service—all interested parties. If it exists, there'll be a lot of people interested in its welfare." And who won't like the idea of its being hunted, particularly if it's a member of an endangered species, Dawn thought.

"Yeah, right," Ray muttered. He turned his ugly

glare on Dawn this time, but she stared right back. He finally looked away. As he took a step toward Lettie, his gaze softened. "Can you join me for lunch tomorrow?" He sounded plaintive as he kept his voice low. "I'll be over at the kids' shelter in the morning finishing up that plumbing work I promised; then I thought we could grab a bite."

"Sorry, Ray. I can't make it. We have that fleet from the rental car agency coming in for tune-ups, don't we, Jonah?"

His grin suggested to Dawn that this was the first he had heard of the mass tune-up. "We sure do, Lettie," he said.

Jonah wanted to run until he dropped. He wanted to climb a mountain till his muscles ached and he was too exhausted to think. He wanted to go to a gym, take out his anger at that nasty, bigmouthed son-of-a-gun Ray Koslowski on a hard, unforgiving punching bag.

Instead, he sat placidly in Dawn's car.

He had not intended to have Dawn take him home, but it worked out that way—courtesy of his officious, unpredictable boss. Earlier, Lettie had insisted on giving Jonah a ride downtown for their "business" dinner, so his car was at home. Then, as they left the dairy shop, Lettie had told Amos that she wanted to visit his animals at the Haven that very night.

The small house Jonah rented was out in the woods. He could have walked home, of course, but it was late. And dark.

And Dawn had offered to drive him.

The inside of Dawn's compact car smelled of her: a no-nonsense scent that was light yet spicy. It felt crowded with just the two of them, yet he was not uncomfortable. In fact, despite the way his anger still swirled inside him, it was mellowing the more he sat.

He felt good—too good—being chauffeured by a beautiful woman. By *this* beautiful woman.

He had not thought, after yesterday, that he would have an opportunity to be alone with Dawn again. But they had taken a walk together after dinner—although, in downtown Eskmont, they'd not actually been alone. Now he really was alone with her. And, surprisingly, he was glad—even though it was torture. She drove him crazy. Made him lose his hard-won control.

But no matter what their differences, just being with her put ideas into his head—ideas that made parts of his body feel more cramped in his clothes than his legs did in this small car.

Dawn's soft, serious voice broke into his thoughts. "I'm sorry about tonight."

"Why? You didn't tell Koslowski to behave like such a jerk."

She sighed. "He's always a difficult person, but tonight he outdid himself. I'm not apologizing for him, though."

"What, then?"

"Lettie and Amos. They were conspiring together, although I don't understand it. There's something between them. You probably know that Lettie and Ray have been an item. But now—"

"Now her item seems to be your grandfather," he agreed with a chuckle.

"And they seemed to use us as an excuse to be together." She hesitated. "I've never seen Amos try to matchmake before. Thank heavens he's not very good at it."

He turned in the car to stare at her. "Was that what it was?"

She laughed. "You didn't notice? I didn't find Lettie or him to be particularly subtle."

103

That certainly would explain Lettie's actions. He should be furious. She had no right to interfere in his personal life.

But their relationship wasn't simply employer-employee. He owed her, big-time. And the idea of her interfering like this, with both her and Dawn's grandfather, pushing them together . . . It was annoying. Very annoying. Yet . . . intriguing.

It was impossible, though. He knew to steer clear of entanglements, especially with Dawn Perry. She wanted to save the world by caging it. And she was a lawyer. And she was judgmental.

But tonight she had run after him when he had stomped out of the restaurant. She'd confided her own emotional secrets to him. She had intervened when that piece of crud Ray Koslowski had insulted Amos and him.

Dawn had also offered him her shoulder to lean on, her ear to bend.

There were other parts of her he wished she had offered as well. He glanced at her. Now that they were on country roads outside town, she was illuminated only by the glow of the meters on the dashboard. She was lovely in that sexy, feminine outfit she had worn that night. Her soft blouse exposed her throat and enough skin around it to tantalize, without actually revealing anything. She was a gorgeous woman, period. Her long, dark hair hung straight over her shoulders. He had touched it before, by accident, so he knew how soft and silky it was.

He wondered how it would feel against his bare skin, while making love. . . .

He cleared his throat and opened the car window a little. He needed to cool off.

He directed Dawn toward his home. It was down a

long, winding driveway shared with a couple of other houses as rustic as the one he rented.

And then they were there. "It's charming!" Dawn exclaimed. "A real log cabin." He had left the small outside light on over the door, and it illuminated the house and the closest trees.

"I like it," Jonah admitted. "You should come back and see it in daylight." *Yeah, right.* Why would she want to come back to his home? And yet the thought stirred him. "There's a stream behind it. Sometimes I just take a chair outside and sit, listening to the water, the birds." Now, why had he told her that? She wouldn't—

"I love to do that, too," she said. "My grandfather's Haven is like that, with a stream nearby, and all the wonderful animals. But there are times when even that seems too . . . well, crowded. I enjoy just hiking by myself. There are some secluded woods behind my house that I particularly like."

"Maybe you and I can go on another hike together," he blurted without thinking. "When we don't have to worry about Amos." The idea of being alone in the woods with her again, at a time when she went with him voluntarily—

"We'll see." Her doubtful tone burst his bubble. Of course she would be dubious. Just because they were being thrown together by kind but crazy members of an older generation did not mean she would want to willingly do anything with him.

What *he* wanted, he realized angrily, was to get her alone, touch her, kiss her . . . make love to her.

She had gotten under his skin.

He didn't like it.

"Thanks for the ride." He knew he sounded curt and ungrateful despite his polite words. He opened the car door.

"Jonah?" Her quiet voice stopped him before he exited.

He turned back without saying a word. He could see concern in her brown eyes, reflecting the light from his cabin.

"Are you all right?"

"No," he said in a growl. And then, impulsively, he took her face in his hands, tangling his fingers in her soft, silken hair. To his own credit, he hesitated for a moment, giving her the opportunity to pull away. To slap him. To scream.

She simply sat there, her eyes watching him through thick lashes. They captivated him, sparkling in the sparse light, searching for answers he could not give.

Her lips parted slightly—and that was all it took. He bent, at the same time pulling her forward. Softly—oh, so softly—he touched her lips with his.

He groaned at the exquisite torture of the gentle contact. Slowly, he moved his bottom lip against hers, savoring the sweet abrasion.

And then he could hold back no longer. He tugged her against him, opening his mouth to kiss her deeply.

Where was the man who had shut out emotion, who had turned away from all feeling? Jonah could find him no longer, for all the sensation he had turned from forever was there, in that kiss. He smelled her faint spicy scent. He tasted the deliciousness of ice cream and Dawn herself upon her lips. He heard her quiet moaning, felt the softness of her breasts crushed against him in the confines of the car, her sweet, sweet lips on his, her tongue touching his. He opened his eyes, but only briefly.

How long did it last? He had no sense of the passage of time, but that kiss was both swift and infinite.

And over much too soon.

And when it was, he wanted to stalk from the car, frenzied from the unwelcome passion it had stoked within him.

He wanted to stay, forever.

He wanted to apologize. No, to demand more. To—

He had no opportunity to decide, for Dawn looked at him with those beautiful eyes in the dim light. They were glazed—did she feel the passion, too? Her eyes were confused.

But they were not angry. "I—Thank you for the evening, Jonah," she whispered. "I'd better get home now."

With that, he slipped out of the car.

Chapter Seven

She was uneasy, this newcomer to the mountain. There was much activity there, where she wandered the woods to hunt. At times, the stalker felt like the stalked.

Already, she had had to abandon a substantial kill. To return to it would have meant drawing close to an area of danger.

Danger. Crouching on a rocky ledge, she felt the cool hardness of stone beneath the sensitive pads of her feet and along her belly. She listened. She swept the forest below with her keen vision. The fur on her back bristled.

Dangerous were these creatures who swarmed her territory.

She would do what she must to protect herself. To remain free and able to hunt the breadth of her territory. To feed.

And yet, there were those among the dangerous intruders that did not threaten. Those beings exuded peace and curiosity instead of fear and hostility.

With them there was a kinship, an urge, a need for contact.

For now, she moved on. Hunting. Searching. Protecting.

She had to survive.

The parking lot at the base of Eskaway was empty early in the morning. *Good!* Dawn smiled grimly as she parked her car and got out. The last thing she wanted was to run into Clemson or one of his investigators—or anyone else, for that matter.

She needed to be alone.

She also needed to hike. To force her legs to carry her along the steepest mountain trails, to work off all that damned excess energy that made her feel as though every drop of her blood had turned into adrenaline.

Shielding her eyes against the surprisingly bright sun of early morning, she looked up. The thickly forested slopes were blanketed mostly with the brilliant new-leaf green of spring. Two Cooper's hawks circled lazily, taking advantage of an updraft.

Dawn did not watch for long. Her legs already marched in place. She had to move.

Although the spring day was warm enough for her to feel comfortable in her blue Penn State T-shirt, the mountainside woods, with all their shade, could get chilly. She knotted the sleeves of her windbreaker around her waist. Then she slipped her lightly filled backpack over her shoulders, locked her car, and strode toward the path.

Where had all her energy come from? She had hardly slept the night before.

Her mind had kept returning to Jonah Campion.

"Oh, Grandpa, what were you trying to do last night?" she whispered aloud. As if she didn't know. He had been attempting to matchmake—for the first time ever. And of all people—to put her together with an ex-con, and one who'd made it clear he would oppose them in the attempt to save an endangered creature. "Why, Grandpa?" she asked as she tromped along the path rising through the woods.

She knew, of course: his damned family fairy tale. That was why her grandfather was all moony-eyed over Lettie Green, too. He had seen a mountain lion, here on Eskaway. He believed now, for the first time, that he was capable of finding true love.

The legend. When Amos told it, with the faraway look in his sharp but wistful eyes, his voice low and hypnotic, she could almost believe in it.

It had to do with one of their ancestors—an Indian princess who had walked these very slopes of Eskaway. Treading a little more slowly, Dawn looked around the trees, the path, trying to see the story through her mythical ancestress's eyes.

In Amos's tale, the Indian princess, whose name was Esk-a-na, had had a lover whose name Dawn could not remember, except that it translated as Lion Slayer. Lion Slayer was as brave as the mountain lion that he hunted. He got into an argument with Esk-a-na's family when he could not afford to pay enough for her hand in marriage. When he died at the hands of her own father on the slope of a mountain, Esk-a-na was so devastated that she wept and foretold that mountain lions would vanish from the area, and until their return no one in her family would find happiness in love.

Dawn reached a fork along the main path and turned right onto the narrower, less traveled trail. Her vision blurred as she pictured Esk-a-na here, in the woods, on her knees over the body of her slain lover, crying out the curse.

According to Amos, Esk-a-na later married the man her father chose for her and had a few kids before the cowardly brave beat her to death. Her mother turned her father out of their lodge in anger at what he had done to their only child. Hence, the Wilton ancestors' disastrous relationships.

"More power to you, Grandpa," Dawn said with a shake of her head. "But leave me out of your legend."

He had reminded her of it nevertheless. Which made her actions the previous night with Jonah Campion all the more inexcusable.

She bent her arms, pumped them at her sides. She took on an uphill pace that punished legs already sore from having spent so much time on Eskaway two days earlier. Keeping her breathing slow and deep at first, she inhaled the damp, pungent scents of the springtime forest. She barely noted the few hemlocks and pines she passed, or the abundant beeches, oaks and maples.

The earthen trail was still muddy from the rain two days earlier, causing her footsteps to sound mushy instead of hard. The overhanging trees held out the sun, held in the moisture.

It was a day much like the one when she had been up here on the slopes of Eskaway with Jonah.

Jonah. The log cabin he rented looked like him: remote and rugged.

She'd had no choice last night but to drive him home. But to have allowed him to touch her, to kiss her, was unforgivable.

And unforgettable.

She had replayed the scene all night, closing her eyes as she lay alone in her bed, between sheets that her own body never seemed to warm.

111

She felt again his lips meeting hers, so softly that he had caught her off guard.

Her breathing speeded up now as her heart rate accelerated. It was from her uphill exertion, and that was all—so she told herself. Yet here, where she'd hoped her mind would empty of all thoughts as she hiked through the forest, she kept recalling that kiss.

The man had been a convict. He looked large and rough; he acted tough and angry. Now he was a mechanic. He worked with the strength of his hands.

And yet his kiss had, at first, been gentle.

If he had come on strong, she would have resisted. Ordered him out of her car.

But only after she'd responded had he deepened the kiss.

It had felt wonderful. So different from anything she'd ever experienced. It had sent currents of something unfamiliar thrumming unevenly through her, sharp yet sweet and altogether too breathtaking. Areas within her that she barely thought of as having sensation suddenly burst into life, as though spring had just arrived and her body had begun to blossom.

And yet Jonah had barely touched her. Thank heavens they had been in her car. Thank heavens there had been no room for anything more, for if there had been . . .

If he had invited her into his house, she would have come to her senses all the more quickly.

Wouldn't she? Of course. She couldn't—she wouldn't—forget Billy. She needed no other man in her life. No more loss. No more hurt.

Lost in her thoughts, her breathing quick but still even, she stopped abruptly as a wild turkey emerged from behind a tree. "Oh!" she exclaimed. It must have been as startled as she, for it hurried out of her way.

She had come quite a distance. Starting off again,

she noticed a trail off to the right that she did not remember. That way, she told herself.

After a while, it led to another face of the mountain. Among the trees, rocks lined the path on both sides, and around them were strewn fallen, rotting logs. A thick green carpet of moss and lichen covered most of them. It was a beautiful area, where the path still rose, but at a gentler angle. It was easy to traverse at the brisk pace Dawn maintained.

By then, her attempt at controlling her breathing had evaporated in the thinning mountain air, and she inhaled and exhaled more rapidly. She glanced at her watch. Nearly an hour had passed already.

Soon she would have to start down again. It was a workday, and she had already spent too much time out of the office this week. Her partner Marnie would not be pleased if she were totally unproductive.

But for now, she still needed to climb. She had to follow this path that lured her onward, higher, as the terrain grew rockier, craggier.

She needed to discipline herself, so her mind would stop wandering onto thoughts she had forbidden. Thoughts of Jonah Campion, and—

She stopped, startled, yet somehow unsurprised. She drew in a breath, even as she tried not to breathe, not to make a sound.

For on a ledge, not very far above her, she saw . . .

The mountain lion.

It crouched, watching her as she watched it: warily, yet with interest.

Dawn did not feel frightened. Despite the animal's taut position, she had no inkling that it meant her any harm.

Instead, it stared at her with keen amber-green eyes, and there was intelligence behind them. Dawn had an impression, somehow, that the animal attempted to impart a message.

Ridiculous. But she recalled Jonah's claim that the cougar had in some manner communicated to him the need to follow. To use its guidance, its direction, to search for Amos.

Only then had they found him.

"Hello," Dawn whispered, oh, so softly. Would her speech scare it away?

Its pointed, upright ears twitched.

The animal was soft, tawny brown, but Dawn was near enough to see the slate gray tips to its hair, even on its face. If it moved, its color would change in the light. Dawn had read that, once, about cougars.

Its face was exquisitely feline, with a pink nose underscored by white fur, and long, dark whiskers. Oh, but it was not a sweet, soft house cat; its thick muzzle suggested the power and ferocity in its jaws.

"Where are you from?" Dawn allowed her voice to rise above a murmur. "Why are you here, on Eskaway?" She did not, of course, expect an answer.

The cougar, long limbed and lanky, rose to a sitting position. Its pink tongue emerged from its mouth, and it lifted one large paw to lick it.

The animal obviously wasn't afraid of her, Dawn thought, any more than she was afraid of it.

Amazing, she thought, to be faced by a wild animal and have no fear that it would harm her.

Or maybe not so amazing . . .

An urge came over Dawn—absurd but compelling. She had to ask, though she would get—could get—no answer. "My grandfather's legend," she began in a conversational tone she would use with a person. "I don't believe in it, of course, but is that why you've come? So someone in our family can finally find true love? If the legend is real—well, I'm all for Amos finding happiness in his old age. He's known Lettie all his life, and suddenly he's interested in her."

The cougar stared, its gaze strangely penetrating, as though it meant to pick apart what Dawn said.

"What?" Dawn's voice was suddenly hoarse. "Do you have something to say?" She wanted to laugh at herself, for the words sounded so bizarre. And yet . . . "I understand now how Jonah felt." She was whispering again. "He said there was something between you. Jonah—"

Jonah. The mountain lion's ears twitched again at his name.

For a moment, Dawn rehashed in her mind her grandfather's legend. She looked at the cougar. Her mind raced to thoughts of last night. Of Jonah.

Oh, no, she told herself fiercely. No way was she going to read something into her grandfather's stupid old story. It had nothing to do with her. She'd had love and lost it. All she felt toward Jonah Campion, if anything, was lust.

She realized she had been glaring at the mountain lion. She shook her head sharply.

At that, the big cat rose and looked over Dawn's head. It surveyed the rocks around them, the mountain below, as though observing its domain.

And then, with a cougar's distinctive snarling scream, it turned, leaped off among the overhanging rocks and disappeared.

"Wait!" Dawn called. Suddenly she felt very, very alone.

Not that she put credence into her odd feelings. Any of them.

The animal had meant her no harm, but that was the only communication between them.

It did not want to impart to her any information—despite her eerie impression that it did.

It had no interest in her family legend. No interest in Jonah, or her—or in anything, except—

"Freedom," Dawn murmured. "I should have asked it, the way Jonah said." Would the cougar value freedom over safety? Or safety over freedom?

She laughed aloud ruefully. Oh, was she a dreamer today! As though the animal could have understood anything she said.

She knew the answer anyway. She sensed the wildness, the need in this cougar to be free. Jonah was right. To cage such a beautiful, wild and proud animal would be a terrible shame.

But it was a shame it might have to live with. And survival was the most important thing. She could sense that the animal was driven to live.

If only . . . if only it could have both.

Dawn looked back at the ledge. She studied the rocks around it. The mountain lion was definitely gone.

And it was time for her to go, too. To return to her world, at the base of the mountain.

"Damn and double damn!" shouted Amos into the phone.

"Look," Clemson said. "I called to tell you what was going on, but if you're going to make trouble, don't bother coming tonight."

Standing in his kitchen, Amos was glad his telephone was attached to the wall. Otherwise, he might have picked it up and hurled it across the room. "Who, me? Make trouble?" He made his voice sound as sweet as molasses pie.

Clemson snorted. "I've got to go. I've an accident report to write up. But like I said, the coroner's report on Sherm is in, and I want to make a presentation at the town meeting tonight. To try to defuse the situation. Everyone is invited, but I particularly thought you would want to be there."

"I do." Amos kept his tone calm despite the way his fist clenched so tight he could feel his short nails dig into his skin. "I appreciate your calling, Clem."

"You'll let Dawn know?" Clemson asked.

"I sure will," Amos agreed.

Dawn was not pleased, when she reached the bottom of the mountain, to see a puddle of something viscous and gleaming oozing from beneath her car. What was it? Oil? Brake fluid?

How should she know? She wasn't an expert.

But she knew who was.

With a sigh, she got in and drove slowly toward Lettie's, watching the gauges to make sure the vehicle didn't show signs of overheating or engine failure or something equally dire.

She felt like hitting something. It wasn't fair that her memories of that wondrous moment with the cougar should be spoiled by something as mundane as car trouble.

And now she might have to face Jonah, too.

Maybe he would be off today, and she would not have to face him. And the legend wasn't real, she told herself. It never had been. It had nothing to do with her.

Jonah and she had made a mistake last night, with that kiss. She just wanted to put it behind her, forget about it. Surely he felt the same way.

He was there, of course. And Dawn saw no sign of Lettie.

Jonah spotted her, too, as she pulled into the parking area just outside Lettie's three service bays.

The look he gave her was wary but not unfriendly. He approached, wiping his hands on a stained red rag.

The short sleeves of his T-shirt were rolled all the way up to his shoulders, exposing the entirety of his substantial biceps. She forced her gaze from his arms to his much-too-good-looking face. His tawny hair spilled over his forehead.

"Hello, Dawn." He spoke so huskily that she could not help remembering their last meeting, despite all her best intentions. "So, to what do we owe the honor of this visit?"

Flustered by her own thoughts, she blurted, "I have a car problem. Why else would I be here?"

His mouth opened as though he were readying an angry retort. Was he going to say something about last night? She found herself worrying her bottom lip with her teeth. Because the gesture reminded her even more of how his kiss had felt, she stopped immediately.

But his face changed into his familiar stony expression. "Why else indeed?" he asked icily. "What's wrong with your car?"

Bracing herself with a deep breath, she described the puddle she had found, and he quizzed her about other symptoms. "It's driving fine," she said. She looked around for moral support but saw neither Lettie nor Fisk. Perhaps they were in the office.

"You didn't have the air conditioner on, did you? It couldn't just have been condensation?"

"It may be spring," she said, "but it's not warm enough for air-conditioning."

"All right," Jonah said. "Leave it here. I'll check it out and let you know what I find."

As he turned away, Dawn had an urge to call him back, to tell him of her experience just now on Eskaway. Her amazing meeting with the mountain lion. Her feelings of connection . . .

It wasn't that she wanted to relate it to Jonah, she

told herself. She simply wanted to share the story with someone—someone who wouldn't laugh at her.

She would wait and tell Amos.

Just then, Lettie appeared from the door to the office, her short red curls bouncing as she walked. She was dressed in blue jeans and a plaid shirt, and she had a grim expression on her wrinkled face. "Ah, Dawn. Glad you're here. Amos just phoned. He left word at your office, too. There's a town meeting tonight. Clemson called it, and he wants you there. We'll be there, too, Jonah." She looked at her employee, and Dawn could tell that she had just issued an order.

Jonah did not seem to her the sort of person who took orders well. She expected him to protest.

But he didn't. "Fine, Lettie," he said mildly.

"Any idea what it's about?" Dawn asked.

"Nothing good, I'm afraid," Lettie replied.

"Well, drat it all, and most especially my conniving buddy Ray Koslowski," Lettie whispered to Amos later that evening. She had donned a skirt and blouse for the momentous occasion of the latest town meeting. And the evening with Amos.

Now she sat beside Amos in the skinny, graffiti-scratched seats of the high school auditorium, listening to Clemson, Ray and others jabber away.

At Amos's side was Dawn. Lettie had made certain that the only available seat with them was at Dawn's other side. That was where she'd directed Jonah to sit. And her big, handsome, ex-con employee always listened to her.

She got a kick out of that kind of power. A big kick, bigger than figuring out what was wrong with a sick car and setting it straight.

But she also liked Jonah. She believed in the guy.

And Amos and she had big plans for Jonah and

Dawn. Together. Though maybe the two kids didn't need too high a flame lit under them. Oh, no. Looked like they were ready to start a major forest fire all by themselves.

She grinned for a moment, then scowled again as she watched Ray with his group of hunting pals. Her dear, departed Arnie had been part of the same group. That was why she'd started seeing Ray after Arnie was gone. They were involved with some of the same charities, too. For a guy who was such a skunk with people so often, Ray was generous with his time, donating lots of work to the needy. Plus, when he wanted to be, the guy could be a perfect gentleman. He was good company, too. When he wasn't being nasty, that was. And Lettie wasn't about to let him parade his faults in front of her without telling him all about them.

She'd have liked to tell him off. That danged porcupine of a plumber was causing trouble, and it riled her.

She had never been one for understatement. Not her. But when she had told Dawn and Jonah that the meeting tonight would be about nothing good, that had sure been one puny understatement about the nastiness that was really going on here. And it was all thanks to Ray. Why didn't he just go fix a pauper's pipes and leave animals to the people who didn't get their kicks from shooting 'em?

"Maybe I should go over there and give him whatfor," she grumbled into Amos's ear.

"It's okay, hon," said Amos. He touched her arm and gave her a big wink.

Lettie couldn't help giving him a teensy smile. Just like that, he'd soothed some of her irritation. Her pulse rate sped up anyway, thanks to his flirtatiousness.

He was a nice man, was Amos Wilton. She had always known it. She'd known him since they were kids. But he had gone off to veterinary school, and she had married Arnie Green. She'd outlasted Arnie, too, and inherited the garage. Amos had also married, couple of times. Then Ray and she had started having dinner together now and then. And then more frequently, until it had become a habit.

Yeah, like a pair of old shoes with a hole in the sole.

Only in the last week or two, she'd noticed Amos again. And he had noticed her. She still wondered why he'd caught her attention right then, after all these years.

And why she hadn't really noticed him in that way before.

Tonight he looked especially handsome in a blue denim shirt, his white hair neatly parted and combed. Sure, his face looked like a city road map now, with all its deep lines. Whose didn't? They weren't kids anymore. But his wrinkles lent him a lot of character. She liked the openness of his broad features, the way his eyes twinkled.

And that wasn't all she liked about him. Who'd have thought that a couple of old fools like them could have had so much fun flirting? And playing touchy-feely games, just like the pair of them were kids who'd just discovered sex.

Oh, yes, she enjoyed being with Amos. Ray and she were just old friends who liked to quarrel a lot. At least that was the way she saw it.

But that could be part of the problem. Drat that Ray! He was trying to get even by making a big stink about something darned important to Amos: that mountain lion.

Not that she was happy that the critter had shown up here. They could be danged dangerous. But as long as this one hadn't killed Sherm, as long as it didn't hurt anyone else—well, live and let live, she always said. She would try to support sweet Amos and his caring for the cougar.

And if Ray did anything really nasty, Lettie would give the big oaf a piece of her mind.

Just try it, Ray Koslowski, she thought. *Just try it.*

Dawn felt the tension in the air in the auditorium as Clemson remained at the podium. He had given the results of the report on what had happened to Sherm Patterson, and it had not satisfied the people of Eskmont.

Clemson waited at the microphone until the ear-splitting sound of feedback subsided before answering the pending question. "Like I said before, the coroner sent me a copy of Sherm's autopsy. There's nothing conclusive about what killed the poor guy, but it was clear his body had been . . . well, out in the elements for a week or better. It had started to decompose. And in the woods, it wasn't any big surprise that some critters had begun to gnaw on him. But there was no indication of any bullet wound or trauma to show any foul play."

Good, Dawn thought, with a sideways glance at the stoic Jonah. That should quiet the people who had thought to blame him for Sherm's death.

"And there weren't any big teeth marks, either," Clemson continued. "Nothing at all to suggest that the cougar got him."

Good for the cougar, too. There was simply no evidence of foul play from any source.

But that didn't stop Ray Koslowski, who stood and strode onto the bare stage. He was a lot taller than the kind, rodent-faced Clemson. Heftier, too, and his pudgy cheeks were puffed out in what appeared to be indignation. But fortunately, Dawn thought, Clemson wasn't intimidated easily. He was the local police chief, and he had no trouble asserting his authority.

For the moment, though, he let Ray have the microphone. "If it wasn't a person—which I'm not so sure about—then it had to be something else. I think it was the cougar."

A rumble of outraged voices began calling from the audience, agreeing with Ray. He was playing to the crowd, and to the media. He had shills here who supported everything he said—his regular hunting crowd, as far as Dawn could tell: Syd Cornelius, Larry Frost and the others.

"We don't need proof it didn't kill Sherm," Clemson argued. "But we would need proof that it *did* before we'd try to get the animal-control people after it."

"You'd rather wait till it kills someone else?" Ray said incredulously. "And what about our area farmers? All their livestock is in danger from this wildcat."

There was another set of supportive hollers from the audience. Dawn noticed some movement out of the corner of her eye. Lettie, looking irritated, had begun to stand.

Amos patted her hand. "It's okay; my turn now." She glared but sat again as Amos rose. "Hey, Ray," he called. "Have you ever ripped out someone's perfectly good water heater just because it was getting old?"

"Well—" the plumber began.

"Don't imagine your customers would like to hear that you cost them that kind of money just because something *might* go wrong, would they?" Amos looked around the audience.

"No way!" shouted Slim Evans. He was Amos's close friend. But others took up the cry, too. Sure enough, Amos got the support he asked for. No one liked the idea of paying for something if it wasn't needed.

"This mountain lion's the same way," Amos continued. "All we need to do is warn everyone it's here, that it could cause trouble if you're not careful to keep an eye out for it. Make sure parents watch their kids up on Eskaway, that farmers keep close tabs on their stock, that kind of thing. If the cougar ever does anything it shouldn't, that's the time to consider having it dealt with. After all, a couple of us have come face-to-face with it, and it hasn't been aggressive at all."

More than a couple of people now, Dawn thought, remembering her own encounter with the beast.

The experience was too personal, though, for her to stand up in front of this crowd to tell her wonderful tale. She'd relate it if she thought it would change anyone's mind about the animal. But sides had clearly been taken already on this emotionally charged issue.

"That's telling him, Amos," Lettie whispered, clapping her hands. Applauding along with her, Dawn had never liked the opinionated old woman more.

The resultant rumblings in the audience, led again by Slim, were mostly in favor of what Amos had said.

"I saw evidence of that big cat first," Slim said with pride.

"It's kind of nice that we've got a cougar back here," said Cissy Calvin, a new high school science teacher fresh out of college. "The area's ecology may be changing for the better."

"Maybe word'll get out, and it'll bring tourists," said Tom Carter, one of Amos's stand-in assistants. He was a chubby young man whose father was one of the oldest members of the Eskmont Chamber of Commerce.

"Foolishness!" thundered Ray from the podium. But before he could say anything else, Clemson took the microphone.

"That's the way it'll be for now," the police chief said, glaring at Ray. "I've checked with a buddy on the Pennsylvania Game Commission. He said cougars aren't protected under state law, since there aren't any in this state." The audience laughed. "But this cat might be protected under federal law, so for now, we'll just keep an eye on things. We'll keep everything nice and peaceful, and let that old cougar who's come to visit just be. Won't we, Ray?"

Ray didn't answer. Dawn wasn't surprised; the overbearing plumber obviously didn't like the way things had gone. This would not be the end of it.

As the crowd dispersed, Dawn picked up her russet corduroy jacket from the back of her chair. Before she could put it on, though, Jonah took it from her, holding it so she could put her arms in the sleeves.

She felt him squeeze her shoulders through the jacket as he adjusted it over her back. For a moment she closed her eyes, enjoying the brief contact. "Thanks," she murmured.

She stepped into the aisle to let the others from her row exit. Jonah remained beside her. He looked great that evening, in a Western-style white shirt with a yoke and black buttons. His light brown hair was combed, but that errant lock in the front threatened to spill onto his forehead.

Amos passed first, then Lettie. The two were engrossed in conversation and looked only at one another.

As they stood to the side, Dawn noticed suspicious, sidelong glances being hurled at Jonah by some of the townsfolk.

"How do they know for sure Sherm wasn't murdered by a human?" she heard one of the farmers say. The man didn't bother to lower his voice as he glared at Jonah. "When someone's been out there that long, it's not easy to tell just what happened."

"Yeah," agreed his companion. "And once a fellow's

been to prison . . ." He left the rest of his thought unspoken as the two strolled away.

Hadn't they listened to Clemson? Dawn looked at Jonah. His jaw was set, his expression furious, but he didn't say anything to these new accusers. He simply stood stiffly, fists clenched, until the crowd had thinned.

"Interesting, isn't it, how the appearance of one animal can cause so much disagreement," he finally said, his tone raw but controlled.

Dawn knew he had decided to pretend those comments hadn't been made. She knew, too, that he was talking not only about the crowd, but about his argument with Amos and her.

She also realized that she wanted to tell Jonah, even more than she wanted to tell Amos, about her sighting of the cougar that afternoon, and how it had made her feel.

"Amazing what just one animal can cause," she agreed. She touched his arm. "Jonah, I'd like to talk to you. Something happened today that—"

"Come on, you two." It was Amos. He stood at the front of the quickly clearing aisle. Lettie was beside him. "We're going for coffee, and we need a couple of chaperones." He looked down at Lettie, and Dawn was certain that the older woman she had always thought of as brash and outspoken was blushing.

Blushing? How adorable! Dawn thought. Could it be that Amos and Lettie had something going besides companionship?

"We'll talk later," Jonah said into her ear, his low, vibrant voice causing her body to hum like the string of a bass guitar. It sounded like a promise. One she wasn't certain she wanted him to keep.

Maybe there should be safety in numbers when she told her story.

Chapter Eight

Damn this narrow-minded small town, Jonah thought as he followed Dawn outside. It didn't matter, once again, that there was no evidence against him. Some people had convicted him, just because he was a stranger, he was an ex-con, and he was here.

Others reacted toward the mountain lion in the same way.

It was no wonder he had felt such an affinity for the animal when he'd seen it on the mountain. They had a lot in common.

He walked slowly through the high school parking lot with Dawn at his side. In front were Amos and Lettie, strolling hand in hand like a couple of kids. The sodium lamps bathed them in illumination almost strong enough to be daylight.

Calm down, he ordered himself. There were people here who didn't accuse him. Lettie, for one. He had to

Linda O. Johnston

shrug it off, just as he had learned to shrug off so much more.

For now, he had to concentrate on what was right in his life. He was free. He was walking beside the most beautiful woman he had ever met.

If it hadn't been so bright, maybe he would have gotten the nerve to take Dawn's hand as well. Perhaps she would have let him, despite the crowd around them pouring into their cars, if she had thought no one could see.

She had let him take her hand on the mountain. She had let him kiss her the night before.

Yeah, then pretended the next day that it hadn't happened. She'd treated him as though the only contact he'd had with her was as her mechanic. What did he expect from a lawyer?

Damn! Once more his temper flared. He determinedly got it in check.

He recalled that, in the auditorium, Dawn had seemed eager to tell him something.

And he wanted to hear it. He had meant it when he said they would talk later. He would find a time to get her alone. He would listen. Then, if they were really alone, maybe he could take her into his arms, kiss her again till she was senseless, then dare her to pretend it was a figment of her imagination.

Brave—and stupid—ex-con that he was.

They reached Amos's truck first. Only three would fit into it. Jonah's car was in the next row. "I guess we're off to the diner again," he said to Dawn. "How about if I drive you there?"

She opened her mouth as though to protest. He grinned despite himself. She never gave up being argumentative. She would probably disagree with him if he told her the exact time—even if it was information from her own wristwatch.

Why did he find her contentiousness so appealing? Could it be the way her eyes glistened, the way her lower lip stuck out so appetizingly . . . ?

He couldn't help it. "If I drive, it'll be your turn to kiss me," he teased under his breath, so Amos couldn't hear. Lettie had already climbed into Amos's truck. "That's the passenger's toll, isn't it?"

He expected her to explode, but she did the unexpected—and he liked it even better. She laughed. "Maybe this passenger can just pay for coffee."

"It's a deal," he agreed, then called to Amos, "See you there." So what if the lights were bright? He slipped his arm around her shoulders as they strolled toward his car. She didn't pull away. He drew her even closer.

He particularly liked it when she matched her pace to his so that their hips swayed together. As though they were joined.

An image of them truly joined, naked in his bed, passed through his mind, and he nearly missed a step, throwing their lockstep off. "Sorry," he mumbled. They had reached his car, and he had to let go to open the door for her.

His body felt miserably alone during those few solitary strides to the driver's door.

The Eskmont Diner was crowded with familiar faces. It seemed that half the people who had been to the town hall meeting had decided to go to the diner afterward.

"There's a place." She pointed to a booth just being vacated, at the far side from where they'd sat the last time. Had it been only the night before? A lot had happened since then.

Dawn had been pressed against Jonah as they had walked through the high school parking lot. The feelings that had been engendered in her were nearly as fiery as those she had felt during their kiss the night before. What was it about this man, this ex-con whom she should avoid like the proverbial plague, that made her want to be close to him?

She'd be close to him now, too. The only empty place in the diner was one of its smallest booths. Amos and Lettie didn't seem to mind; he put his arm around her as they squeezed in together.

Dawn could ask for a chair at the end of the booth. But the aisle was narrow. She would only get in the way.

"Are you comfortable?" she asked Jonah as he slid in beside her, hoping, since he was a lot larger than the rest of them, that he would complain. Then they'd have to wait for a larger table.

"This is just fine." He fitted his hip tightly against hers. Though she was five foot eight, he was so much taller that she could have rested her head against his shoulder.

Was it the crowd of people that made the diner seem so crazily warm all of a sudden? Or was it the delightful crowding of Jonah against her in this booth?

They ordered coffee for four and two pieces of apple pie to split. Then Dawn was prepared to tell the amazing thing that had happened to her since the previous night. She could not keep it to herself any longer.

"I saw the mountain lion today," she announced softly, so only those at her table could hear.

"Really? Where? How?" Her grandfather half-stood with excitement, squeezing Lettie into the side of the booth.

"Sssh," she replied with a laugh. "I'm not ready to share it with anyone but you. Yes, I really saw it. Up on Eskaway. It was an amazing experience, and—"

"What were you doing up there?" Jonah asked, his voice low. "Were you with any of the investigation team?"

She knew, from his ominous expression, that what he actually wanted to know was if she had been alone. "No," she said lightly. "I took a hike up there on my own." *To try to escape recollections of that little kiss you gave me last night*, she thought as she glared back at him. *The one that nearly incinerated my insides*.

"After Amos's incident, and what happened to Sherm, I would have thought you would know better than to go by yourself," Jonah said. "You could have fallen into a pit. Or worse."

"You're too new to these parts to understand." She knew her voice was testy. "I've hiked on Eskaway since I was a kid." What right did he have to tell her what to do? To worry about her . . . ?

"Children, let's get back to the subject," demanded Lettie. "Don't know about the rest of you, but I want to know all about Dawn and that mountain lion. Where was it? What did it do?"

Grateful for once for Lettie's straightforwardness, Dawn meekly obeyed and told her story—at least how she had spotted the cougar, observed it, then saw it spring away. She did not attempt to relate where her imagination had strayed: how she had felt a connection with the animal, as Jonah had mentioned. And how she could not help but think of Amos's quaint family fairy tale, and wonder, as she thought of Jonah, if there was a grain of truth to it.

"How did it make you feel, Granddaughter, to see that magnificent beast?" Light glowed in Amos's brown eyes again, and he looked the way Susie had described him: as though he had seen a stairway from heaven. "When it stared at me, down in that pit, I was enthralled: a wonderful, welcome stranger to our mountain. . . . I felt as though I had been handed a special gift."

Dawn looked at Jonah. "Is that the way you felt, too?"

His smile was genuine. It lit his entire face and made Dawn want to grin in return. "I could not have phrased it so eloquently, but yes. And you? What did you feel?"

Dawn bit her lower lip. There were too many things she did not want to say. She began, "I'm not sure I can describe how I felt. It was . . . well, personal. But I was struck by the beauty and power of the animal. The way it looked at me as though we both were just as significant in the scheme of things—not like I was food, or an enemy, but an equal." She hesitated. "It was wonderful. And I remembered then what you had said, Jonah." She took a sip of coffee, her eyes on the man beside her.

"What?" he asked softly. For a moment, Dawn felt as though they were alone in the room, talking only to one another. She had an urge to stroke his rough cheek, to smooth away the furrows that pain, and life, had dug next to his mouth.

"That I should ask the mountain lion its opinion. Of whether it wanted to remain free."

"What was its answer?" A muscle worked in Jonah's throat, and Dawn knew her response was important to him.

"Yes," she replied. "That animal did want to be free. It *needed* to be free."

Jonah straightened. She was certain he searched for words to express his pleasure that they were in agreement.

They weren't, though. Not entirely. "But there was more." She braced herself against the argument she knew would come. "I had a feeling somehow that, no

132

matter what, life was important to it. That the most important thing of all was survival."

She sensed, rather than saw, Jonah's tension. "More important than freedom? You can't be sure that's what it wants. It's what *you* want." His voice was tight, and he took a swig of coffee.

Dawn sighed. She did not want to oppose him, but their disagreement seemed insurmountable. "In a perfect world, it could have both: freedom and survival. That's what I'd wish for it. But you were there tonight, Jonah. You saw those rabid animal-haters like Ray Koslowski, and the farmers worried about their livestock. The law be damned; they'll be after the cougar as soon as they can. I only hope it will survive long enough for Amos and me to get permission to place it in the Haven."

"Then even after seeing the mountain lion out in the wild, you're going through with your scheme to cage it?" Jonah barely spoke above a whisper, but Dawn felt as though he screamed at her. His eyes blazed with fury, and his large hand, clenched around his coffee mug, appeared about to crush it. If she were on the outside of the booth's bench, she would leave, escape from the tension at this table.

"Yes," she said calmly, hoping that he would somehow see through his emotion to her perfectly rational argument.

But he didn't. "Excuse me," he said through gritted teeth and began to stand.

"No, excuse us," Amos said, rising and helping Lettie out of the booth. "We have a big night ahead. We're going dancing."

Lettie looked at him for a moment as though he had suddenly lost his mind, then grinned. "Yeah, I guess we are. Don't know when we'll be back."

"Dawn, call the Haven for me before you go home."

Amos handed her some change. "Make sure from Susie that everything is all right. Jonah, I'm trusting you to get her home safely. Don't send any search parties for us this time; I'm not sure where the nearest place is where we can dance all night, but we'll find one. Good night, children."

Then they were gone, leaving Jonah and Dawn alone together at the table. Dawn's car was still at Lettie's shop. She was at Jonah's mercy.

No. She would never be at his mercy. "Look," she said, "I see a lot of people here that I know. I can grab a ride home. You don't need to—"

"You were entrusted to my care." He did not sound at all pleased. "Let's finish our coffee; then you can make your call."

Dawn had to hand it to him; he made a tremendous effort to be calm and cordial. He finished their entire slice of pie, praising its delicious taste both to her and to their waitress. Dawn had lost her appetite.

But then they had no reason to sit in the thinning crowd any longer. It was time to go.

"I'd better make my phone call," Dawn said. Jonah let her out of the booth, and she headed for the pay phone.

She should have guessed, when she got Susie on the phone, what the outcome would be. "Oh, Dawn, thank heavens you called!" Amos's assistant sounded frantic. "I thought your grandfather would be home long before now. I called the high school, and the custodian said the town meeting adjourned an hour ago. Dawn, can you get Amos here quickly? Someone brought a fawn in. It's been hit by a car, and it needs help right away."

Of course Dawn could not locate Amos. And of course Susie had tried calling the Haven's vet, but he was off

134

on a house call. Not even Amos's other primary assistant, Tom Carter, was available.

That was why Dawn had insisted that Jonah take her to her grandfather's animal sanctuary.

"I'm not sure what I can do," Dawn said. "Maybe just give Susie and the fawn moral support until Doc Knerr arrives. Amos had veterinary training, too, you know; that's how he came to run the Haven."

"No, I didn't know," Jonah said. "Did Susie say how badly the fawn was injured?"

"No. I don't think she could tell."

They arrived at the Haven ten minutes later. Jonah had broken more than one traffic law to get her there in a hurry, and she was grateful.

As soon as he parked his car, Dawn raced into the house. She found Susie on the kitchen floor, cradling an animal in a blanket. The room was filled with the metallic odor of the blood soaked into the covering.

Susie's long, yellow hair was caught up behind her head with a clip, and her eyes were wet from crying. "I don't know how to help," she said with a sob. "This little guy is breathing so slowly; he's hardly moving. He's got a big gash on his leg, too. I've tried to stop the bleeding and keep him warm, but—"

"You're doing just fine." Dawn knelt beside Susie. To her surprise, Jonah was right beside her. He had taken off his shirt, and his V-necked white T-shirt revealed a smattering of tawny chest hair.

He unwrapped the blanket from around the young deer. It eyed him listlessly, obviously too hurt to flee. Jonah removed a lump of bloody cotton from the animal's flank to reveal a long cut. The wound was still bleeding.

"He's in shock," Jonah said. "Get me some more blankets, will you, Susie, and some soft, clean rags. And how about mixing up a little sugar water. Oh, and

135

Linda O. Johnston

I'll need a needle and some white thread, if you have it, and antiseptic. If you have anything especially for animals, that's best, but something for people will do, too. I've no idea what other medicinal supplies you have here for the animals, but a topical anesthetic would help, too."

Dawn looked at him in amazement. "How do you—"

He did not let her finish. "I don't know how quick a deer's pulse is supposed to be, but it seems fast to me. Let's keep him calm. Will you help?"

"Of course, Doctor," Dawn said, but the sarcasm she had tried for disintegrated when she saw a look of fury pass over his face. "Here." She took the fawn and cradled it on her lap. It struggled, but only a little.

Susie returned with some of what Jonah had requested. Quickly, he took the clean rags and swabbed the seeping blood from the fawn's leg. "You did a good job of stanching the flow of blood, Susie," Jonah said. She gave him a grateful smile.

"Dawn, give him a little sugar water now," he said. "That will get his blood glucose level up a bit." She complied. Fortunately, the animal seemed to like the sweet mixture and allowed her to pour a few drops onto its tongue, then a few more.

In the meantime, Jonah threaded the needle, dabbed on some Cetacaine—a topical anesthetic that smelled like bananas—and some antiseptic, then began stitching up the cut. The fawn began to kick, but it was too weak to move very much. Soon the gash had been closed, and Jonah put some additional antibiotic on the area. "If you have anything to bandage this with, it would help a lot," he told Susie.

In a while, the fawn was bandaged and trying to stand. It obviously felt better. "Looks like I'll have to prepare an area to keep our little friend," Susie said, "though I'll keep him in the house for now. For a while before you got here, I didn't think he'd make it." The large-boned woman gave Jonah a big grin. "Looks like you fixed him. Thanks, Jonah." She gazed at him adoringly, which made Dawn want to slug her.

Jonah seemed oblivious of Susie's devotion. He shrugged, though his expression appeared relaxed. "Glad I could help."

How was he so knowledgeable? Dawn wondered, not for the first time since they had arrived at the Haven. She asked as they left the house.

He looked uncomfortable. "Just some training I picked up a long time ago."

"What kind?" she pressed, wondering what it was he seemed to be hiding.

"Medical," he said. They stood outside now, and the air was cool. Or did Dawn just feel chilled because of Jonah's bleak expression?

"Tell me about it," she urged gently, embarrassed that she had called him "Doctor" so sarcastically before. Whatever had happened must have affected him deeply for him to act this upset.

His shoulders were hunched beneath the unbuttoned white shirt he had put back on. She could almost feel his pain. She touched his arm, but he drew away. "I was a medical student when I was arrested," he said. His chilly stare raked her face, as though he searched for her condemnation.

"I see," she said, though she was not sure she did. He had been a medical student, and he had been arrested for embezzlement. Why hadn't he gone back to medical school? Why was he now an auto mechanic? Maybe he liked fixing cars better than healing people—and yet he had seemed proud and relieved that he had helped the fawn.

With one hand on the house's doorjamb as though

for support, he answered some of her unspoken questions. "I had lost one of my scholarships and needed a job, so I'd gone to work in the offices of a supermarket chain. They're the ones who accused me of embezzling. Then, when I got out of prison, I had no money for medical school, no means to get scholarships or even a good enough job. Besides"—he started down the front walk—"I no longer had any interest in helping people."

"Wait!" Dawn caught up with him. She had no idea what to say to soothe him, though she wished she could hold him, make the hurt reflected in his voice abate. She gently tucked his arm against her side. "Jonah, I'm sorry. It was none of my business, but—well, the way you treated that poor fawn . . . for whatever it's worth, I think you'd have made a good doctor. Maybe you still can. You could—"

"Forget it," he interrupted. But his voice was soft, and he looked down at her, his gaze no longer remote but intense. "I don't need it anymore. But thanks."

He touched her cheek. For a moment, she thought he was going to kiss her, and she closed her eyes. But he let go and began walking away. "I'll take you home now," he said.

"Not yet," she said. She didn't think he should be alone then with all his memories of lost opportunities. Besides, she wanted to remain in his company. She didn't try to figure out why; she just did. "You can't come to the Haven without looking around." She led him down the path toward the animal enclosures.

To her surprise, he came along with no argument.

But what would he, a former prisoner, think of all the incarcerated animals?

He was still being punished, damn it. He would be punished every day for the rest of his life, and there wasn't a thing he could do about it.

138

But the punishment of remaining in Dawn Perry's presence a while longer was one he could not bear to end. He knew what she thought of ex-cons; he had seen it in her eyes when they'd first met. She was a lawyer. He had come to despise lawyers. Law was, nevertheless, a theoretically noble profession, one that could command respect. A profession of which Dawn was proud.

No matter what he thought of it.

He might have been a doctor, but he wasn't. And she could never care for someone with a menial job, like an auto mechanic.

But, despite his better judgment, he was attracted to her. Too attracted. She made him remember he was alive. To her, though, he was just someone handy in emergencies, for finding her missing grandfather and saving an injured fawn.

Punishment.

Still, as absurd as it was, he wanted to be with her. And so he allowed her to take him to the area where the animals at her grandfather's Haven were caged.

Seeing them in their cages would only add to his penance. But he could take it.

He had, somehow, taken everything else.

But he was surprised when Dawn led him first into a barnlike structure and turned on the lights. It was big and airy, and it contained a number of small habitat areas.

Yes, most were behind chain-link fences or glass. But the animals had toys, and small running streams. They had company, for none was alone.

A few were bandaged. Dawn led him over to an enclosure where a beaver watched them listlessly. She opened the small door. The animal limped over to her so she could scratch its head. She reached into a sealed plastic container beside the enclosure and pulled out something green, which she gave to the beaver. "It's cabbage," she explained. "Sir Dammo, here, enjoys it." She paused. "Amos names only the animals he thinks will never be well enough to release back to the wild. Giving one a name makes it seem domesticated."

There was a family of raccoons. One enclosure contained rabbits, another minks. There were more, too—too many to visit all of them, but Jonah could see that each type of animal had a small habitat clearly designed to accommodate its own species and make it feel at home.

Dawn had names for only a few that they visited, but as she reached inside to stroke even those without names, none tried to rush for freedom. All seemed pleased to be handled and given treats, for she did not neglect any of them.

The animals here at the Haven clearly were well cared for, and with love.

"So Amos does release some?" he had to ask.

"Sure," she replied. "That's the main idea. He brings them here only if they're ill or hurt or threatened. Then, as soon as they're able, he sets them free again." She appeared hesitant but said, "That would be his intention with the mountain lion, you know. If it ever seemed safe, he would let it go. Or maybe he would send it somewhere out west, where they're plentiful and where people haven't overrun their habitat as much as they have here. If there is any such place." She motioned to him. "Come with me, and I'll show you more."

She led him into another, larger building. "This is where our mountain lion would go." She pointed to a large, empty area. "First, Amos would have the right kind of environment built. I know the Haven isn't like being up on the mountain, being free—but, oh, Jonah,

140

it's such a wonderful animal. I know now how you felt, as though there were a connection with it. And I understand how important freedom is to you. But I couldn't stand it if one of those miserable hunters killed it. The mountain lion has to live, Jonah, don't you see?"

He did see. That was the thing; for the first time, now that he had seen the Haven, he understood more what Dawn and her grandfather had in mind for the mountain lion. Yes, it would be in captivity. But it would be made at home, cared for, loved.

It was a far cry from his own prison experience.

Still, it would not be free. "I understand better now, Dawn," he said, cupping her soft, smooth cheek in one hand. "I do. Just as you understand my opinion better, now you've seen the cougar. I want that animal to live. I can't even tell you how much I want it to live. But to confine it, even here—I can't be sure that it would want *itself* to live. Do you see what I mean?"

He held his breath. It was important, damned important, to him that they reach agreement on this. Surely, she had to realize that life without freedom wasn't life. He knew that. He had experienced it. She could not confine that mountain lion, deprive it, if not of its life, then of its will to live.

She nodded, but her head drooped so that she was looking at the floor. Her lovely, long black hair fell beside her face. "I do see, Jonah. And I know how much this means to you. But I'm afraid this is something on which we will never agree. I have to save the mountain lion's life. Now that I've seen it, that's even more important to me. I'm sorry, Jonah, but I'll do whatever it takes."

Chapter Nine

Dawn lived only three miles from the Haven, so the ride home was short.

And uncomfortable. She was aware of Jonah's tense form beside her in the car. His hands gripped the steering wheel so tightly that his knuckles gleamed white in the faint light inside the car.

He'd seemed angry with her after their conversation in the large-animal barn. Disappointed in her, too, she imagined.

That hurt. Despite her attempt to explain her opinion, he simply did not agree.

She was frustrated with him, too, for his single-minded intolerance. But she forced herself to be understanding, to a point.

He, who had lost his freedom for a while, valued it above all else. Above life, perhaps.

But that did not mean that all creatures felt the same way. If they did, no caged beast would survive.

No man would survive imprisonment. They would find ways to end it all, to end their own existences.

Jonah had not done that himself—thank heavens.

Neither, she was certain, would the mountain lion.

"Turn right here, then left," she directed, her voice a stark intrusion into the uncomfortable silence. "There." She pointed. "Third house on the right."

She glanced at her home as if through a stranger's eyes. It was a hundred-year-old redbrick Victorian house; two stories, with a large porch in front and a peaked tower on one side. Compared with Jonah's small but charming log cabin, it was a mansion in size. It had been her family home. She had remained there with Amos when her mother had gone off with her umpteenth husband, then stayed by herself when Amos started the Haven. Now it was hers alone.

He pulled the car up in front and stopped. "Good night, Dawn," he said softly. It sounded to her like good-bye. A permanent one.

She didn't leave the car. Instead, she looked at him. In the dim glow from the streetlight a few houses down, she could see he was staring straight ahead. The crags of his rough, handsome face were deepened by his frown, exaggerated by the faintness of the light.

She hated to leave things like this. "Will you come in for a cup of coffee, Jonah?"

No answer.

"I'd like you to."

He looked at her. His habitual stony expression, at least, was gone. It had been replaced by a look of deep sadness that nearly broke her heart. "Why? So you can try to convince me that your way is right, that the mountain lion must be incarcerated?"

"No, so I can try to convince you that we can agree to disagree. For now, it doesn't matter what either of us thinks. Amos and I may not get the permit." She

143

hesitated, and her next words spilled out with a cry. "Or that damned Ray Koslowski may kill it. I don't think I could stand it if that happened." To her dismay, tears rose to her eyes.

Damn! Getting emotional in front of Jonah was the last thing she had intended. "Good night," she said, then exited the car, meaning to run inside.

But she did not get far before he was beside her, his arm around her shoulder. "I'd like that cup of coffee," he said.

He should have refused. The last thing he wanted was to be alone in Dawn's house with her, arguing about something upon which neither of them was going to compromise.

The place felt like her, though: charming and substantial on the outside, neatly decorated on the inside. There were touches that spoke of her profession: in the entry foyer there was an oil painting of the scales of justice held by the traditional blindfolded lady, and in the living room there was a built-in bookcase filled with leather-bound law volumes.

The reminders that she was a lawyer warned him even more than recent events to stay away from her. A warning he'd yet to heed.

"Come in here," she called, and he followed her down a hallway into the kitchen.

This room was one he could get used to. It was large and homey, with copper pots and red chili peppers strung from the wood-beamed ceiling, a large double-ovened stove, a cooking island in the center complete with a small sink for cleaning vegetables, and a large wooden table in a windowed alcove at one end. A faint aroma of cinnamon hung in the air.

"Have a seat." She motioned toward the table. Standing at the counter near the large side-by-side refrigerator, she ground some beans in an electric grinder, then poured water into a coffeemaker, which she plugged in. He soon smelled the fragrance of brewing coffee. He began to relax.

"This is a wonderful room," Jonah said. "Do you use it much?"

She laughed, a wonderful, joyous sound that made his heart soar. He had, without even trying, elicited that moment of happiness from her. "Is that an oblique way of asking whether I cook? Yes, actually, I do. Very well; just ask Amos. And if you're trying to finagle a dinner invitation, you'd better play your cards right."

He teased her right back. "And what cards are those, Ms. Perry?"

She pretended to ponder, furrowing the black, arched brows over her exotically shaped eyes. "Let's see. First you need to stop contradicting me. People whom I grace with my superior cooking skills don't give me a hard time."

"Like Amos?" he asked.

"Well, he's my grandfather. He's an exception."

He wondered, suddenly, who else she cooked for. Were there any men in her life? Something dark and leaden lay heavy in his stomach at the thought.

But of course there would be men in her life. She was a wonderful woman. Gorgeous. Kind. A professional woman who undoubtedly had a lot of friends. A professional *lawyer*. He felt himself scowl. What the hell was he doing here?

"Jonah, is something wrong?" The bantering tone had left her voice, and she took a few steps toward him on the red-tiled floor.

"I'd better skip the coffee." He rose to his feet. "I'm sure Lettie has a big day planned for me tomorrow."

"Sit down," she ordered, taking a chair at the table

145

beside him. "I have plans for you tonight."

He obeyed and sat, then looked at her. He couldn't help it; he lifted his eyebrows suggestively, as though she had just propositioned him. "Plans?"

Her clear complexion reddened in a blush. It was an enchanting reaction, and he found himself smiling and drawing almost involuntarily closer.

"Not those kind of plans," she said grumpily. "I want us to reach an understanding, as I said in the car. We don't have to agree with one another, but we do—"

"All we have to do . . ." He let his voice go deep and soft, a caress. And then he followed it with his hand in her hair, along the bones of her jaw. ". . . is this."

Foolish, was his last coherent thought. He drew nearer yet, touching her lips with his. Gently again, the way he had begun to kiss her the last time. Wondering, since the plans she alluded to did not include this, if she would push him away.

But she did not. Nor did she, apparently, want him to be gentle. Things escalated quickly, as though they both had been starved and offered each other sustenance. In moments they were standing. Her arms were wrapped about him, her body tight against his. Oh, lord, what that body was doing to him! He felt himself harden, and he pressed against her, wanting her to feel him, too.

"Jonah," she murmured into his mouth, writhing against him. He thrust his tongue between her sweet lips, forging his way past them so he could taste her deeply.

How had he ever thought he had lost his libido? Maybe he had just not had a woman like Dawn in his life.

He did not have her now, not really. But for this moment, he would enjoy having her close. Closer.

Refusing to take his mouth from hers, he pulled her

blouse from her slacks, let his hand move up. The soft, smooth skin of her back was hot to his touch. He kneaded it, felt the indentation along her spine, and moved upward. He maneuvered his hand to unfasten her bra strap, then moved his caress to her shoulder blades. He heard himself groan. If innocent parts of her body elicited such an erotic reaction from him, then how would it feel to touch her—

He did not speculate further but let his fingertips range to her front and caressed the glorious mounds that were her breasts.

"Oh, Jonah," she whispered raggedly. "I do have a bedroom."

"I want to see it someday," he said in a growl, "but not now." He pulled her to the floor and fastened his mouth on hers again.

What was she doing? Dawn wondered fleetingly as she felt her bared back rest upon the hard, cold floor.

Making love with this man. Fiery, passionate love. She could set the floor, the entire kitchen, on fire with her own body heat.

Jonah's kisses were incredible. His mouth molded against hers. He used his lips, his tongue, to torment, to taunt, to stimulate.

His hands were magnificent, stroking and kneading as though he were a master chef and she were un-formed dough. One hand cupped her breast. She arched into it. She heard her own sharp intake of breath as his thumb rasped against her nipple, stim-ulating it to peak against his touch.

He broke their kiss. Disappointment surged through her—but only for a moment. She glanced down to see his thick, tawny hair as he lowered his head. And then her nipple was in his mouth. The sweet sucking sensation, concentrated in a single sensitive area, surged liquid heat through her entire body.

"Jonah." She moaned, holding him close, wanting him closer still. Jonah. She had not let anyone near her this way for years, not since her first ineffective efforts to find peace after Billy. Even then, even with her sweet Billy, had she ever felt such unbridled, ecstatic passion?

She'd no time to feel guilty about such traitorous thoughts as wave after wave of arousal surged through her. She felt an ache down below that cried for Jonah's touch.

His hands were on the waistband of her trousers, unfastening them. She shuddered deliciously, her need growing with his every stroke.

But it was unfair. She wanted to feel his skin against her. She pushed him away to unbutton his shirt. She felt her pants drawn down her legs even as she pulled his shirt from his chest.

She gasped. Stopped moving. Stared.

Jonah's strong, hard chest had a long, puckered scar from his clavicle down to the end of his rib cage.

"Oh, Jonah," she whispered, her breathing ragged. "What happened to you?" She reached one shaking hand toward the scar, intending to touch it, wanting to erase it and the pain of the wound it evidenced.

"Prison happened to me." Despite his erratic breathing, his voice was suddenly hard and distant. "I wasn't the meek, dumb college kid the others expected. They showed me what they thought of anyone who dared to show guts. They tried, in fact, to gut me." His laugh was mirthless.

"Oh, Jonah, I'm so sorry," she whispered. "No one should have to suffer like that." Sorrow welled within her for this man and what he had gone through.

"Not even convicts, you mean?" This time his chilly

tone sent a shiver down her back. "Prisoners? People you lawyers have sent to jail?"

"Jonah, I didn't mean . . ." Her voice trailed off as he sat up. She watched him button his shirt.

Suddenly, embarrassingly aware of her own nearly undressed state, she sat up and pulled her clothes on. Whatever passion she had felt had fled just that quickly, to be replaced by—what? Mortification? Fury? How dare he make assumptions about what she was thinking?

Jonah was standing now, with the stony expression on his face that she had come to know so well. He tucked his shirt into his trousers.

"Damn it, Jonah." Dawn's voice shook. "You're blaming me for your imprisonment, because I'm a lawyer. You were the embezzler. Excuse me, *alleged* embezzler. *Convicted* embezzler. I didn't put you into prison." She took a deep breath. "I didn't cause your scar."

"I'm not blaming you," he contradicted. "You had nothing to do with the fiasco that's my life. But this was a mistake. I got carried away. You're a damned sexy lady, Dawn Perry." His gray-green eyes bored into her, but they were as cold now as the winter sky in a snowstorm. "I won't bother you again."

He left her there, sitting alone in her kitchen.

Jonah tried, on his drive home on the dark country roads, to still his shaking. To steel his mind against any thought, as he had learned so painstakingly to do years before.

But thoughts of Dawn Perry, and what almost had been, threatened to send him spiraling over the edge—of the road? Of madness? He wasn't sure.

Still, he forced himself to concentrate on his driving. To keep his speed reasonable. Even though everything inside him wanted to break loose, to speed, to drive as recklessly as his furious thoughts made him feel.

Dawn was right. He'd somehow blamed her, blamed the whole damned legal system on her. Stupid, uncouth ex-con that he was.

Never mind that he hadn't planned on being alone with her tonight, that he hadn't planned on finding himself, irresistibly, in the heat of a near-uncontrollable passion with her. He should have been prepared for this moment. He should have thought about what would happen the first time he made love with a woman after leaving prison.

Not that he hadn't thought of sex a lot in prison. He'd even come near to propositioning a couple of willing women right after his release. But memories of all that had happened to him, including the faithlessness of his former girlfriend, had interfered. Not even the physical release, the mindless pleasure, of emotionless sex could convince him to get that close to anyone. He'd wanted nothing to do with women.

Until Dawn Perry.

Of course his scar—the visible one—would be a sharp reminder of what he had been through. Of course any woman would notice it, would comment, would express dismay, or repugnance, or, worst of all, pity.

But he especially could not take Dawn's pity. It had enraged him.

And in spitting out that rage, he had lost his opportunity for fulfilling the fiery, sensual promise of that evening that had begun and ended on her kitchen floor.

Damn it, he'd blown it. He had lost, perhaps, a chance at redemption.

He should have been prepared.

Well, he would have plenty of time now to prepare. There would be no next time with Dawn Perry. There would be no further loss of control, no more unrestrained passion between them. She would want nothing more to do with him.

It was better that way. He had been right in what he had told her. It was a mistake. Nothing should have happened between them. He didn't need her. He didn't need any woman.

He slammed his hand hard against the dashboard and soaked in the sudden, agonizing pain.

It was nothing compared with the agony in his heart.

Lifting her head from her pillow, Dawn blinked in the darkness of her bedroom.

Her body ached all over. It felt empty. Unfulfilled. She had enjoyed every moment of their lovemaking. She had wanted more. Much more.

She writhed in bed at the recollection of Jonah's kisses. His touch.

The way he had begun to undress her and then himself.

Then she had seen his scar. She had done nothing wrong. She had merely reacted to seeing it. And he had withdrawn from her.

She felt furious.

She felt hurt.

She had lain in bed for hours, forming retorts to hurl at Jonah the next time they met.

No. It would be better if she avoided him.

How dare he judge her that way? How could he possibly know what she was thinking?

Surely he didn't expect her simply to ignore that huge, conspicuous scar on his chest? And then for him to react the way he had—well, he could take his attitude and his scar and . . . well, he knew what he could do with them.

Sure, she was a lawyer. She was proud of it. She had a great respect for the legal system. And if the system had mistreated Jonah, well, she was sorry. But it wasn't her fault.

She knew that the legal system she revered wasn't perfect. She had lost cases, now and then, that her clients should clearly have won. She knew of situations where innocent people were, occasionally, wrongly convicted of crimes. Was Jonah truly one of them?

Well, how should she know? He hardly talked about it.

What if he *had* been innocent? For a moment, she imagined herself in his place. Arrested, subjected to the indignities of incarceration and a trial. Convicted and sent to prison.

She imagined being attacked by other inmates, and cut in some horrible fight that resulted in that scar. "Oh, Jonah," Dawn said aloud, shaking her head sadly.

No wonder he wanted the mountain lion left free. Why should it be caged for the follies of people? It had done nothing wrong.

But captivity could save its life, she reminded herself, and that was the most important thing. A mountain lion had returned to Eskaway. That part of Amos's fairy tale had come true. And the rest of the legend?

If it were true, the Wilton family could now find true love.

That meant maybe Amos would find happiness with Lettie.

Dawn's mother, Amos's daughter, might finally be happy with husband number five. Or was it six?

And Dawn? Dawn had found love once, with Billy. She needed nothing, no one else.

But a disloyal thought still nagged at the corner of her mind: with Billy she had never experienced the passion she had merely tasted last night with Jonah. They had just been kids.

If Billy had lived, would their love have lasted?

Of course it would have. How could she think otherwise?

"Billy?" Dawn said into the darkness, twirling strands of her long, dark hair between her fingers. "What would have happened to us?" She had never questioned her relationship with her lost love before. But what if it had been an immature one?

What if the legend were right, and she now had the opportunity to experience true love?

An image of Jonah Campion's rugged face came into her mind. Not with his usual, stony look, but a laughing one. And then the smile disappeared, to be replaced with pain. And anger.

She had made assumptions about him because he was felon, just as he'd made assumptions about her, as a lawyer. Maybe neither was fair. . . .

Well, it didn't matter. Amos's legend was a myth.

Jonah wanted nothing more to do with her, just because she'd dared to show compassion for his scar.

Well, the heck with him. For all she cared, he could take one of those cars he worked on and drive it till it dropped.

She'd had Billy. And no matter how bitterly her unfulfilled body complained, she didn't need anyone. And most of all, she didn't need Jonah.

Chapter Ten

The telephone rang. Groggily, Dawn reached for it. It had awakened her. Sometime after light had begun to show in the sky, she had actually fallen asleep.

Maybe it was Jonah, calling to—what?

Apologize for the previous night? That was as likely as if he were calling to invite her to have a picnic at a prison with him that afternoon.

"Hello," she said.

"Are you still in bed, Granddaughter?" Amos's cheery voice was not what she needed right now.

She groaned. "I'm getting up now. What time did you and Lettie get in last night?"

"None of your business." He chuckled with self-satisfaction. "But I'm calling to thank you for taking care of the fawn last night. Susie's a caring soul, but she doesn't deal well with the gory stuff."

"No problem," Dawn replied. "But you're thanking the wrong person. Jonah's the one who helped. Did you know he was studying to be a doctor when—" She hesitated. Darn her, she couldn't even say the words. She forced them out. "When he was arrested and convicted." And imprisoned. And had his body slashed in prison, and had his mind damaged even worse.

Drat him anyway! Even an apology might not help. He'd had the effrontery to blame her last night, in the throes of the most incredible lovemaking she could imagine, for his wrongful conviction.

Wrongful conviction . . . Not *alleged* wrongful conviction. Was she really beginning to believe in him? Without even knowing his story? Well . . . maybe. He confused her.

"Yes, Lettie told me some of Jonah's sorry history. Poor man lost a lot because he was trying to help someone, though he never talks about that part of it. Come to think of it, Lettie says he never talks about much of it at all."

Trying to help someone? Dawn's curiosity had already been piqued about Jonah, but now it was stimulated like crazy. How could she get him to—

"Anyway, the reason I'm calling is that we have another little problem with our wild friend."

"The mountain lion?" Dawn's heart plummeted to the floor. Surely it wasn't injured—or worse. Ray Koslowski had not gotten to it, had he? He couldn't have.

"What other wild friends do you have? Never mind. Yes, our pal the cougar. Turns out that the reason our dear vet, Dr. Knerr, was unavailable last night was because he was at Syd Cornelius's farm. Seems that one of Cornelius's milk cows was killed last night by something big that started eating her. From what Knerr says, it was probably our mountain lion. Now Cornelius is fighting mad."

"He wasn't too pleased about the mountain lion at the town meeting, either, as I recall," Dawn said.

"Like the other farmers, he was afraid this would happen. Now Ray has a bunch more locals on his side. They're thinking about how to rid our area of this horrible scourge."

"Oh, no. Grandpa, we'd better move fast to get the okay to put our friend in the Haven."

"I was thinking that, too, but I was wondering how you'd feel. Remember, Jonah doesn't want us to. Aren't the two of you getting pretty thick?"

Dawn could hear the gloat in Amos's voice. "No, your conniving and matchmaking with Lettie aren't working. We hate each other's guts." She tried to sound as angry as she'd first felt the night before, but it had softened, leaving a sense of loss at things left undone.

"I'm sorry, honey," Amos said. For a moment she considered telling him what had happened, then caught herself. She could hardly tell her grandfather that she had been all set to make love to a near stranger the night before but that he'd called it off right in the middle, after baring his scar to her.

She sighed to herself. "Nothing to be sorry about. Anything but animosity between us would be impossible. The two of us are total opposites. We have nothing in common."

"You've both seen the mountain lion," Amos said gently.

"Yes," Dawn said. "Except that. Oh, yeah—and we both like trout."

When she hung up, she stood, thinking about the angry farmers. And the cougar, who was only doing what it needed to do to survive: kill.

In the Haven, it would be brought food. Dawn imagined that a mountain lion would eat a lot. Thank heaven, Amos had suppliers who would provide fresh meat daily.

Then she thought about Jonah. Would this new development matter to him? Before, the main danger to the mountain lion had come from the small group of people who enjoyed hunting for hunting's sake, and who did not mind taking a chance with the legalities: Ray Koslowski and his ilk.

But now the farmers, too, would be after the wildcat. And she suspected many law enforcers would look the other way even if this predatory cougar were a member of an endangered species—particularly if someone caught it in the act of trying to kill livestock.

She had to act fast, Jonah notwithstanding. She had some business to take care of this morning, but then she would get right on it.

She dressed hurriedly, then remembered she was still without a car. With some trepidation, she called Lettie's shop. Might Jonah answer? If so, should she tell him off or just pretend nothing happened?

Fortunately, the owner herself picked up the phone. "I'll hurry the guys to finish," she said, "but I suppose you need a ride to your office. Why don't I just send Jonah, and—"

"No, thanks," Dawn interrupted. "It's a beautiful day, and I'm not far from town. I was planning to walk anyway."

That was a lie. Though she enjoyed long walks, she never took one while dressed in a suit for work. But there was always a first time.

The office was only two miles from her home, and she wore her athletic shoes, carrying her high heels, purse and briefcase. By the time she got to the office, Marnie was fuming. "Where have you been? I was afraid I'd have to cover for you. You're due in court in half an hour on the Evanod joyriding case."

"I have plenty of time," Dawn replied. "It's not as if the court were on the other side of town."

She made it to Judge Foltz's courtroom with five minutes to spare. There, she met up with her client, Agnes Draper, a thin beautician who wore her own bleached blond hair like someone from the forties.

Clemson walked by as Dawn greeted her client. "Come see me later, when you're free," he said. Dawn did not have time to wonder why. The court appearance was about to begin.

She represented Agnes in a suit against Stan Evanod, a neighbor whose teenage son Louis had "borrowed"—and wrecked—her car. This was one time Dawn wished she had followed the legal career she had originally planned for herself: in a prosecutor's office somewhere. But though she had attempted it as her first job, her emotions had gotten in the way. And so she had sought justice instead by representing people in civil actions, seeking compensation for wrongs done to them.

In this case, loudmouthed Louis had been arrested by Clemson. The police chief would testify in this suit if it went to trial, and had also participated in the criminal action against Louis, who was anything but contrite.

Clemson had told Dawn that the kid had plea-bargained and had gotten a few hours of community service. It had been a first offense, after all.

Billy's murder had been, too.

Now Louis's family was represented by a smug and snotty insurance defense lawyer who figured he could get rid of this case for a measly thousand or two.

Not if Dawn could help it.

But the judge had called a mandatory settlement conference. And after a couple of hours of hearing the worst part of her case—even knowing the judge was doing the same to the opposition—Dawn recommended to Agnes that she take their last offer. "It'll buy you a nice, new car to replace the Chevy you lost," Dawn explained in the small room where they'd gone to confer. "That's what their offer is based on."

"I could get my brother-in-law Sal to come," Agnes said, pursing her lipstick-reddened lips contemplatively. "He'd swear that the new car closest to the wrecked one would cost another three thousand dollars. Would they offer more then? After all, I'm losing money at work. I can't fix my customers' hair when I'm in court."

"I don't believe in . . . exaggeration in court," Dawn said firmly. "Or even in a settlement conference." Or anywhere else, she thought. Exaggeration? Lies! That was what she'd meant. But she didn't want to alienate her client.

"Okay, then," Agnes said. "I'll take it. Thank you, Dawn." She smiled happily and pumped Dawn's hand.

After the formalities were concluded, Dawn began walking toward the police station, which was several blocks away. She wanted to talk to Clemson. As usual, after helping a client, she felt pleased and actually proud to be a lawyer.

Would Jonah agree?

She doubted it. The legal system had its flaws, and that was what Jonah focused on. One of its imperfections—and good parts, too—was compromise.

In her line of work, the law didn't vindicate, nor did it exonerate. It simply compensated—sometimes, and not always enough.

Not even the stiff sentence handed down to Billy's killer could have brought her fiancé back, but at least the young murderer had had to suffer the consequences of his horrendous act.

But nothing could compensate Jonah for what he had endured, if he hadn't been guilty.

Linda O. Johnston

What had he done to help someone that had gotten him into such trouble?

As though Dawn had planned it, Lettie's garage loomed on the opposite side of the street from where she now walked. Or maybe she *had* planned it, subconsciously. She could have called Clemson, after all. Despite his request, she didn't need to go to see him. Or she could have taken another route that could have taken her only a block out of her way.

But she was already there. All she did was look at the large, double-bay garage as she hurried by. Her little green car was parked in one of the service bays. A loud drill-like noise emanated from the area, but she could not see whether the work was being done by Lettie or Fisk . . . or Jonah.

She should stop in to see when her car would be ready. And then she could say to him . . . what?

That she forgave him for the previous night? But he hadn't asked her to.

That she was sorry she'd mentioned his scar? Heaven knew she *was* sorry. But what had he expected? It was obvious. She had noticed it. Her reaction had been natural: curiosity, and even a little compassion. His overreaction had been his problem.

Then why did it bother her so much?

She sped up, not wanting Jonah to see her as her anger began sparking again. What could she possibly say that wouldn't cause another argument? But she glanced back—hoping, despite herself, to see him.

There was no sign of him. She began thinking about how she would explain her work this day to him—if she ever saw him again. She had used the legal system he despised to get compensation for her client. It had worked for Agnes. Hadn't it? But Agnes had lost money on the deal. Time, too. And what about the defendant? Had he learned anything?

Thrill to the most sensual, adventure-filled Romances on the market today...

FROM  LOVE SPELL BOOKS

As a home subscriber to the Love Spell Romance Book Club, you'll enjoy the best in today's BRAND-NEW Time Travel, Futuristic, Legendary Lovers, Perfect Heroes and other genre romance fiction. For five years, Love Spell has brought you the award-winning, high-quality authors you know and love to read. Each Love Spell romance will sweep you away to a world of high adventure...and intimate romance. Discover for yourself all the passion and excitement millions of readers thrill to each and every month.

Save $5.00 Each Time You Buy!

Every other month, the Love Spell Romance Book Club brings you four brand-new titles from Love Spell Books. EACH PACKAGE WILL SAVE YOU AT LEAST $5.00 FROM THE BOOKSTORE PRICE! And you'll never miss a new title with our convenient home delivery service.

Here's how we do it: Each package will carry a FREE 10-DAY EXAMINATION privilege. At the end of that time, if you decide to keep your books, simply pay the low invoice price of $17.96, no shipping or handling charges added. HOME DELIVERY IS ALWAYS FREE. With today's top romance novels selling for $5.99 and higher, our price SAVES YOU AT LEAST $5.00 with each shipment.

AND YOUR FIRST TWO-BOOK SHIPMENT IS TOTALLY FREE!

IT'S A BARGAIN YOU CAN'T BEAT! A SUPER $11.48 Value!

Love Spell ⊕ A Division of Dorchester Publishing Co., Inc.

Get Two Books Totally
FREE —
An $11.48 Value!

▼ Tear Here and Mail Your FREE Book Card Today! ▼

PLEASE RUSH
MY TWO FREE
BOOKS TO ME
RIGHT AWAY!

Love Spell Romance Book Club
P.O. Box 6613
Edison, NJ 08818-6613

AFFIX
STAMP
HERE

A few minutes later, in the combined police station/post office, she hurried past the people buying stamps. Clemson was in the station alone, leaning on the tall counter filling out papers. Eyes narrowed and lips pursed over large teeth in concentration, he resembled a beaver more than ever. His thick shoulders were hunched as he wrote.

"Clemson?"

He looked up. "How'd you do in Agnes's case?" he asked.

"We settled." She could not tell him the terms, since they were confidential.

"You don't sound thrilled."

She wasn't. Not then. *Damn Jonah Campion!* Without her even seeing him today, he had made her question her judgment.

She sighed. "I'm concerned now that the consequences were too light, since in the criminal action, the kid plea-bargained his way to community service, and he also got away fairly lightly under the settlement of the civil action. I just hope he doesn't think he's gotten away with something with his joyride and goes off to do bigger and better things."

"Not all kids who act up are murderers, Dawn." Clemson's voice was gentle. He knew about her Billy. Everyone in Eskmont did.

But Louis Evanod had admitted to what he had done and had gotten off. Jonah had, perhaps, not been guilty, had somehow tried to help someone. And he had gone to prison for . . . how long? Dawn didn't know.

There was too much about Jonah's situation that she didn't know. And what she did know had hurt her.

Not wanting to talk about Agnes's case further, Dawn asked, "What did you want to see me about?"

"Your mountain lion," he said, holding his head as

though it hurt. "This situation is escalating."

"Then you've heard about the problem at Cornelius's farm."

"Heard about it? I investigated it. Something big got that cow. Could very well be your cougar. And Cornelius is fit to be tied, ready to go kill himself a cat. He says no court on earth will convict him for protecting his property."

Dawn leaned on the counter defeatedly. "At least he didn't kill it last night." She looked up in alarm. "Did he?"

Clemson shook his head. "No, far as we know the cougar got clean away." He reached over and patted her hand. "I know why you and your grandpa are so anxious to save this animal, Dawn. We were out celebrating after a Penn State football game some years ago, and Amos told me. Who knows, but maybe it's true, what with him now seeing Lettie. And the whole town's buzzing about you and Jonah."

Dawn felt herself redden. She pretended to look for something in her briefcase while she got her emotions under control. "You would think everyone would find something more exciting to 'buzz' about," she said. "Something real. I'm grateful to Jonah, of course, for helping me find Amos. And since then, Amos has been throwing Jonah and me together, to try to make his silly story come true." He hadn't, of course, gotten them together in her kitchen the previous night, when she had thought she would burst from need of Jonah. The very recollection caused her to tingle way below. But it had ended so abruptly. So unfairly. She sighed. It was bad enough she kept thinking about Jonah. Why was everyone talking to her about him? "You'd think if Amos meant to matchmake, he would do it with someone more suitable."

"Jonah's a good guy, Dawn." Sincerity resounded in

Clemson's tone. "There are things about what happened to him that he won't talk about, but I've heard from some people close to the case. There was more than met the eye, or the court."

"What happened, Clemson?" Dawn touched his arm. Maybe she would get an answer. "Amos said he was protecting someone. Is that true?"

"You'd better get it straight from the horse's mouth. He's made Lettie and me promise to stay quiet."

Dawn recalled Lettie's exclamation that Jonah had been convicted for something he hadn't done. No matter what she had promised, Lettie was Amos's source for information. Clemson obviously knew the story. Why was no one telling *her?* And could she really believe, without knowing the facts, that a man convicted by a court of law was innocent?

Maybe this time she could. Maybe this time she wanted to.

"Back to your cougar," Clemson said. "Are you and Amos working on getting the okay to take it to the Haven?"

"I don't know about Amos," Dawn said, "but I'm about to get busy."

When she got back to her office, she phoned Amos first. No, he had not yet called his contact at the Pennsylvania Game Commission. He was too busy with the fawn. Then there had been a hawk that needed his attention, and a food order that hadn't come in.

In other words, he did not want to deal with bureaucratic details, as usual. Oh, he did a great job of schmoozing recalcitrant officials when he needed something. But finding out what was legal and how to handle it—that was not his forte.

But it *was* Dawn's.

She made a few calls, then did a little legal research.

And when she was through, she sat at her desk with her head in her hands.

"Dawn, have you seen the Smithson file?" Marnie asked as she burst into her office. "Oh," she said. "Sorry. You look as though you've just lost a major case." She looked at Dawn expectantly, obviously wanting an explanation. She was wearing a black pants suit, and with her long blond hair flowing behind her and the bow of her white blouse tucked under her petite chin, she resembled a cute toy penguin. The scent of Poison wafted through the office.

"No, I haven't lost anything. At least not yet. But I'm not quite sure what to do."

Her partner plopped herself down on one of the chairs facing Dawn's desk. "Tell Mama Marnie all about it."

Dawn hesitated, but only for a moment. Maybe explaining what she had learned would help her solidify the possibilities and come up with a plan. She looked down at her notes. "It's about the mountain lion."

"Why am I not surprised?" Dawn glanced up to see a belligerent expression on Marnie's pretty face. "If it were something that might earn us a little money—"

"We're doing fine in the income department." Dawn kept her tone light, not wanting to start another fight on this subject that had always been a hot spot between them. "And I've had a referral on a personal injury case on behalf of a poor, injured child against a great big toy manufacturer with great big insurance that—"

Marnie laughed and raised hands with long, pink nails, as though warding off Dawn's words. "Okay, kid. That's not the issue here. Tell me about your great big mountain lion instead."

Dawn relaxed, letting her mind roll through the calls she had made earlier.

With each, she had thought of Jonah. What would he have asked? What would be his reaction to the answers?

How could he keep the mountain lion free?

But more important was how could *she* keep the mountain lion safe?

"Well," she said to Marnie, "I phoned a contact at the Pennsylvania Game Commission, then someone at the closest office of the U.S. Fish and Wildlife Service."

She had learned a lot in those calls, mulled everything over in her mind afterward. This would be a good test: how could she explain it simply? Marnie would understand the complications, but not everyone Dawn needed to deal with would.

"First, there's Fish and Wildlife," she began. "They'll get involved only if the animal at issue was a migratory bird or a member of an endangered species. Some types of cougars are endangered, and others aren't. The only way to tell is by genetic testing, which involves getting hair or nail clippings, maybe even anesthetizing the animal."

Jonah would love that, Dawn thought. Capturing the poor beast. Scaring it, taking small body parts, just to get information. And it still wouldn't guarantee saving its freedom—not to mention its life.

Marnie shifted impatiently. "Can't you just assume the one that showed up here is endangered? After all, mountain lions are supposed to be extinct in Pennsylvania."

"That's actually a good reason to suppose our mountain lion *isn't* endangered," Dawn said. "The woman at the game commission said there are a lot of sightings of cougars in Pennsylvania, but they're usually wrong: a footprint that turns out to be a bobcat, for example. The few that are real have been animals that escaped from zoos or private menageries. And they mostly are western cougars, which aren't endangered."

Removing her dark suit jacket, Marnie draped it over the back of her chair. "So let's look at it the other way. Do you want this one to be endangered or not?"

Dawn sighed. "I'm not sure. If it's endangered, it's protected and can't be hunted—at least not legally. Possibly not even if it's eating livestock. But I don't think Ray Koslowski and Syd Cornelius are going to let a little thing like the law get in the way of killing it."

"And there's nothing at all standing in their way of hunting it if it's not a member of an endangered species. So it'll be killed whether it's endangered or not."

Dawn nodded at her partner. "That's why I want to bring the cougar into the Haven."

"Okay, then." Marnie leaned forward, her blond hair catching on her shoulders. "I know you'll want to do things right. What do you need to do to put the beast in the Haven?"

Dawn looked again at her notes. "My contact at the Pennsylvania Game Commission said that they're unlikely to give clearance to take a cougar into the Haven if it's really a wild animal that's somehow shown up here. To put it into the Haven, we'd have to prove it was formerly in captivity and that we have the former owner's permission to keep it."

"There you go," said Marnie, starting to rise. "You just need to show it was someone's pet puma, then hide it away in the Haven. What could be simpler?"

"Simple?" Dawn felt her jaw drop in astonishment. "Well, I suppose Amos has enough contacts to find out if it has escaped from a zoo somewhere. But if it *was* someone's pet, keeping it may have been illegal, so the owner might not admit it." Frustrated, she stood and began pacing. "The problem is time. It will take a while to rule out all possibilities. In the meantime, Ray and the others could shoot the animal."

Marnie had reached the door. "Sounds like an emergency to me. Like I said, you just need to show it belonged to someone. Quickly."

Dawn looked at her partner. Marnie's softly penciled eyebrows were arched higher than usual, and she regarded Dawn with amusement.

"I'm sure," Marnie said very slowly, "that you can figure out a way to do it quickly."

Dawn froze, her hand touching her desk. "You mean lie about it?"

Marnie's manicured hand rose to her mouth in a parody of shutting it physically. "I said no such thing," she said, moving her hand. "I would never suborn perjury. You know that." But her tone was still deliberate, as though she were speaking to a backward child. "Anyway, I still have to look for the Smithson file. Let me know how things go."

No, Dawn thought, staring at the closed door. Her partner would not suborn perjury, but she did tend to skirt the borders of what was ethical. And unless someone were under oath, a simple lie wasn't necessarily perjury.

Dawn shook her head. No, that wasn't *her* way. She would talk to Amos, see how quickly they could find out if anyone had misplaced a mountain lion recently. And hope the animal survived long enough to get its owner's permission to capture it.

And if the owner could not be found? Or if there were no owner? Somehow, Dawn thought the latter to be true. The mountain lion she had seen had appeared too at home in the wild to have been someone's caged pet.

Cages. Lies and law-breaking. The concepts swirled

167

around in her mind—and reminded her, as nearly everything did lately, of Jonah Campion.

What would he do in this situation?

He would be glad that legally capturing the cougar was so complicated, but he would not want it to die. She was sure of that.

Her car had been in Lettie's service bay before. Surely enough time had passed for it to have gotten fixed. Maybe she would go find out if it was ready.

Chapter Eleven

"Hello, Jonah."

The soft voice behind him might as well have been a shout, the way it startled him. Not that he jumped. He had learned years ago how to hide physical evidence of all emotion, even surprise.

On the other hand, maybe surprise was the least of the emotions invading his mind. Last night, as he had lain wide awake in his bed, he had flogged himself in his mind for the way he had reacted; Dawn had done nothing wrong. He'd been the one who'd gotten out of line. Way out of line.

He had imagined their next meeting hundreds of times, alone in the dark as his body ached with unslaked passion. This morning, he had fantasized even more encounters here, as he'd worked. Each time, he had practiced in his head infinite variations of the cool, offhand apologies he might make for his asinine overreaction.

But now that she was actually here, none came to mind.

"Hi, Dawn." *Good*. Though his mouth was dry, his tone was casual as he straightened from bending over a car's engine. He turned toward her, aware of how dirty his work jeans and T-shirt were.

She was dressed as a lawyer, in a navy business suit that only emphasized the differences between them. But it was nothing like a man's suit. No, this one was tailored so that the hip-length coat nipped in at her slender waist, displaying her curves. Her long hair was parted on one side and hung loose, framing her beautiful face.

"Lettie didn't call," she said, "but I was in the neighborhood and thought I'd check whether my car was ready."

No mention of last night. Still, she was thinking about it. He was certain of that, for she looked unsure of herself. Her head tilted quizzically, as though she waited for his next bit of lunacy. A small, wry smile teased the corners of lips so luscious that the very sight of them reminded him of the kisses they had shared.

No, he thought, he had been wrong a moment earlier. He had not learned to control the physical evidence of all emotion, or else he would not now feel the insane tightening of his groin.

"I think your car's all set," he said gruffly. *Damn*. That wasn't the way he wanted to play it. He should be contrite. Friendly, at least. Instead, hiding his discomfort, he made himself sound polite, all business. "I'll have to look at the paperwork to be sure. Wait outside the service bay, please. Lettie worries about liability when customers come out here."

Besides, he thought, this was not somewhere for Dawn Perry to be—not in this place of engines and oil and dirt. She was an immaculately dressed professional woman. She earned her way by using her brains, not her hands. A lawyer. Perfect . . . and part of the hated system.

Way out of your league, Campion, he dug at himself as a reminder. As if he needed one after the way he had acted last night.

But though she obviously was at home in an office or in court, she'd had no qualms about getting dirty on the mountain, while looking for Amos. And she had said she enjoyed hiking. She had gone back to Eskaway alone to see the mountain lion.

She had even seemed to enjoy their rough, erotic foreplay on the floor last night. Until she had seen his scar.

He took a deep breath against the reminder of his pain—and the anger that he now directed unswervingly toward himself.

She was no one he could stick into a box like an auto part and label with precision. That made her even more appealing, damn it. He enjoyed puzzles.

She walked around the old Mazda he had been working on, exiting to the pavement outside the shop. She looked up at the sky. "It's a perfect day, isn't it?"

He had to hand it to her. Even after their last emotional encounter, she was able to make polite conversation. "Great weather," he agreed. A perfect day? He had few of those, but this one had certainly brightened up with her presence.

Get real, Campion, he scoffed internally. *The woman's presence has nothing to do with you. She hasn't forgotten last night. She just wants her car.*

He wiped his hand on an oily rag and walked toward the office. Not that he needed to. He knew the car was ready. He had worked on it himself, had let his own hands range over the engine of Dawn's car, twisting caps and testing seals.

It had been torture.

Not that he believed her perfect hands had ever wandered in the same areas that his filthy fingers touched. But he knew that the auto belonged to her. That she had entrusted something important to her well-being to him.

No, not to him. To Lettie Green. And he was only Lettie's flunky, who happened to be lucky—and dumb—enough to be doing the work.

This morning, Lettie and Fisk had gone to rescue a customer whose engine had overheated, leaving Jonah by himself. That was another sign of how much Jonah owed Lettie. She trusted him enough to leave him alone at her business. She allowed him in her office, where the books and cash were kept. She expected he would not steal or embezzle. And of course he wouldn't.

Going through the motions, he looked in a folder on Lettie's desk. The paperwork was there. He returned to the shop. "Guess Lettie didn't get around to letting you know, but your car is done."

"Great! How much do I owe?"

Jonah ran her credit card through the machine, then got her keys. "It's outside, at the other side of the office."

"I saw it. Thanks."

That was it. She could take her car and drive off now—out of the repair shop and out of his life. There was no reason for further contact between them. It was better that way. He'd have no further opportunity to make an ass of himself.

But she did not leave. She stood beside the cash register near the door. "Jonah?" Her dark brows were knitted, and her teeth worried her lower lip.

"What?" He kept his voice calm with what felt like superhuman effort. Was she about to make peace with him, to institute the discussion about last night that he felt unable to broach?

"It's our mountain lion," she replied.

Of course it would be. What else would she want to talk to him about?

She looked around the shop. The service bays were filled. "I know you're busy, but I found out some things today and wanted to tell you. Ask your advice."

He stared at her. The worry in her dark, glistening eyes looked sincere. "I'd have thought," he said dryly, "that I'd be the last person whose advice you would want about that."

"It's as important to you to save it as it is to me. Even if we disagree on how to do it."

He nodded slowly in acknowledgment. "Tell you what." He looked at the clock on the wall. "Lettie and Fisk are due back in fifteen minutes. When they come, I can take a break. I'll meet you at the diner. We can grab a cup of coffee." And maybe by then, he thought, I'll have figured out what to say.

"It's a date." Her smile brightened her beautiful face. Despite everything, Jonah wanted to take the few steps to erase the gap between them. He wanted to pull her into his arms, and—

Yeah. Pull that well-dressed lawyer against his greasy clothes.

Besides, she only wanted his advice about the wild animal. After last night, he was sure that the last thing she would want to experience again was his touch.

Despite the fact that he was touched by the very sight of her.

"See you then." He turned his back toward her. He had cars that needed attention.

*   *   *

173

"What did you learn?" Jonah leaned back in the booth at the diner. They were off in one corner, and at this midafternoon hour there were not many patrons in the restaurant.

Dawn sat across the table. She had pulled her long, black hair back from her face and fastened it at the nape of her neck. The style was severe, but it emphasized the perfection of her facial features. Her full, rosy lips pursed slightly as she took a sip of hot coffee. He thought he smelled her softly spicy perfume.

He was unmoved. Uninterested. He had decided, during the brief time he waited for this meeting, that he would hear her out, then offer any advice he thought pertinent. Perhaps he'd offer a cool acknowledgment that last night should not have occurred—any of it.

That was all.

Once more, he had gotten his emotions back under control.

He watched as Dawn took a sip of coffee, then another. She took a deep breath, then began, "Jonah, about last night—"

"I apologize," he interrupted. "I'm sure that's what you wanted to hear. I take back the accusations, and everything else as well. It was all a mistake, but it could have been a worse one if we'd gone any farther." He felt nothing at all at her wince, the hurt in her eyes. He didn't let himself.

"All right, then." Her tone was brusque, and she studied her coffee cup. "I spoke with a couple of governmental agencies about how best to protect the mountain lion." She described her phone calls, then said, "So if it's an endangered species, it's supposedly protected and can't be hunted. But we can't prove it, and I'm afraid Ray and the farmers will shoot first and worry about explanations later."

Jonah nodded. "So you still want to bring it to the Haven to protect it." He knew his voice was as cold as the cola he sipped. Did she think giving him this information would somehow change his mind?

"I know you don't agree. But I also know you care about the mountain lion. And—I probably shouldn't admit this to you, but after my discussions today, I'm not sure I'll get clearance to bring it into the Haven anyway."

She told him that, to capture and shelter the animal, she might have to prove it had been domesticated and belonged to someone. "Amos is checking around, but since it may have been illegal to keep it, we doubt we'll find someone to admit it was theirs. Besides . . ." Her voice trailed off, and she toyed with a straw.

"Besides what?" he asked.

Her eyes rose to meet his. They were luminous, and their exotic angle made her appear wistful, almost sad. "I think it's wild, don't you?"

"Yes," he said immediately. "And that's all the more reason to leave it free."

"Free to die?" Her voice was soft and sorrowful.

He hesitated. No, he did not want the animal to die. Nor did he want it to spend its days in a cage, wishing—

What? Did it have enough consciousness to yearn for freedom, the way he had?

He had come face-to-face with the mountain lion, had looked into its fierce, golden green eyes. Had felt . . . something. Yes, on some level, he did think it was aware enough to value its freedom above all else—maybe even life.

"Yes, free to die." He emphasized the last word, purposely leaving no room in his tone for argument.

"Jonah, I—"

"If you were hoping to change my mind, you haven't. You can't."

Her nostrils flared slightly, and he knew he had angered her. "No, I know better than to try to move you, Mr. Campion. You've made up your mind, no matter what is best for the animal. Maybe I'm just as stubborn, but your goal is its freedom; mine is its survival. I was hoping, when I saw you, to ask . . ."

Her voice trailed off, and she appeared flustered.

"To ask what?" he demanded.

She sat up straighter, then stared him squarely in the eye. "To find out what happened to you. I gather that you've told some people around here about your crime. Some say you didn't do it, and others say you did it to help someone. Which was it?"

A lancing pain pierced his insides, and his vision clouded as he stared at Dawn Perry. So much for believing he had his emotions back under control. *Damn!* This woman knew how to get him where it hurt.

He did not want to talk about his past. And obviously he had talked too much. Too many people knew pieces of what had happened. The little good that had come out of his imprisonment might be undone if the truth was known by the wrong people.

"Jonah?" Dawn's uncertain voice broke through his trance.

"I thought we were talking about the mountain lion, Ms. Perry. My criminal past has nothing to do with saving the animal, and in any event it is none of your business." He slammed some money down on the table and stood.

But before he stalked away, he thought he heard Dawn say very quietly, "What I'm afraid of, Jonah, is that you're wrong."

* * *

176

What had she expected? Dawn demanded of herself as she searched through a file drawer in her office. That Jonah would genuinely apologize for the night before and transform into a different person? Maybe he would agree all of a sudden that the mountain lion belonged in the Haven? And then he would spill his guts about why he had chosen to break the law.

Of course, it would be a marvelous, altruistic reason. Any lies he'd told had been utterly, obviously necessary. His justification would be so clear, so earth-shattering, that it would convince her it was all right for her to lie to save the cougar.

At least, she thought, she'd been able to focus first on her car, then on the mountain lion, when she'd been with him. That way, she didn't have to think about how uncomfortable she was. She had very nearly made love with him. He had seen her virtually naked. She had seen him with only his shirt off. And look what trouble that had caused.

She found the file she was looking for and slammed the drawer shut.

The noise must have been audible outside her closed door, for in a moment it burst open. "What's going on?" Marnie asked.

Dawn nearly shouted, "None of your business!" but she caught herself. She leaned against the file cabinet, hanging her head. "Just having a temper tantrum," she admitted with a shrug.

"Well, have it later. Right now there's someone in the reception area who wants to see you."

"A client?" Dawn asked the empty space where Marnie had stood. She took a deep breath to make certain she was calm, then left the room.

And stopped. The person in the reception area was Jonah.

Dawn froze.

"Would you care to explain what you meant?" His tone was conversational, as though they were continuing the discussion that had ended so abruptly before.

"What I meant by what?"

Dawn noticed that her secretary, Lil, an efficient young thing fresh out of secretarial school, was looking from Jonah to her and back again—though her admiring gaze mostly remained on Jonah.

He had changed into a clean beige shirt and blue trousers. He looked great. But it was more than seeing his clothes that sent small flutters of pleasure through Dawn; it was seeing *him*.

She shook her head at her folly. "Come into my office," she said.

She closed the door behind them and motioned him to a seat. "Why are you here? I thought you wanted nothing to do with me."

"I'm here to apologize." He seemed nearly to choke on the words, and she managed to keep herself from smiling. Quickly, he continued, "And I wanted to understand what you meant about my being wrong. What I recalled saying was something like my unsavory past is not your business, and that in any case it has nothing to do with saving the mountain lion. Which part of that isn't correct?"

Dawn took her seat behind her desk, wanting to return to his perfunctory apology. It might be an easier subject to tackle with him. She put the file she was carrying down on a pile and straightened it. How could she answer? "I . . . I wanted to find out what would make a person commit a crime," she said uneasily. She couldn't explain the entire thing: that she had been thinking hard about what Marnie had said, wondering whether, if she found someone at a zoo or other menagerie to back her up, she could lie to the government to save the mountain lion. "What pushes a person to lie?"

Jonah stiffened as though she had struck him. His face was again shadowed by his old, stone-hard expression. "A person does what he has to," he said, not denying, this time, that he had committed a crime.

Was it really as simple as that? She ached to know Jonah's story—but, as defensive as he was, he clearly was not about to tell her.

"Tell you what," he said. "I still don't think the mountain lion belongs in captivity, but maybe we can get it some better legal protection while it's free if we can prove it's a member of an endangered species." He had changed the subject. Or, rather, between the topics of the mountain lion and himself, he had focused on the animal. But what he had suggested . . . had Dawn heard right?

"You'd rely on the system?" She looked at Jonah in amazement.

His tawny eyebrows slanted inward, as though he were irritated. "I didn't say that. But maybe having the cougar declared endangered would be better for it."

Maybe from his perspective. If the animal were found to be a member of an endangered species, then it might be even harder to get it into the Haven, even if Dawn lied—for not only the state, but the federal government, too, might get involved.

Did she want that?

But such a finding might have advantages, too. "If the mountain lion is proven to be a protected species under the law, I might be able to use the legal system to get injunctions against Ray and Cornelius and anyone else who has threatened it," she said slowly. "They don't care if it's endangered; Ray has already made that clear. But if they were personally and expressly enjoined from hunting it, they'd have to know that they would be watched. If they hurt—or killed—the animal, they'd be subject to federal prosecution."

"That's the general idea," Jonah said.

Maybe, just maybe, a temporary restraining order, followed by a permanent injunction, would act as a deterrent. Unless, like Jonah, they decided to commit the crime despite the law.

Why had Jonah . . . ?

That was getting her nowhere. "Okay, how will we prove the cougar is a member of an endangered species?"

"Tomorrow is Saturday," Jonah said. "I have the day off. Let's go onto Eskaway and locate that cat. We'll see if we can find where it sleeps and get some fur or something else that can be used for DNA analysis."

"I'm not sure that's a good idea," she said, "being up there ourselves." The last time she had been alone with him, they had nearly made love on her kitchen floor. And what a humiliating mistake that had been. Nevertheless, the idea sent warning tingles through her—and a strange, slow heat. But being close to him wasn't her only concern. "I don't trust—"

"Forget it," he interrupted, standing as if to go. His broad chest rose and fell unevenly beneath his shirt, and his fists clenched at his sides. "Of course you shouldn't trust me." He spoke through gritted teeth. "Bad idea. See you around."

"You didn't let me finish, Jonah."

His gray-green eyes stared daggers, but he did not move.

"I don't trust Ray or Cornelius or the other crazy hunters," Dawn went on. "They're probably running around on Eskaway with guns, and being up there until we get a restraining order may not be safe. Maybe not even after we get one."

He visibly relaxed, and Dawn nearly smiled. After

all that had happened between them, perhaps he was justified in expecting her to insult him or hurt him.

She hadn't intended to before. And now? Now she wanted his input. His help. Maybe even his confidence.

"We'll find a way to corral Ray and the others," Jonah said. "But first, we need proof this cougar is endangered. Without that—"

She finished his sentence. "We won't get a restraining order. You're right. And I'm with you."

She only hoped she would not regret it.

"What do you mean you don't think they're right for each other?" demanded Lettie.

Amos walked around her square kitchen table with the blue checked cloth over it. He put an arm around the dear, outspoken woman with whom he had been spending another wonderful evening. Until now. "Now, Lettie—"

"Don't 'Now, Lettie' me, Amos Wilton," she said, standing to face him.

Lettie was half a foot shorter than he, but she was still a powerhouse of energy, and, with his arm still on her shoulder, he could feel her trembling with indignation. She wore a pretty red dress that evening; no one could tell by looking at her that she was a champion auto mechanic.

"You know full well that my Jonah and your Dawn make a perfect couple," she continued irritably. "Just like us."

Amos nearly laughed aloud. "Yes, Lettie," he said meekly. "Exactly like us." Fighting all the time. Disagreeing on everything. Yes, that had to be true love!

Her hands were on her hips. "Are you insinuating that there's anything wrong with our relationship?" As she tapped her foot on the floor, her red curls bobbed slightly about her face.

Amos drew her into his arms. She remained stiff as he nibbled at her neck, but she smelled good—like fresh soap. "There's nothing wrong with our relationship that a little lovin' won't cure, sweetheart."

He felt her relax, just a little. "But—"

"Shush. Let me explain. I just meant that I'm not sure my stubborn granddaughter will ever open those sweet brown eyes of hers enough to really look beyond his prison record to the real Jonah. And he doesn't help much, by insisting that no one talk about what happened to him."

"I shouldn't even have told you," Lettie grumbled, though the sound was beginning to be a little more like a purr as he rubbed her back.

Amos glanced around the small kitchen in the house that Lettie had lived in since she married Arnold Green more than forty years ago. Poor Arnie hadn't been able to keep up with her, but he'd been a good provider and had left her the auto shop.

"You can tell me anything, Lettie." He moved his mouth around to find her lips. They were willing, yielding—and they tasted mighty fine.

"Oh, Amos." Lettie sighed after a while. "Why didn't you ever ask me out before?"

"I didn't think your friend Ray would approve." Amos realized he sounded testy. But he didn't like Ray Koslowski. He'd always found him an overbearing fool, even before their current feud.

Lettie pulled away. Her tone was quarrelsome again. "Ray's not really a bad sort, Amos. In fact, he can be a dear. He just has a different opinion about wildlife than you, that's all."

That wasn't all, but Amos was not about to rile Lettie any further. She still sounded sweet on the guy, darn it all.

He pulled up the sleeve of his plaid flannel shirt and looked at his watch. "Look how late it's getting. Guess I'd best hurry home."

Lettie took a step toward him and eyed him flirtatiously. "Amos, are you jealous of Ray?"

This was not a game he enjoyed. "Should I be?"

"You're the one whose mountain lion came back here to Eskaway. If it hadn't, you might never have paid attention to me, and maybe I'd still have been with Ray."

"Maybe," he agreed, taking her hand. He owed the mountain lion. So did she, though she didn't realize it. How could she care for a contentious, self-centered, animal-killing maniac like Ray Koslowski?

Amos should have asked her out before, if only to save her from that man.

But it was time they got off the subject of Ray Koslowski, before Amos said something he regretted. Or didn't regret. "I'm glad you, at least, believe in my family legend about the mountain lion."

"I may believe in the legend angle," Lettie grumbled, "but that doesn't make the animal any less dangerous. It killed a cow already. I just hope it does its magical thing and disappears again before a person gets hurt."

"Or that we can get it into the Haven before *it* gets hurt," Amos chided gently. He sighed. "I just wish Dawn believed in the legend."

"What about Patty? Has your daughter felt any effects?"

"She's a hard one to reach. She travels a lot with this latest husband. I'll have to ask Dawn if she's heard from her mother." Amos led Lettie from the kitchen, turning out the light.

"While you're at it," Lettie said, "ask Dawn why she's

such a disbeliever. I mean, it all makes sense to me. Jonah didn't come into her life till the mountain lion's return, and—"

"Like I said, she's not recognizing there's anything between Jonah and her. And who's to say whether he's the right one?"

"Amos!"

"Look, Lettie," he said, leading her into her living room. "It's only been a few days. And it won't make any difference to us, will it, if things don't work out between them?"

She sank down onto the beige overstuffed sofa and held out her arms to him. He sat beside her, cuddling her against him. Gosh, did she feel good!

"No," Lettie said. "But I wish Jonah could feel as happy as I do now. He deserves a little joy in his life."

"So does Dawn," Amos said, "but they're the ones who'll have to let it come to them, and I'm afraid they're both too set in their ways."

"Oh, young folks!" Lettie made it sound like an imprecation. "What do they know?"

"Not as much as we do, honey. Smarts come with age." Amos sought her lips again.

The next morning, Dawn walked carefully through the carpet of delicate ferns, peering around a tall pine. "Do you see anything?" she asked Jonah, who hiked the slopes of Eskaway beside her.

"Yes," he said. "I see you."

Feeling herself flush despite the coolness of the shade, she looked up to find him watching her. How had she ever thought his gray-green eyes to be cold? They burned now, so heatedly that she wondered if they would set the hillside on fire.

She made herself laugh. "And I see you, and the forest, and an awful lot of bugs. But no mountain lion."

"No," he agreed. "No mountain lion."

They had come up the mountain a different way this time, a shortcut to the rocky area where she had spotted the cougar a couple of days earlier. They had started off staying far from one another, but when she had stumbled on a root, Jonah's arm caught her waist to steady her. For the last hour, they'd walked side by side.

It felt natural, hiking through the forest with him again. It was as natural as the sweet, clean scent of the outdoors, the calls of the birds about them, and the brilliance of the green moss on the logs flung here and there about the forest floor.

Natural, but uncomfortable, too. Jonah was being nice today. Too nice. She did not want to feel as though being with him was becoming a pleasant habit. Or worse, an addiction.

She might start wanting a repeat of that evening on her kitchen floor. One that his scar wouldn't stop.

Trying to distance herself from him, she said argumentatively, "We've been hiking quite a while. Don't you feel anything that says which way we should go? You're the one the mountain lion gave directions to."

"It's drawn you to it, too." Jonah's retort was mild. "Maybe it's your turn to get the call today. Let me know when the phone rings, will you?"

She glanced up again. He grinned mockingly, and the expression lightened many deep hollows on his fascinating face. A lock of his pale brown hair had fallen over his forehead and was now damp with the sweat of exertion from walking uphill for more than an hour. She wanted to push the hair back, out of his way, but she didn't.

"Sure, I'll tell you," she grumbled.

"I'll tell you, too," Jonah said. His voice had grown serious.

"About what?"

"About me. And why—Hey, look!" His hand reached out, and he pointed ahead of them.

They had reached a rocky clearing. There, standing majestically atop a boulder, was the lion.

Dawn drew in her breath. It was magnificent! It stood erect and proud, its tawny, multihued coat glistening in the light filtering into the clearing. The sun was at its back, and dust motes swirled around it, giving it the appearance of flickering in a radiant mist. Its head was raised, and it seemed to regard them with interest, ears cupped forward. It showed no fear, nor did it appear ready to attack.

"Hello," Dawn said quietly. Maybe she had not heard it calling her, but she certainly sensed its presence now with more than her vision. Dawn wanted something from the animal—something that would prove it was a member of an endangered species. But there was more. She felt as though the cougar wanted something from her in return. What? She yearned to reach out to it, to pull from it the answers. All answers . . .

She glanced at Jonah beside her. He was staring as though mesmerized, his brows lowered in concentration. Was he attempting to communicate wordlessly with the animal, too?

Was he succeeding?

If only she had that ability. But she, apparently, did not. And so she asked in a low voice, "Will you show us where you sleep? Can you leave us something to show us who you are, what species you belong to? And tell me what *you* want. I'll try to help."

It did not understand her, of course. But on some level she had the feeling once more that it wished to communicate. She would have laughed aloud at herself, if she did not fear scaring the cougar away.

Besides, her impression was far from humorous.

"Please," she whispered. Slowly she walked toward it, only half-aware of Jonah at her side.

"Careful," he murmured. "No matter what we feel for it, it's still a wild animal."

Dawn nodded in agreement but did not stop her advance. Her grandfather had taught her that staring for too long into an animal's eyes was construed as a threat, since many beasts looked hard into the faces of their prey before attacking. So Dawn averted her eyes slightly as she kept moving forward. The leaves beneath her feet were brittle, and her steps created a crisp rushing noise.

She felt no fear of the animal. Would it allow her to get close enough to run her fingers through its pelt, drawing out loose hairs that could be tested for its DNA content?

Dawn drew nearer.

"It's time to go, fellow," Jonah said. "Let us check where you've been standing to see if you've left any fur behind."

The animal reacted as though it had understood him. It turned and began walking slowly away.

"No," Dawn cried. "Wait!"

She increased her pace only slightly, for fear of scaring the cougar. She stopped where it had been standing but, glancing down, saw nothing that she could pick up and carry.

"Please wait," Dawn repeated, following as the animal walked slowly through the trees.

It turned its head, as though looking back at her. Then it opened its mouth and bared its fangs, as though warning her to stay away. It let out a loud, snarling scream.

187

"I don't mean you any harm," Dawn said. "Please."

But, reaching a tree, it began running, and by the time Dawn got where she had last seen it, it was out of sight.

Chapter Twelve

"He *does* value his freedom," Dawn said softly to Jonah.

They were walking slowly back down the mountain, using a different trail from the one they had taken to find the cougar. "Maybe that was what our friend the mountain lion was trying to communicate to me."

"Maybe," he agreed. "What did you feel?"

Dawn shrugged. "I can't explain it. But the way he moved away so easily, then dared us to follow—oh, I know I'm not making sense, but . . ."

"You're making a lot of sense. Believe me."

"Then you felt it, too?" She turned to study Jonah's face. They were in shadows again beneath tall trees, so it was difficult to read his expression. But when he looked at her, she saw conflicting emotions; there was pain behind his eyes, yet he smiled.

"I've felt it all along," he said, "though I guess shrinks would call it 'projecting.'"

"Do you mean that you projected your own emotions onto the mountain lion?"

"More or less. I just wish we'd figured out a way to get a little fur."

Dawn nodded. "We're back where we started from. We've no evidence that can prove whether it's endangered."

The last time they had been on this mountain together, Dawn had been frantic about Amos. Jonah had found him for her. And that was not the only reason she had begun to care for him. For she *had* begun to care for him, damn it—despite all her confusion. Something about Jonah drew her like a magnet. But there were still things that repelled her, huge things in the path of letting herself go with him that she could not ignore. His defensiveness, for one thing. And his criminal record. Perhaps, though, they were things that could be gotten around, if she had all the facts.

She clenched one fist so that her nails bit into her palms. She might enrage him, but she had to ask. "Jonah, will you tell me now?"

He did not play games with her. "About why I went to prison?"

"Yes. Please."

All she heard for a long while were their footsteps, some birds, the distant sound of water from a mountain stream. Finally he spoke. "You'll understand, when I tell you, why it's important that the story stop here. Too many people already know, and if what happened gets back to the wrong person, it'll cause hurt that's unnecessary. Especially after all that's happened."

She held up her hand with two fingers extended skyward. "I won't tell anyone else. Scout's honor."

"And I suppose you were a scout, Ms. Perry."

"For one year—until I tried to earn a merit badge for crocheting and found I had no patience for it."

His half-smile was ephemeral. He stared ahead as they continued down the slope, as though seeing the past before him.

Impulsively, Dawn grabbed his hand, but he did not seem to notice. His was cold, barely gripping hers in return.

"I was a medical student. I had done well and was awarded several scholarships, but one source ran into financial difficulty and dried up. I needed money."

Was this, then, the answer? Dawn wondered, feeling her shoulders stiffen in unwilling repugnance. He needed money, and so he had taken it—just like any other thief?

No, that couldn't be all. If it were, why did so many people believe in him? How could he mislead so many?

"My sister was married to a certified public accountant who worked in Philly for a large corporation. He told me about a job opening in his department for a clerical type, someone to enter figures into a computer. The hours were flexible, the pay decent, and I took it."

"Is that the company you were accused of embezzling from?"

His grip tightened slightly. "Yes. Apparently the thefts started when I did. An auditor caught it, and by then there were nearly fifty thousand dollars unaccounted for."

Dawn let out a small whistle. "Wow." Jonah released her hand and increased his downhill pace, as though to catch up with whatever he was chasing. Dawn sped up till she reached his side.

"Yeah, wow," he said. "Everyone was suspected and

examined. I was the new kid, and the evidence all pointed to me."

"But—"

"But I didn't do it. Of course, that didn't stop your wonderful legal system from convicting me. I was there, I was new, there were unexplained discrepancies in my accounts, end of story. But I was not the only one with access to those accounts. And I had no increase in income, no overseas bank account, no change in lifestyle. No one could figure out where the money was. I swore I didn't do it. But someone had to hang for the loss, and it was me."

Dawn stumbled over a fallen branch and grabbed Jonah's hand again to right herself. "Sorry," he said. "Am I going too fast?"

She shook her head, wishing she could bring some color back to his pasty cheeks. He appeared drained of blood, of emotion.

"That's not the whole story, is it?" she asked gently.

He gave a quick shake of his head. "No. I knew who the thief was but couldn't say anything. I counted on the system not to convict me, since I wasn't guilty. I didn't think I had to hand over someone else to be cleared. And even if I'd known—"

"Even if you'd known you'd be punished, you could not have said anything." Dawn guessed the rest of the story. "It was your brother-in-law, wasn't it?"

He nodded. "My sister is four years older than me. She had three kids at home then, all under five years old. She'd taken some liberal arts classes in college but got married without graduating. She'd worked as a store clerk till they started having children—a minimum-wage job. She had no way to raise those kids on her own, and I'd no way to help her then. I couldn't point a finger at her husband."

"And he let you go to prison, rather than confessing."

Jonah's hand suddenly gripped hers so hard it hurt. "Yes. I think the statute of limitations has passed, so he couldn't be convicted now, but there's no sense in accusing him. He had a gambling problem—didn't even use the money for his family. He owed it to others. My sister never benefited from a penny. After all this time, she has another toddler at home now. She still couldn't make it on her own, and she might leave him if she knew the truth. As it was, she was righteous enough not to stand by me. Can you believe it? She was furious with me for robbing her dear husband's company. She said she was glad our parents hadn't lived to see the day their only son was exposed as a crook." His laugh sounded as though he were choking.

"Oh, Jonah."

"And then there was my so-called girlfriend. We'd talked of marriage, and she suspected the truth—but she wanted nothing to do with a convicted felon."

Dawn used the hand he held to stop him and pull him close on the trail. Then she did what she had wanted to before; she reached up to smooth a wayward hank of hair from his face. "I'm so sorry," she whispered, not sure what it was she apologized for: for not believing in him, for the legal system she defended, for the miserable way the world had treated him—or for all of the above.

He clasped her elbows and used them to draw her close. The agony on his face was painful to see, and she closed her eyes.

His lips on hers were rough and punishing, but she did not draw away. Instead she tried to soothe him with her own kiss, trying to draw away his sorrow, his hurt.

His body hard against hers, he thrust his tongue

inside her mouth, and she met it with her own, nearly falling from the way heat flooded her. "Come on," he said. He nearly dragged her the rest of the way down the hill.

He handed her silently into his car. What was he thinking? Did he need to be alone, after what he had revealed? But that kiss—it had stirred her. Deeply.

She tried to break the silence when he got into the driver's seat. "Jonah, you don't—"

"Forget it," he demanded. He turned the key in the ignition, threw the car into gear, and started down the road at a speed that made Dawn pray that Clemson and his deputies were nowhere about.

It seemed like mere moments until they reached her house. Or was it hours? It was still daylight, midafternoon. Dawn said, "Would you like to come in? We missed lunch. I could make us something."

"If I come inside your house," he said in a deep voice as raspy as coarse-grade sandpaper, "it won't be for lunch."

She stared at him, trying to ignore a lava flow that moistened her insides. "Come in," she invited again.

This time they made it to her bedroom. Nervously, Dawn wondered what Jonah thought of it. After she had lost Billy, she had assumed she would be alone forever, and so she had made her room a feminine enclave, one that did not invite men. Its walls were pale lavender, and the bed wore a beige coverlet with piles of pillows at the head in lacy shams of blue, purple and pink.

Maybe Jonah didn't even notice, for the moment they stepped inside the room he used his foot to slam the door shut. Then he grabbed her. She shivered with anticipation.

His kiss was again rough, unyielding. He began unbuttoning her shirt with one hand, and his touch on her breasts even outside her clothing made her gasp.

He stopped for an instant. "Are you sure you want this?" he demanded against her mouth.

She wasn't sure of anything at that moment—except that she did not want to stop. "Yes, Jonah. Please."

In moments she felt her blouse being yanked from her body. He used his hips to urge her backward until she collapsed onto the bed. She lay on top of her cool, feminine coverlet feeling like a vixen in heat as Jonah reached behind and undid her bra strap. In moments, her upper body was bared to him, and he wasted no time in taking advantage. Lying beside her, he covered one breast with a hot, trembling hand, kneading it, then massaging the nipple with his thumb until it peaked. She drew in her breath and looked at him.

His head was even with her breasts. His light brown hair was long enough to spill around him, and she watched as he reached for her breast, took it into his mouth. She moaned at the sweet sensation as his tongue assaulted it, then helped to suck it into his mouth. "Oh, Jonah," she said in a whimper. She inhaled the aroma of shampoo mixed with sweat and sex.

She was hardly aware of his ridding her of her pants, for she was too busy pulling at his clothing. But passion made her awkward, and he had to help her.

He seemed to hold his breath for an instant as he pulled off his shirt. She hesitated, unsure how to react. Their eyes met for an instant. He looked defensive . . . vulnerable. This time she said nothing, but touched his scar gently, then placed her lips on it. She heard him inhale deeply, then reach for his belt buckle. She, too, began to breathe once more.

He had a wonderful body—not that she was surprised. The manual labor at the car shop must have helped, for his pectoral muscles, even marred by the scar, matched his biceps in bulging firmness. He had a line of light, curly hair that swept down his chest and beyond, expanding at his abdomen to form a nest for the protruding maleness that showed that he was as excited as she. She blinked at the sight. She was not a virgin, but her experience was limited and had been long ago. He was beautiful everywhere, and the sight of him nearly made her whimper with desire.

She couldn't help it. She touched him, gently at first, and was rewarded by hearing him moan. Emboldened, she wrapped her hand around his length and showed him a rhythm that she desired for a song yet to be sung.

He stopped her for just a moment, and as she heard the crackling of cellophane she thought both with amusement and embarrassment that he had planned this. Or maybe he did this a lot, with many women, and was always prepared.

She hated that idea.

But she had no time to dwell on it. His mouth returned to hers, and, tasting the unrelenting demand of him once more, she closed her eyes. She lay still as he moved on top of her. He was large and heavy, but she reveled in his sweet weight.

And then she felt him touch her there, where she needed soothing, where she craved contact. She gasped, feeling her body buck as his fingers explored her. And then it was no longer his finger but his sex that entered her, probing, unrelenting.

She lifted her hips to meet him and felt him fill her fully. She felt no pain—just building ecstasy. "Oh, Jonah." She moaned as he plunged his tongue into her mouth again.

His body moved slowly at first, as though testing the

feel. It was wonderful, but it was not enough. She rose to meet his gentle thrusts, then encouraged him by creating a faster tempo.

It was as though she had ignited a fuse, for in moments he drove in and out of her with a fervor that matched her own wild hunger. She heard the sounds of passion fill the air, whether from him or her or both, she did not know. She felt heat and moisture and wonder, and then—

And then she flew over the edge, hearing a shout fill the room as she called his name.

Dumb, Campion, Jonah thought as he lay uncomfortably under the feminine covers on Dawn's bed. She was beside him, her warm back pressed against his side.

Very dumb.

But oh, so necessary. He had wanted Dawn Perry from the moment he had first laid eyes on her, as she had skipped fearfully around Clemson's police station demanding help to find her grandfather.

And up on the mountain today, after spilling his guts to her, he had needed release—and this was the very relief that he had craved. To be with Dawn, to touch her, to taste her, to feel her everywhere, engulfing him.

He had gotten what he had wanted. No, he had gotten a sample of what he had wanted, for now that he had experienced lovemaking with this woman, he wanted more. A lot more.

But first he had to say something. Break the silence. Was she upset? Angry? Embarrassed?

"Jonah?" Her voice was a muffled whisper, and he turned to face her. She had one hand tucked beneath her face on the pillow, and her gorgeous black hair was spilled all around her. She looked like a sleepy child.

No, not a child, for as she raised her eyes to look into his, there was desire there. What? Hadn't she had enough?

He hunkered over and put his arms around her, pulling her naked body tight against his. Damn, but it felt good: those curves, that soft, heated skin. . . .

"Yes?" he murmured into her sweet-smelling hair.

"I'm not—I mean, it was a long time, and I haven't—"

He laughed. "Do you have something you want to ask about the birds and the bees? I thought you knew all about wildlife, Ms. Perry."

"There's wildlife, and then there's *wild life*." He could hear the smile in her voice. "And what I want to know has to do with powers of rejuvenation."

That took him aback.

"Do you mean—"

"I mean, how long does it take before we can do it again?"

Her very words started his blood flowing downward. He could feel it pumping through his veins, feel himself growing hard.

"Oh, I'd say about another minute." He rolled on top of her and began kissing her.

Dawn lost track of how many times they made love that weekend—for Jonah stayed all night Saturday and into Sunday.

"Isn't the auto shop open today?" she managed to ask once while they were resting, as daylight cast a mellow glow into the room through the closed beige draperies.

"Usually not on Sunday, unless there's a customer

with an emergency. And then Lettie will call. I'll check my answering machine."

She held her breath while he did. He sat at the edge of her bed with a towel around his slim, masculine waist in an attempt at modesty.

He pushed some buttons, then hung up. "Guess nobody had anything to say to me today," he told her.

"Maybe not," she replied, "but I have a lot for you to do."

"More?" His tawny brows were raised in a show of incredulity that she did not believe for an instant.

"More," she demanded, and he dove for her, the towel slipping to the floor.

Much later, they showered together for the second time, her long hair tucked up beneath a lacy cap. When they were finished and she had slipped on her blue chenille robe, she offered, "If you don't mind cholesterol, I can whip us up one heck of an omelet. And if you do mind, I have some salad fixings."

"I'm hungry," he said. At her look, he laughed as merrily as she had ever heard him. "For food, that is. For now. You do the omelet, and I'll fix the salad."

He put on his trousers, and as they ate at her kitchen table in the windowed alcove, she admired the breadth of his chest—notwithstanding the scar that marred its handsome, masculine contours.

He noticed where she was staring, and she saw his relaxed facial features begin to harden, as though he were throwing up a wall between them.

She shook her head. "No, Jonah," she said as though answering a question. "Let's neither of us talk about your scar. But I do want you to know it doesn't bother me. Neither does your past." That was not entirely true; she was quite bothered by it. But not because she did not believe in his innocence. Instead, it was

Linda O. Johnston

because of the disintegration of her own innocence. Naïveté, rather. After Billy, she had wanted so much to believe in the inviolability of the legal system that she had turned her back on anything that hinted that things could go wrong.

But she could not, would not, turn her back on Jonah. Never again. Yes, he was a convicted felon, and perhaps that might always bother her. But she realized now that she was falling in love with him.

One of life's little ironies, she thought. Dawn Perry, attorney extraordinaire, advocate of victims, defender of the legal system, was falling in love with a hardened ex-con.

Although at the moment, he was far from hardened—anywhere. He smiled at her, and she loved the lightness in his gaze. His words mirrored her thoughts. "Here you are, having brunch the morning after in your own kitchen, with a crook. And here I am, having a great time the morning after with a lawyer, of all things. Maybe our mountain lion *is* magical, like your grandfather believes."

"Maybe," Dawn said with a smile. "Though I'd hate to tell the cocky old son of a gun. He'd rub it in from now till forever."

He took a sip of coffee from one of her Penn State mugs. "I haven't really heard his whole story. What does he think the cougar's return means?"

Dawn closed her eyes. Did she really want to explain it to Jonah?

Yes, she thought. She didn't really believe in it—or at least she hadn't before last night. Or this morning, as she sat reveling in everything that Jonah made her feel. Were they destined for one another?

That she did not know. But just maybe . . .

"It's a long story," she finally said. "A family legend, really, that Amos claims he heard from his own grand-

200

father. It's an explanation for a run of bad luck for the Wiltons, and now the Perrys, but—"

"But you don't want to tell me." Jonah's voice was flat. She was hurting him again.

"It's not that," she said quickly, bending over the table to touch the back of his sinewy forearm. It was tense, and she squeezed it gently. "Let me refresh our coffee; then I'll tell you the whole absurd tale."

She took her time crossing her tiled floor, her slippers making scuffing sounds. She remembered how their first lovemaking had started—and ended—several days ago right there, beneath her hanging copper pots. And now it was all so different.

She refilled their mugs, then sat down again. "You shared the skeleton in your closet with me; I guess it's my turn." She looked away from his face, not wanting to see his incredulity as she explained Amos's story. Instead, she looked out the window into her garden, where daffodils and irises were blooming along the path to her garage. "I think it's a hybrid of several area legends, though Amos doesn't admit it. But the way it goes is this: As you may have been able to tell from my features and the color of my hair, the Wilton side of my family is descended partly from Native Americans."

"Yes," he said quietly, reaching over to stroke her prominent cheekbones tenderly with his thumb. "I'd wondered."

She reveled in the feel of his callused fingers against her skin. He was arousing her again, even with such a sweet, innocuous touch.

She made herself go on, though her voice was hoarse as she related the family legend.

She stopped once to look at Jonah. He was watching her with curiosity in his features, that was all—no scornful skepticism.

And so she continued, relating the story of the Indian princess Esk-a-na and her doomed romance, her doomed life, her family curse.

She paused when she'd finished. "I don't do a good job of telling it. Amos puts in names, dates, sound effects; you'll have to ask him."

"I get the gist of it," Jonah said. "So in your family, no one has found happiness in love for all those generations?"

Dawn shrugged. "Amos certainly didn't; he was married and divorced twice. My mother is on husband number six now, I believe."

"And you—is that why you haven't married?"

She smiled grimly. "Not really. I didn't believe in the legend. I like to think that if Billy, my fiancé, had lived, we would still be happy together."

That made Jonah frown. He took a long swig of coffee. "I see. And he was murdered."

She nodded.

"Then you did not find happiness in love, though maybe for a different reason from your grandfather and mother."

She stared at him. "Do you believe that story?"

He shrugged his broad shoulders and looked out the window. "There is a mountain lion back here after all these years."

But that wasn't all there was to the legend. A mountain lion's return was supposed to mean that members of her family could find their true loves. Was Jonah obliquely saying that he loved her?

She knew she was falling in love with him. She had already admitted it to herself. She believed she might finally be able to put Billy, and all that he had meant to her, to rest.

But she was not certain she was ready to admit her love to Jonah. Or to hear that he loved her.

Mountain lion or not.

"Let's finish here," she said. "I'll do the dishes later. Not that we haven't been getting our exercise, but I feel like taking a walk. There's a nice wooded area behind my garage. Are you interested in accompanying me?"

"I'd accompany you anywhere," said Jonah with a smile. "Within reason."

Jonah enjoyed their peaceful walk. The woods behind Dawn's house were not as thick as the forests of Eskaway, and for a while the two of them followed the course of a glistening stream.

The breeze was cool, and he lifted his face into it, feeling it gust through his hair. He had been delightfully warm, for a long while, there in Dawn's bedroom, but now he had to return to reality. Maybe.

He rubbed the stubble on his chin. He would have to move shaving paraphernalia into her home in the future. If they had a future.

A short one, at least, he hoped.

A bird sang overhead, and Jonah looked up into the canopy of leaves above them, searching for it. "This reminds me of the woods behind the house I rent," he said. "It's great."

"I think so," Dawn said. "I always have." She closed one eye, then sighted along her arm beyond her pointing finger toward a branch where leaves fluttered in the breeze. No, it was a small, brown bird that stirred them. "A wood thrush," Dawn said with satisfaction. "There are a lot fewer of them now than when I was a kid. They're growing more scarce, the more civilization moves in."

"Then you lived here when you were growing up?" Jonah asked. He could envision her as a wide-eyed, dark-haired child in coveralls, studying the birds in these woods and helping her grandfather save injured animals. It was an impression of her that he liked much more than the aloof, professional attorney.

Although she had been far from aloof with him this weekend.

"Oh, yes, I've lived here a long time," she said. "Amos inherited the house from his father, who grew up there, too." She spoke fondly of the place. "Of course, I don't know where our Indian ancestors used to hang out. Maybe it was even on this same property."

"I envy your deep roots," he blurted out, then regretted it. He sounded maudlin, ridiculous. He cleared his throat. "I mean—"

"Isn't it great?" She smiled at him, a great, big, excited smile that lit her entire beautiful face. The smile warmed him to his very depths and drew an answering grin from him. She hadn't seemed to notice how stupid his comment had been.

Or maybe it hadn't been so absurd after all.

"Most people in the United States measure their time here by the arrival of some ship or airplane within the last couple of centuries. My family really belongs here."

He did envy her that. Imagine, if he could put down roots in this area as well. Raise kids here . . .

Helping Dawn over the rocks and along a twisting dirt path, he held her hand. He did not want to let it go. He did not want to let *her* go.

Dumb, Campion, he told himself over and over. He was falling in love with the woman beside him, the woman who refused to believe in her grandfather's fairy tale, because she was much too practical. She was a woman who, in her disbelief, would convince herself that the only man she would ever love was the dead, sainted Billy.

Just as well, Jonah thought bitterly. He had to control his aching heart, just as he had learned to control the rest of his emotions. He had nothing to offer Dawn.

But if he were to run into the mountain lion down here, he would ask it to work harder to convince her of its magical qualities.

Whether it was true or not, Jonah wanted Dawn to believe in Amos's legend—for that way, just maybe, she would let herself care, just a little, for Jonah himself.

"It's wonderful, isn't it?" Dawn pulled him down onto a large boulder beside the stream.

"What is?" He sat beside her on the hard rock, one arm around her shoulder, holding her close. The water bubbled melodically, and he inhaled the fragrant humidity of the air.

"Just being here. To be able to wander outside without thinking of any problems."

He considered asking which problems she was avoiding.

"I do understand, you know," she continued.

"Understand what?"

"About your need to see the mountain lion free."

"Then you'll help to keep it loose?"

Dawn hesitated, her dark brows knitting as she considered her answer.

His heart fell. Even now, after seeing the mountain lion again, feeling their connection with it, she wasn't willing to concede—

"I'll try," she finally said.

He grinned at her. Her words had sounded like a promise, and he knew she was a straight-shooting lawyer. One who never lied. Hadn't her grandfather told him that?

"We have to get that evidence, you know," she continued. "Our best avenue is still proving that it's a member of an endangered species, to get the legal system on our side. Then, if we can scare Ray and the rest enough that they could pay through the nose, even go to jail, if they harm our wild friend, maybe they'll forget about hunting it."

Hallelujah! Jonah thought. She *did* understand. He pulled her closer, then used one finger to tip up her chin. The kiss he gave her was not nearly as passionate as many they had shared previously—but it was enough to stir him yet again. As he broke it off, he looked at his watch. "It's still afternoon," he said. "Maybe we should go back to your house soon, and . . ." He let his voice trail off.

"And what?" Dawn's tone was teasing. She knew exactly what he meant.

"And this!" He stood and took her into his arms, letting his hands rove over the areas that he had learned from practice were her most erogenous zones.

"Mmmm," she murmured against his lips. "Are you sure you have to go back to work tomorrow?"

Laughing, he began leading her down the path, toward the direction from which they had come.

Thanks, mountain lion, Jonah's mind called. He expected no reply, and got none—except that suddenly a feeling of apprehension flooded him.

He shuddered, trying to understand the source of his unexpected uneasiness. It was just his imagination, he told himself. He had learned that whenever he thought things in his life were improving, he was always, invariably, wrong.

But this was different. And in a surge of overwhelming fear, he stopped and took Dawn again into his arms. This time he didn't kiss her, but merely held her close.

"Jonah? What's wrong?"

He did not attempt to answer—but he did not let her go.

Chapter Thirteen

The newcomer to the mountain stalked quietly, uneasily, despite the familiarity of her usual paths. Her pointed ears turned to and fro as she listened for strange sounds. Her vision was extraordinary even in the dark of night. Now, in the pale light of dawn, she could see even more as she watched for any movement that might mean prey—or danger.

For the danger was increasing. She sensed it closing in.

Another kill she had cached below the leaves had been stolen. It had been an easy kill from among a group of placid animals just outside the forest. But the beings that visited her mountain had thronged around it. Their voices had been raised; she had heard them from a great distance.

Much was at stake. She would let nothing stand in her way. . . .

There. Noises. She stopped abruptly to listen.

Linda O. Johnston

The sounds came from the direction from which she had just come. She had to return. Now.

As swiftly as her strong legs would carry her, she ran through the underbrush. And then a sound exploded through the forest, a sound louder than any she had ever heard.

It was followed by a softer one, so low that it captured all her attention.

It was time to follow her instincts. Time to protect her own.

Time, if necessary, to kill.

"Granddaughter? I'm at Centre Community Hospital, right near the Penn State campus. You need to—"

"The hospital? Grandpa, are you all right?" Dawn was already standing at her desk, grabbing for her suit jacket.

"I'm fine. But you've got to get here right away. The emergency room. All hell is breaking loose."

Dawn was surprised to see Jonah in the emergency-room waiting area. But she shouldn't have been. It looked as though all Eskmont was there. Others, too. Television cameras were set up all over the place.

Dawn pushed toward Jonah through the crowd, making her way around the rows of upholstered wooden chairs. She noted with pleasure that he put his arm possessively around her shoulder. He was dressed in clean work clothes: jeans and a flannel shirt.

It was early Monday afternoon. He had left her first thing that morning, without explaining his odd behavior earlier. "I *can't* explain it," he'd insisted. "But I know something's wrong."

And he'd been right, for here they were, at the hospital.

"What's going on?" she asked him. "Do you know?"

His expression was grim. "It's Ray. According to his hunting buddies, he was mauled by the mountain lion."

Dawn's legs wobbled. "Oh, no. When? What happened?" She took a deep breath to brace herself, inhaling the odd combination of hospital emergency room smells: air-conditioning, a touch of antiseptic, and fear.

"From what I've been able to gather—"

"Dawn! Come here." Amos was at the far side of the crowd. Around him were Lettie, Clemson, Syd and others—including Larry Frost, Susie's uncle who was one of Ray's hunting cronies, and Ezzie Foreman, the reporter for the *Centre Daily Times*. As usual, Ezzie had a notebook in his hand, and he wrote in it fast and furiously.

"Syd was supposedly with Ray," Jonah said. "He'll have more information than I do." He took her hand, and together they wended their way toward Amos.

"I can't believe it," Syd was wailing. His weather-worn face attested to his having been a farmer for more than thirty years. He wore a bright green jacket that said JOHN DEERE on the back, and his gray hair had receded behind his ears. "It was the most horrible thing I've ever seen. That damned cougar just sprang out of nowhere, landed on Ray's back and knocked him down. It started biting his neck. I shot into the air—I was afraid of hitting Ray—and then the crazy thing just up and ran away."

Horror seeped through Dawn, hurting her head like a drink that was too cold. She looked at Jonah. His old, stone-hard expression had returned, but now she could read it better. He was blocking out emotion, yes. But there, behind his eyes, was the torment he was trying to hide.

What have you done? Dawn silently asked the mountain lion. How could they save it now? *Should* they save it?

"How's Ray?" Her voice was so raspy she was not sure anyone would understand.

"He'll live," Clemson said. "Not too serious, thank heavens." His beaverlike face was angry. "Damned cat."

"Poor Ray," Lettie whispered. Dawn watched Amos try to put his arm around her, but she pulled back. "Didn't I warn you that dratted animal was dangerous?" She walked away.

Dawn had never seen her grandfather look so bereft. She hurried to him. "It'll be okay, Grandpa," she said, though she knew she was lying. What could be okay from all this?

The mountain lion that Amos had believed heralded the salvation of their family had shown its true, savage nature. The stuff of Amos's legend had turned out to be as ephemeral as dandelion seeds in a gale.

Lettie—the woman Amos believed would turn his love life around now that a mountain lion had returned to Eskaway—had instead turned her back on him because of that same animal. She *had* been dating Ray. She apparently still cared for him. Perhaps she even blamed Amos, indirectly, for the attack on her former boyfriend.

But Dawn still had Jonah at *her* side. "What should we do?" she asked softly.

"Let's—"

The crowd noise suddenly swelled. Dawn looked around. Ray Koslowski stood in the door from the emergency room's reception area. His round face looked pale. His shirt was off, and white bandages swathed his fleshy torso. He wore a neck brace. But he was alive. And he did not appear badly injured.

The media swarmed toward him like hornets whose nest has been disturbed. Ray lifted one hand, and the people in the emergency room grew silent. "Well, now, that was an experience to tell the grandkids," he said, wincing. "Since I've lived to tell about it. But, gosh darn, that hurt." He looked pitifully toward Lettie, who then joined him. His shirt was buttoned wrong, and she fixed it.

"Looks like you need a little TLC, Ray," she said.

"I really do, Lettie," he agreed, giving her a little hug that made him moan. She clucked her tongue and shook her head.

Clemson approached him. "Glad you're okay, Ray." He held out his hand, and Ray shook it. "Soon as you're up to it, come to the station so I can make a report."

"I'll be there when I settle up with the folks here, to tell you what you want to know," Ray said. "Don't want to forget anything. Hey, Clemson, tell you what. Why don't you call another town meeting for tonight? That'll give me time to rest up a little and to give everyone who's not here notice." He glanced around the crowd, and his gaze lit on Amos. The corners of his mouth turned up in a grin that reminded Dawn of a used-car salesman who had just palmed off his lot's worst lemon. "I think it's time to talk again about what to do with that devil cat that tried to take my gosh-darn head off."

Jonah followed Dawn back to her office in his car. His heart thudded dully in his chest the entire way, and he wanted to shout in frustration. The whole town would be up in arms now against the mountain lion. From what he had seen of the group at the hospital, even those who had supported its freedom before had now turned a hundred and eighty degrees in their opinions.

He parked and met Dawn at the door to the pharmacy on the first floor of the building housing her law firm. "I don't know, Jonah." She appeared as despondent as he felt. Her lovely face was flushed, and the life seemed to have left her eyes. "I'll try to call a few people, do some research, but—"

"Hi, gang." Marnie Wyze hurried up to them. Dawn's blond partner carried a briefcase nearly as big as she was, and Jonah automatically reached out to take it from her. "Thanks, big boy," she said, "but the stuff in here's confidential. I just won a summary judgment motion in the Shaller case!" She looked at Dawn as though expecting accolades, but her partner's dismal smile looked as though Marnie had told her she had just eaten rotten meat. Her own proud grin vanished. "What's wrong?"

"Come upstairs," Dawn said. "We'll tell you about it."

"And you want to save this animal?"

Dawn hated the incredulous tone of Marnie's voice, though she could understand it. Jonah and she had gone into Marnie's office to explain what had happened, and her partner now sat behind her desk, leaning toward them as though they were clients with the craziest story ever.

But Marnie was a sucker for crazy stories. And for finding creative ways around problems.

"What if Ray hasn't told us everything?" Dawn countered. "He's a hunter, after all. Maybe it was self-defense."

Marnie snorted.

"Look," Dawn said with a frustrated sigh. "I just want to hear more about what happened. For now.

But killing the cow was an act of survival; the mountain lion needed food. And then all those angry men went traipsing up the mountain to shoot it. Maybe it just wanted—"

"Who knows what a dumb animal wants?" Marnie demanded. "If I'm not mistaken, there have been plenty of stories from out west where mountain lions are plentiful, where they've attacked joggers or, worse, kids. Unprovoked attacks."

Jonah spoke for the first time. His voice was low, and although he sounded defeated, the anger behind his controlled tone made Dawn wince. "It's a wild animal. It will act wild. But everyone is losing sight of the fact that it's a kind of animal that's extinct here, in this area." He leaned forward, clasping his hands between his knees. "You're both lawyers. Use the law to protect it."

Dawn had somewhat gotten over her surprise that Jonah was asking the legal system he despised for help. Still, she wished she could prove to him, by doing what he asked, that it wasn't all bad.

But the answer, as with anything in the law, was not simple. She stood and squeezed Jonah's taut shoulder in an attempt to be supportive. "We can do our damnedest, Jonah, to prove it's endangered, then make sure Ray and the rest know about it. The problem is that, even if we succeed, there's an exception under the Endangered Species Act that allows even protected animals to be killed if they're endangering human life."

"You already figured that proving the animal is endangered wouldn't save it," Marnie confirmed.

"There must be a way to protect it." Jonah stood abruptly.

He was right. There had to be something. If only Dawn knew what.

213

"And keep it free," he added. Before Dawn could respond, he stated, "I need to get back to work."

Dawn followed him to the outside office door. She felt as though her heart were being torn in two. "Jonah—"

He turned. She could have wept at the sorrow she saw on his face. It mirrored her own. "It's not over," she said. "The lion is still alive. But maybe we shouldn't be so eager to save it; it did attack a man."

"The man was a hunter."

"Yes," she said softly. "And the mountain lion is a symbol, I think. To Amos and you. And yes, even to me. We don't want to believe it's vicious and evil. But we could be wrong."

"We're not, Dawn," he said fiercely. And then he took her into his arms. His kiss was quick but firm, and it sent shivers through her as she was reminded of their wonderful weekend together.

Had it ended only a few hours ago?

"You'll be at the town meeting tonight?" she asked.

"Nothing could keep me away."

Dawn sat at her desk, her hand poised over her telephone.

Was what she was about to do right?

Yes, damn it, it was. She reached for the receiver, then hesitated. Again.

After what she had felt, had sensed, had understood about the mountain lion when Jonah and she had seen it on Eskaway, Dawn wanted the animal to be free. Just as she had told Jonah.

But alive and in captivity trumped free and dead, no matter what Jonah thought.

Yes, but she had told him she would do her best to use the legal system to keep it free. If she did anything less, Jonah would think she had lied to him.

But she hadn't. She never lied. At the time she'd promised to help keep the animal free, she'd been totally serious.

That had been before the attack on Ray. Before circumstances had changed.

Besides, she wasn't committing to anything yet. She was just exploring the possibilities.

Determined, she reached for the phone.

Her first call was to Amos. "It's a long shot," she said, "but what if this mountain lion really is an escapee from captivity? That would put us a step closer to being able to bring it in." She grimaced as she said that. As Amos put her on hold, she sighed aloud. "Oh, Jonah. For someone so bitter and cynical, you're such a dreamer."

"What's that?" Amos was back.

"Just talking to myself. Have you found anything?"

Fortunately, he had a fax machine at the Haven, for the list of Pennsylvania wild-animal parks, zoos and shelters was more extensive than she had imagined. He even had information about a few private collectors.

She had to prepare for a trial that would commence the following week, but knew she would not be able to concentrate. Not with this hanging over her.

Her next calls were to the U.S. Fish and Wildlife Service and the Pennsylvania Game Commission. Again, she explained to her contacts what had happened, invited them to the meeting that evening. Isabelle Moravian of the game commission had already heard of the attack on the news and was quite interested in what had happened. No, though she had asked around, she still hadn't heard of any cougars that had escaped from local menageries. She would try to be there that evening.

The man from Fish and Wildlife said, unsurpris-

Linda O. Johnston

ingly, that he would defer to the state unless it were shown that the cougar was a member of one of an endangered species, but to keep him informed.

Dawn started with the closest facility that housed a mountain lion: Penn's Cave in nearby Centre Hall, which had a cavern toured by boat as well as a wildlife sanctuary. But their cougar was alive and well and right where it belonged.

She went next to the first name on the list: Aardvark to Zebra, a small preserve in Erie County. "No," said the curator of animals, "we have never had a mountain lion here, let alone one that escaped recently." He did, however, give her some additional places to call—most of which were already on Amos's list.

For the next hour, she placed calls all over the state. She even tried a few shelters in neighboring areas as far as New York, New Jersey, Ohio and southeastern Canada. She learned of other places to try, but the few mountain lions in area zoos or private collections were the nonendangered kind from the west, and they were tucked safely into their enclosures.

"How's your trial preparation going?" Marnie had popped her head into the room.

"Slowly," Dawn admitted. She had just hung up after a conversation with someone at the Pittsburgh Zoo. She did not want to admit that to her partner.

But Marnie's blue eyes widened skeptically, and she folded her arms in front of her. "You don't mean to tell me you're actually going through those damned boring depositions, do you? When there's a mountain lion to save?"

Dawn blinked. Her partner never ceased to surprise her. "I thought you didn't believe in saving it."

"What I think and what you think seldom match. But you're as tenacious as I am for a cause you believe in. So go to it, partner." She turned, then pivoted back again. "And if you want to brainstorm ideas, you know where I am."

Dawn smiled. Marnie and she might not see eye to eye on a lot of matters, but her partner had a good soul.

Dawn turned back to her list, made some more unsuccessful, frustrating calls. And then she called Bertram Alexander.

Bertram was an outspoken television talk-show host who lived near Philadelphia. He was well known as a collector of wild animals, though there were rumors that he had come by some of his protégés in unorthodox ways. If he had lost a cougar, he would probably have announced it on national television so the public would help him get it back.

To her surprise, after she told her tale to someone on Bertram's staff, she was put right through to the man. Once more she explained what she was doing.

"So this mountain lion attacked someone and will probably soon be hunter bait?" Dawn did not watch Bertram's show often, but she recognized his distinctive, mellifluous British voice.

"Yes," she said.

"And did the gentleman"—he emoted the last word so that it sounded syrupy yet sarcastic—"provoke the attack?"

Dawn sighed. "I wouldn't be surprised, but I couldn't prove it. You didn't lose a mountain lion, did you?"

"From what I gather, you may not be able to save this cougar unless you capture it right away and place it into your grandfather's Haven. Is that correct?"

"Afraid so."

Jonah's scowling face passed through her imagination, and she decisively cast the image aside. The most important thing was to save the animal, then worry about its long-term home. She would just have to convince Jonah that capturing it was in the cat's best interest. Surely, after all that had happened, he would come to understand.

"And the only way you can easily do that is if you determine that it was from a nonendangered species and that it escaped from someone's possession?"

"Yes," she agreed. She was starting to become impatient with Bertram's questions. Why didn't he just answer hers?

"Well, in that case," he said, "yes, I did lose a mountain lion. Let's see. I named it Harry, I believe, and one of my trainers was neglectful enough to leave the lion's cage open at dinnertime—er, when shall we say it escaped?"

Dawn was silent, though her pulse raced. This man had not lost a mountain lion from his collection. She was sure of it. But he was willing to lie to save its life. To tell whatever governmental bureaucrats that might be involved that he had owned the lion.

She knew it was a lie. And if she filled out the paperwork, she would have to lie, too.

Just as Marnie had suggested. And Dawn had rejected.

Before.

Now she had a credible person willing to put himself at risk to save the mountain lion. Could she refuse to go along?

"Thank you, Mr. Alexander," she said quickly. "I'm not sure this is your animal." She had to play along for now, while she decided what to do. She wouldn't accuse him of bending the truth; after all, he was doing it for her.

No. He was doing it for the mountain lion. For "Harry."

"I want to make a few more calls first, just in case

it escaped from someplace closer. Finding its way here from your place—it's outside Philadelphia, isn't it?—might have been difficult. But I'll call you back if it seems like the right one." She might as well go along with the charade. "Did yours have any distinguishing marks?"

"Well," he said in his cultured voice, "suppose you tell me what distinguishing marks yours has, and I'll let you know if mine had them, too."

Thanking him profusely, Dawn hung up. She sat with her head in her hands for a long time afterward.

What was she thinking? She could not consider this as a solution. She was an officer of the court. She could not suborn perjury. She could not *commit* perjury.

But perhaps neither she nor Bertram Alexander would have to take an oath, to that "Harry" had come from Bertram's collection.

And if they did, if the mountain lion's life depended on it?

It was still a lie. Even Jonah hadn't lied about the crime he had been accused of committing. He had simply not told the entire truth.

She would just have to come up with another way. Fast.

The auditorium was filled. People stood in the aisles and behind the many rows of seats. Their grumbling did not sound friendly.

Jonah glanced around. He had come early enough to watch for Amos and Dawn to arrive so he could sit with them. At the moment, he was saving them seats, since they stood by the door waiting for someone. They spoke quietly together, heads tilted toward one another, Dawn's dark hair contrasting with the white of her grandfather's.

The media was there, too—like the miserable excuses for news crews who'd hounded him after his arrest. During his trial. *Vultures!*

Lettie had come with Ray. The guy was limping and using a cane and milking his injury for all he was worth. Lettie, the officious woman that she was, also had a kind streak, as Jonah knew. She seemed to be mothering Ray. And by the way Amos assiduously avoided looking at her, Jonah could tell how hurt he was.

Clemson and a couple of his officers stood, uniformed, on the stage, surveying the crowd with their arms folded, their eyes watchful—as though daring someone to step out of line.

But as far as Jonah was concerned, the line had already been crossed. This was no longer a friendly crowd half-concerned with saving a poor, endangered creature.

This creature had drawn blood—and now these people wanted it to pay.

"Okay," Clemson finally said into the microphone. "Ray, come up here and tell everyone what happened."

Lettie and Ray were sitting in the first row. Ray rose painfully to his feet, using a walking stick. The dark blue sweater he wore emphasized his bulging stomach—as well as the white collar holding his injured neck stiff. Lettie helped him up the stairs onto the stage.

Jonah glanced at Amos. The poor old fellow looked as though someone had stuck him in the gut with that walking stick. Dawn must have noticed her grandfather's pain, too, for she patted his hand on the wood armrest.

In a moment, the shriek of microphone feedback filled the room. Unlike some of the audience, Jonah refrained from holding his ears. And then Ray began speaking.

"I guess you all know some of what happened or you wouldn't be here." He went on to explain how he had been attacked by the mountain lion. It was much the same story that Syd Cornelius had related to them at the hospital: an unprovoked nightmare.

Jonah did not believe it. But how could he prove otherwise? Ray had been injured, so everyone sympathized with him. His witness was Cornelius, whom Jonah took to be an upstanding citizen of the area.

When he was through with his story, he looked pitifully toward the audience. "Better that it was me than one of your kids."

A collective moan rose from the crowd. And then a couple of people in the middle stood and began to clap. Soon the auditorium resounded with a standing ovation for Ray.

Jonah did not rise. Neither did Amos or Dawn, nor a few other people here and there. Did they mistrust Ray, too? Or were they just supportive of Amos?

Ray lifted his hands, quieting the audience. "Thanks," he said. "I guess you'll all understand why it is that I have to go back to the mountain to find that devil cat, to take care of it. Soon as I'm better."

"Yeah!" a few voices shouted. Others called out that they would go with Ray—including Cornelius and Larry Frost.

"Now hold on a minute." Amos rose to the stage.

Jonah noticed for the first time that there was someone new standing with Dawn: a young woman in a red sweater and slacks, wearing athletic shoes. Was this the person they had been waiting for?

"Before you all get too excited," Amos said into the microphone, "there's just a little problem here—the law. I want to introduce someone from the Pennsylvania Game Commission, Ms. Isabelle Moravian."

Dawn led the sporadic applause, then came to sit beside Jonah. "I've never met Isabelle in person before, but I've spoken with her over the phone. She didn't promise to come, but here she is. Maybe there's hope yet."

He had asked for it, Jonah thought: help from the law. But he'd be a darn fool to believe that, this time, there would be an easy, legal solution.

Isabelle Moravian picked up the microphone from its stand and began pacing the stage energetically. Her walnut brown hair was in a pixielike cap on her head. She looked like a young kid, but Jonah was soon convinced she had experience enough to know her stuff.

"How do you do, ladies and gentlemen," she began. "I'm a wildlife conservation officer with the Pennsylvania Game Commission. I want to tell you first that I was sorry to hear about Mr. Koslowski's mishap. Now, I'm just here to give you a little information. If this animal is a member of an endangered species, the U.S. Fish and Wildlife Service would have jurisdiction rather than us at the state. But I've spoken with someone at the service. Right now, both agencies will assume that this cougar is a nonendangered western species that somehow wound up here, and therefore the state game commission is in charge. But just in case, you need to know that there are severe penalties for disobeying the Endangered Species Act, and you, Mr. Koslowski, need to be aware of them."

"But the damned cougar attacked me!" Ray, standing beside his front-row seat, did not need to speak into the microphone to be heard throughout the auditorium.

"I understand." Isabelle leaned toward him on the stage. "The thing is, if it were an endangered species, then you couldn't just hunt it, even if it's a threat to human safety. That's for an employee of the Fish and Wildlife Service or our state commission to do. We're authorized to remove animals, even if endangered. And before we'd kill it, we'd have to do an evaluation as to how dangerous it is. If the threat is minimal, we would just try to capture and release it someplace else."

Release it someplace else. The words resounded in Jonah's mind. Maybe this was the solution. He would need to show somehow that this mountain lion fit within the jurisdiction of the state, then convince this officer to have it captured—very briefly—and released someplace where it would be in less danger. Somewhere that it could remain free.

He glanced at Dawn. She was looking at him, her eyes sparkling. She must have had the same idea. He smiled at her.

But Ray's scoffing interrupted Jonah's thoughts. "What're you supposed to do when you're being mauled by a mountain lion? Wait for a bureaucrat to come save you?"

That brought an uneasy laugh from the audience.

"No," Isabelle said. "If you're in immediate danger—well, even if it's an endangered animal, you can defend yourself."

"I see." Ray sounded humbled, but Jonah was not fooled. The man would not let this go, he was certain. "And if this one isn't endangered?"

"Well, once again we'd need to evaluate the circumstances. If it's a definite threat to humans, we would have to destroy it. Otherwise, we might just capture it, let someone with an appropriate wildlife rehabilitator license, like Mr. Wilton, there, take it into his shelter."

"Could it be hunted?" Ray asked. "If it weren't endangered, that is. And if it was a threat to people."

"Probably," Isabelle admitted. "But before you rush out and kill it, I'd like to say that our official position is that you should leave it to us. Plus, I'd suggest you review appropriate safety rules and not just run up on the mountain shooting guns."

"Oh, that goes without saying. Thanks, Ms. Moravian." Ray pivoted to look at the people there, playing to his audience. Then he sat down again.

The meeting continued. People—including reporters—asked Isabelle a lot of questions.

Eventually it was over. For the first time Jonah believed the mountain lion had a chance for survival, particularly if the game commission stayed involved. But if Ray chose to take the risk that the animal was a western cougar, not on the endangered species list, he might put together a hunting party.

And if he killed it, if it disappeared, no one would ever find out if it was subject to federal protection.

Jonah would have to devise a plan to deal with that.

Correction. Dawn and he could work together to decide how to keep the animal alive and free.

For that wonderful, sexy woman he was beginning to care for—a lot—well, they were on the same side now. She had said so.

"Would you like to go to the diner for something to eat?" he asked Dawn. She was beaming, and her smile warmed him as thoroughly as if he were drinking sweet and creamy hot chocolate.

"Sure," she said. "In a little while. Grandpa, you come, too."

"All right," he grumbled.

But for the moment he did not stay with them. He edged over toward where Ray stood, surrounded by supporters—including Lettie.

Isabelle Moravian had a crowd around her, too. Jonah accompanied Dawn to talk with her.

"Thanks so much for coming," Dawn said, shaking Isabelle's hand. "It meant a lot, getting real information to the people. Maybe everyone will calm down a bit."

"You're welcome," Isabelle said. She looked expectantly at Jonah, and Dawn introduced them. Jonah was amused to see the irritated expression in Dawn's eyes as Isabelle asked him who he was and what his interest was in the cougar. The wildlife conservation officer seemed just a touch flirtatious, which did Jonah's ego a world of good. "If you have any more questions, or if I can help at all, just give me a call." She gave Dawn a business card first, Jonah noted, but she pressed one tightly into his hand, as though inviting him to use it.

He would, of course—but only to work with the state game commission on a scheme to save the cougar. But he had no intention of telling Dawn that. A little jealousy never hurt anyone. He smiled to think that Dawn cared enough to be jealous.

When Isabelle left, Jonah followed Dawn to where Amos stood, not quite in the group surrounding Ray, but not far from Lettie, either.

"Ready to go, Grandpa?" Dawn asked.

"Soon!" Amos said.

Jonah stood beside Dawn, waiting. Then the group broke up. Everyone headed for the door.

"Like to come to the diner for a bite?" Amos asked Lettie.

"No, thanks." She sounded angry, irritable. Poor Amos, Jonah thought.

While the group dispersed, Amos hung back. Soon only Lettie, Syd Cornelius and Larry Frost remained in Ray's crowd. They began walking toward the door. Jonah noticed that Ray's gait and posture had much improved in the last hour or so—but not enough to lose Lettie's sympathy.

"So what are we going to do, Ray?" Syd asked. "We can't just hunt the cougar. What if it's endangered?"

"I'm not worried," Ray said. "That Ms. Moravian seemed to think it unlikely. And even if it is—well, any animal can be killed in self-defense." He turned and smiled evilly toward Amos. "Even your mountain lion. And gosh darn it, I have a premonition." He raised his hand dramatically to his forehead and closed his eyes. "I think I'm about to be attacked again."

Chapter Fourteen

"I think it went as well as could be expected," Dawn said, looking at Jonah. He sat beside her in the diner's booth, tall and tawny haired, and looking wonderful in his blue work shirt and jeans. If the business at the town meeting hadn't been so serious, she could have spent her time watching him.

But he frowned at her words. "The meeting went fine," he agreed, "but our buddy Ray made it clear that he's going to stop at nothing to kill the mountain lion."

"He'd already decided that, curse him," Amos said in a growl. "No matter what the legalities. I'd like to take him out on that mountain myself, and then—" He stopped and sighed. "Then nothing. There's nothing I can do."

He sounded so despondent that Dawn reached across the table and stroked the back of his flannel-clad arm. She knew that, as much as he cared about the mountain lion, his frustrations ran much deeper.

Linda O. Johnston

To Lettie. They'd been a pair for several weeks. Amos had stolen her away from Ray.

And now, out of sympathy or something else, she had allowed Ray to steal her right back.

"Things will work out," she said, wondering why people always resorted to platitudes when they had nothing helpful to say. "They always do."

"Right." Her grandfather straightened himself in the booth facing her. He had worn his newest plaid shirt, and his gray hair was slicked back with a fragrant tonic. He had spruced himself up something wonderful for the meeting, and Dawn had never loved him more. "So what do we do now?" he asked.

Just then their waitress Bette arrived with their food. "How is Carleen?" Dawn asked. She had not seen the young woman anywhere since Amos had found her father's body up on Eskaway.

"She's hanging in there," the large waitress said. Her heavy, almost masculine features looked sad. "It's tough on her, though. She knew her dad drank too much, but she'd expected to have a lot longer with him to complain about his bad habits."

"Please let her know we're thinking about her."

Bette nodded and walked away.

Dawn had ordered roast chicken, and it looked and smelled delicious. But the aroma of Jonah's cheese steak sandwich, with its nest of scrumptious grilled onions, made her mouth water even more.

"Here, Amos," Jonah said. "I can't eat all of this. You take half."

"I've extra chicken, too," Dawn urged.

Amos, claiming his stomach was upset, had ordered only hot tea. Dawn figured he had simply lost his appetite. Unhappiness in love did that to a lot of people.

She had not been able to eat right for months after Billy was murdered.

"I'm not hungry," Amos insisted. His brown eyes seemed even more sunken than they had been earlier, and his complexion was pasty.

"Are you feeling all right?" Dawn asked in alarm.

"I'll survive," he said. "Now, let's get back to what's important. Saving that mountain lion."

She didn't know whether to be pleased or saddened by his devotion to the animal.

He wanted to save it anyway, even though he had become unlucky in love once more. Or maybe he thought that, if he saved the cougar, the family legend would spring right back into effect.

Poor Grandpa, Dawn thought. She was glad she had not started believing.

Her eyes traveled once more to the handsome man beside her. Well, maybe she had begun believing just a little. After all, no one had come into her life for all these years until the mountain lion had appeared. She had wanted no one. But despite that, now there was Jonah.

Whom she had made love with.

Whom she was, despite herself, starting to love.

Was she letting herself in for more heartache, as after her loss of Billy? She hoped not. But how could she expect otherwise between volatile Jonah and herself?

"So what are we going to do now?" Amos asked again, interrupting her thoughts. "Till the state takes a position on what to do about the mountain lion, we need to make sure it doesn't stray into the path of Ray and his rowdies."

"Maybe we can convince Isabelle to get the game commission to set a culvert trap right away to protect it until something else is decided," Dawn said, forcing her mind back to the business at hand. She didn't look at Jonah, didn't want him to even imagine what she'd been thinking.

"Did Isabelle say where they'd release the cougar once they caught it?" Jonah asked, his voice so ominously quiet that it stung Dawn. She recalled all too clearly that the trust between them was tenuous at best. "It'd be done quickly, I assume."

Dawn remained silent for a long moment, trying to determine how best to answer Jonah without angering him. "Even if the state got involved," she finally began, using the neutral tone she used to explain alternatives to clients, "it could take a while to decide where to release it. First they'd need to determine its genetic makeup. They wouldn't want to release an animal with the DNA of an eastern cougar, the kind still found only in parts of Texas, in an area where there are western cougars. And then there are all the political considerations. I mean, even if there already are mountain lions in an area, people nearby may object to releasing another one that could hurt people, kill livestock. So it would be a hard decision. . . ." She let her voice trail off, not quite willing to continue to the logical conclusion: that the cougar might remain in captivity for life.

But Jonah clearly knew where she had been heading. "So if it's trapped, it may never be released." His words sounded as though he had swallowed an icicle. "Is that what you're saying?" Dawn found herself cringing beneath his scowl. "But you're still planning on capturing it?"

Where had he been during the meeting? Didn't he understand?

"Jonah," she said patiently, "Ray is planning to kill it. He's determined, and he's a skilled hunter. The only way to save it now is to take it in. And now we might be able to get the Game Commission's help."

"You said you understood that the mountain lion needed its freedom." Jonah's voice was hissed under his breath from between gritted teeth.

Dawn closed her eyes, letting her head drop so her chin rested on her chest. She did not want him to see the tears in her eyes.

"I do understand," she said hoarsely. "And if there were a way I could see to protect the animal and let it stay free, I'd jump at it. But I still think it's more important to save its life than to let it die wild."

She felt the booth seat rise as Jonah stood. She didn't look up, but she flinched as his napkin hit the table, followed by some money.

"Don't count on catching it," Jonah warned. "It can live free—right here." And then he was gone.

Dang it all! thought Amos, watching the tears pour from his granddaughter's eyes.

Oh, the poor young thing was trying to hide it, keeping her head down as she pretended to eat. But he knew she was only going through the motions.

The stomach just didn't work right when the heart was broken.

"I don't get it," he finally said. "The legend and all. Once the mountain lion came back here, our family was to get lucky again. Do you suppose the old curse stays in effect as long as the cougar's in danger?"

"Oh, Grandpa." Dawn finally looked up. Her pretty cheeks were wet, and her eyes had red rims. "Don't you get it even yet? A fairy tale can't make people happy. You decided to get amorous again once you saw the cougar. That's why you started seeing Lettie— to *make* the legend come true. But if that was the only reason you were attracted to her, it was doomed to failure."

"But Dawn, honey, the story was real. Lettie noticed

231

me for the first time in all these years. And you and Jonah—there'd been no one you'd even looked at twice after Billy. Did *you* just start seeing Jonah to try to make the legend come true?"

"Of course not." She sniffed, wiping her face with a tissue from her purse.

"Then what's your explanation?"

She shook her head, and the lovely black hair that she had inherited from their Native American ancestors flowed around her face. "I have none. There is none. I was just attracted to Jonah because he's a good-looking man. I stupidly let down my guard. But he has too many demons inside that your fairy tale can't exorcise. He has an overdeveloped need for freedom." Her sigh was deep and soul-wrenching. "But we're all prisoners of something, and he can't understand that."

Amos looked at her sadly. "And what keeps you captive, Granddaughter?"

She looked at him blankly for a moment. And then she whispered brokenly, "Loneliness."

He should have known better, Jonah thought. Everyone he had ever known had betrayed him.

Why had he thought beautiful, kind, sexy—conniving, lawyering—Dawn Perry would be any different?

He turned the steering wheel so his car screeched around the corner. Home. He was heading toward his rented sanctuary, where he would have time to think about this.

To try to figure out a way to save the cougar and its freedom, by himself. For he was the only one who cared.

"Why the hell does it matter so much?" he demanded aloud. "It's only an animal." A ferocious one at that. There was no dispute, after all, that it had attacked Ray Koslowski.

But why had it attacked? Jonah had confronted it in person not once but twice. The first time he had been alone. The cougar had looked wary, ready to spring. But it hadn't.

Instead, it had seemed as though it had wanted to communicate with him.

And then he had seen it again. With Dawn.

Before he knew the gist of her family legend.

Once he had heard her story, he had dared to imagine that it *was* true. That the coming of the mountain lion to Eskaway meant that Dawn's family could find love.

That Dawn could find love.

With him.

"Hah!" he shouted. He would never love a woman who turned her back on all that was important to him. Yes, the mountain lion might be a symbol, but it was a vital one to him.

It was free.

He had not been able to keep himself free, but he would keep the cougar free.

He knew he was being stubborn. Maybe even crazy. On some level, he realized Dawn had told only the truth. She wasn't the kind to lie, even about little things. Even to make people feel better.

She had pointed out clearly that the only alternative to the cougar's going into captivity right now would be, quite possibly, its death.

He had thought of killing himself in prison. After all, he had already lost everything that had meant anything to him. Death might have been preferable to that hellish existence.

Now that he was out, his past followed him.

Haunted him. Kept him all alone, a mechanic in a tiny, backwater town.

Still, did he wish now that he had died in prison? No! He was certain about that. He valued his life, such as it was. He still had his health. He still had, however foolish, hope.

But what would have been best for his life, his dreams, would have been never having been imprisoned at all.

He wanted that for the mountain lion.

Maybe he could use his indescribable connection with the animal, whatever it was, to communicate with it somehow. Drive it farther into the mountains. Convince it never to get close to man again.

Right. But he had to do something. He would figure it out. He would keep that mountain lion free.

His intractability on this issue had already cost him whatever might have been developing between Dawn and him, but that was all right. It had to be all right.

He *would* keep the cougar free.

"You look as though you lost your best friend." Marnie stood over Dawn's desk, her arms crossed. This morning she wore a shocking pink pants suit, but with a tailored blouse and a scarf tied about her neck she still managed to look professional.

"I suppose I have," Dawn admitted. She had thought about nothing else all night—except how she was going to make sure the cougar was captured quickly and safely.

"So your big romance with that grease-monkey hunk is off?"

Dawn levered herself up from her chair by pressing her fists on her desk. "It wasn't a big romance. And I find your referring to him as a 'grease-monkey hunk' offensive."

"You wouldn't care if you didn't *care*." Marnie's grin was nearly a smirk.

There were times that Dawn felt the urge to throttle her petite, smart-mouthed partner. This was one of them.

But she restrained herself. She took a deep breath, then sat down again. "You're probably right," she admitted, straightening her black-print peasant skirt. "But it's over now. He has this fixation on freedom, no matter what the cost."

The phone rang. "Excuse me." Dawn picked up the receiver. She had left a message for Isabelle Moravian earlier and hoped this was her return call.

It was. "Thanks for calling back," Dawn said, raising her brows in apology to Marnie. Her partner left her office. "I want to confirm how long it'd take before your office could set a culvert trap for the mountain lion. I'd hate to see it killed before we even tried, and—"

"Oh, Dawn, I'm sorry. I'd love to help. I saw at your town meeting last night what you mean by the lynch-mob mentality you described to me. But as I told you, we're understaffed right now, and every single one of the wildlife conservation officers, even the part-time deputies, has too much to do."

"But I'll help. Amos, too. Maybe we can—"

Isabelle interrupted. "Without knowing its hide-away or its hunting grounds, it wouldn't do us much good to use a trap. Or even to patrol. There's too much territory for so few of us to cover, and it would take too much time."

"I know, but . . ." Dawn's heart sank. She'd been counting on the game commission's help. "Well, can I trap it myself, put it into the Haven, at least temporarily? Will you at least give me clearance for that?"

"Possibly, but I can't do it right away."

Damn! Didn't she understand that time was of the essence, that the mountain lion's life was at stake? But it would do no good to gripe at the beleaguered bureaucrat. Dawn took a deep breath and asked, "What's the quickest way, then, for me to catch the cougar legitimately?"

"Well . . ." Isabelle drew out the word as though she were thinking. "As I've suggested before, you might do some checking into its possible source. We get reports of mountain lion sightings practically weekly. The legitimate ones are usually escapees from menageries, zoos, those kinds of places. If you find the animal's owner and get his okay—"

"—then you'll give me clearance. Okay. Thanks."

Dawn put the receiver down slowly. What should she do? The busy game commission was unlikely to act fast enough. Dawn could do as Jonah wanted, let the animal remain free—and probably die at Ray Koslowski's hands.

Or she could call Bertram Alexander. He would profess that the mountain lion was his. He'd give her permission to put it in the Haven.

He'd lie to protect the cougar, as long as she lied, too.

Oh, Jonah, she thought. *I wish your way weren't so dangerous. It'd be a heck of a lot easier on me.*

But the lines were drawn between them. If she couldn't have Jonah because of their insurmountable differences, then at least she could try to save the mountain lion.

"Thanks, Susie," Dawn said. She stood in the Haven's utility shed behind the house, where Amos kept his veterinary supplies.

"I don't know, Dawn." Susie Frost's shrill voice sounded dubious. A Pittsburgh Steelers sweatshirt hugged her large-boned body, and its gold lettering added to the contrast that her stringy yellow hair made against the black. "Sure, my uncle is tight with Ray and intends to hunt the cougar with him, but whether I can get him to tell me when Ray is ready to trundle off to the hills—"

"I know," Dawn admitted. "It's a long shot. But I'm heading for Eskaway first thing tomorrow, and it would be great to know if I'm going to have hotheaded hunters up there, too."

"Not to mention a dangerous cougar," Susie added.

Dawn raised her eyebrows. "You're not frightened of it, are you? I'm hoping, after all, to make it the newest addition to the Haven." No matter what Jonah thought. Her decision had been made.

The only question remaining was what she should do to capture it most quickly. Her choices seemed too limited. Too repugnant. She could either catch it illegally or she could lie about where it had come from.

There had to be some other way.

"I won't mind having the cougar here." Susie interrupted Dawn's unhappy thoughts. "As long as you sedate it first, then keep it in a cage."

She eyed the kit that Dawn held in her hand. Inside were a few first-aid supplies kept in the trail kit for dealing with injured animals to be brought into the Haven. They included a hypodermic needle and a couple of small bottles of tranquilizer. Amos, with his veterinary training, had prequalified to capture and treat many kinds of animals.

"You're sure you don't want to try one of those tranquilizer guns?" Susie continued.

Dawn did not even want to think about a gun. Even one that would sedate, rather than kill, the mountain lion.

She had faced it before, after all. She had not felt

threatened. She would just get close enough to touch it, and then—

And then would it attack, the way it had with Ray? If she thought that her imaginary connection with it would completely protect her, then she was as nutty as her grandfather.

"Tomorrow I'm just going to see if I can find where it hangs out. If I can, then I can tell the game commission where to lay its trap, and maybe they'll get involved. I'm just taking this"—she patted the case with the hypodermic—"as an added precaution."

"Well, you be careful," Susie said. "Meantime, tomorrow I'll work with Amos, like you said. I'll ask Tom Carter and the other assistants, too. We'll all work hard, start fixing up that side of the large-animal barn to be as nice as possible if you catch the cougar."

Not *if*, Dawn thought grimly. *When*. But the biggest question still remained. *How?*

"I'd like some time off."

Lettie looked up from her paperwork. Right in front of her desk stood her great big ex-con employee—the one who was hanging out these days with Amos Wilton's granddaughter.

She'd been glad to help set that little romance into motion. Now she wasn't sure it had been such a great idea. But what did she know?

She'd gotten herself all excited about that danged family legend of Amos's and let herself get involved. Worse, she'd done it when all the time she'd known that the darn beast was a dangerous creature that could hurt people, not cause them to fall in love.

That made her scowl. It was a good scowl, too good to keep to herself. She turned it on Jonah.

"And just why do you want time off?" she grumbled. "Aren't I keeping you busy enough?"

He had the nerve to laugh. "I could work twenty-four hours a day here and still not keep up, Lettie. I think everyone in Centre County comes here to get their cars fixed. How do you attract them?"

He was resorting to flattery, was he? "I do a good job, reasonably priced," she retorted. "Quick, too. But I can't stay quick if my help takes time off. What are you up to?"

She could see the young man bristling. *Well, let him.* She was his keeper, of sorts. She'd taken him on here when no one else would.

Not that she wanted gratitude. But she had a stake in the guy and how he got along here.

"I just have some business to attend to," Jonah said.

"It wouldn't have anything to do with that damned cat, would it?" Lettie rose. She clutched a pencil so hard in one hand that it was in danger of breaking in two.

"Yes, it's because of the cougar." He acted reluctant to admit it. *Good.* He obviously knew she wasn't too happy about that animal and what it was doing to the town.

She let that good scowl of hers grow deeper. "I want to give you some advice, Jonah."

He obviously didn't want to hear it. But she didn't give him a choice.

"Ray's my friend, and he was injured by that damned cat." She took a few steps toward him around the desk. "Amos is also my friend. And the cougar means something to him. It's about a family legend. Maybe Dawn's explained it to you." She waited for Jonah's nod. "For a while, I let myself get caught up in it, too. Believed in the magic. But being with someone takes a lot more than some Indian legend." She glared at Jonah, daring him to contradict her. He didn't. He couldn't. She was right. He nodded again.

239

"I didn't intend to get smack-dab in the middle," she went on. "But it's happened anyway, curse it all. Far as I can see, no one can win. I'm mad, really mad at Amos for taking the lion's part when Ray was hurt. Ray's a man, after all, and the lion's only a beast. But now that gosh-darned Ray's out to kill it. It's not just because he's afraid it'll hurt others, or even in sport. It's 'cause he's angry. He knows the animal's death will hurt Amos, and he's mad about the way I've felt toward Amos. That's why I'm ticked off at Ray, too—for wanting to kill that animal for the wrong reasons." She sighed. "I don't understand any of this, but the smart thing would be to stay out of it. Altogether. That's my advice to you." She looked up at him, raising her eyebrows. "Maybe you, young man, can keep your relationship with Dawn Perry, even if Amos and I don't see eye to eye."

Jonah snorted. "Too late for that," he muttered. The poor guy was obviously trying to act as though he didn't give a damn. He wasn't succeeding, though. "Now, can I have tomorrow off?"

What else could she do?

"Okay, Campion. But watch your step."

"Thanks, Clemson," Dawn said. "I appreciate your letting me borrow these." She fitted the orange neon vest over her denim jacket and gestured with the cellular phone.

"You didn't give me much choice." The police chief stood beside the desk in his cramped, institutional gray office, glowering at her. The place smelled like mildew and stale coffee. "I really don't want you up there traipsing on Eskaway—"

"We've gone through that already," Dawn interrupted mildly. She recalled sadly how Jonah had last bawled her out for going to the mountain alone. That had been back when he'd cared about her, if just a little.

"Let me finish." Clemson interrupted her sorrowful thoughts. "I don't want you there at all, but if you're going to go anyway, you should least be visible to those damned stubborn hunters." He looked at her earnestly, the grim expression that tightened his lips emphasizing his severe overbite, making him look even more like a beaver. "You're sure Ray's going up there already? I thought it would take him a while to recuperate."

Dawn sighed, resting her blue-jean-clad behind on the edge of his desk. It was early morning, and she'd had to come in a side door to the police station; the adjoining post office would not open for hours. "So did I. I thought I'd have a day or two to go and see if I could find where the mountain lion hung out. But Susie said she'd heard her uncle was on his way up to hunt it. I really hoped I could turn the whole thing over to the game commission to handle." Maybe then, if she'd had no more to do with it, Jonah would have ultimately forgiven her.

But without a location, the game commission wouldn't get involved.

And she was simply dreaming if she thought there was a chance she and Jonah could ever make amends.

"You still can turn the matter over to the state." Clemson sounded hopeful. A static-filled call came over the large radio on a stand near his desk, and he listened for a moment, then shrugged and turned back to Dawn.

She picked up their conversation again. "I'd like to count on Isabelle and the others. But that will depend on whether I get enough information and—"

"And whether that troublemaking cat lives long enough," Clemson finished.

*   *   *

Walking up the winding path onto Eskaway Mountain that he had last come down with Dawn, Jonah was not sure what he was going to do.

It depended, he supposed, on whether he saw Ray and his crew first, or the mountain lion.

He hoped it would be the hunters. He could stay with them. Distract them. Make enough noise to cause the cougar to flee into the forest.

Ray wouldn't like that. And that was all the more reason Jonah looked forward to it.

But if it were the mountain lion?

The animal had once found a way to communicate with him; it had shown him the direction to go to find Amos.

What could Jonah, in return, communicate to the cougar?

Nothing, of course. Absolutely nothing.

To think otherwise would be to buy into Amos's stupid supernatural legend.

Jonah knew far better than that, no matter how much Dawn haunted his thoughts.

He inhaled deeply, smelling the humus beneath his feet and the sweetness of the flowers that grew in a clearing surrounded by trees. The air was cool, this early on a spring morning, and humidity hung in the air like a tangible endless curtain. It had rained a little the previous night, though, and once more the trail was mushy.

Jonah felt the strain on the muscles of his legs as he forced himself to maintain a grueling pace uphill. His back, too, strained under the weight of his full backpack, complete with a thin goose-down sleeping bag. He intended to stay up here for as long as it took. He was not certain of his destination—but he knew it waited for him somewhere on the upper slopes.

Birds sang in trees all around him. Wood thrushes? Who knew? He wished, for a moment, that he had Dawn along to identify them.

"Right," he scoffed aloud. That was all he needed. Instead of being able to scare the mountain lion deeper into the woods, Dawn would try to get near it. Charm it.

As she had charmed him.

Then she would throw a net around the animal and keep it caged forever.

"Forget that!" He practically shouted the words, and a bird in the tree nearest him was startled and flew away. "Forget that," he repeated under his breath. If he were going to be effective up here, he would have to choose when to be loud—and when to be silent.

He continued on quietly for a while, into a large stand of trees that grew surprisingly close together, turning the morning into shadowy twilight. He found that he was enjoying the sights and sounds of the forest, and the freedom.

Oh, lion, he thought. *You can settle for nothing less.*

And then he heard a noise.

He stopped for a moment, listening. Nothing. Had he imagined it?

He remained motionless for a long while, just in case. If it were the hunters, and they had heard him, believed he was their quarry, they would do something to flush him out.

But nothing happened.

Okay, he told himself. *It's just your imagination.*

Still, he started off again. Slowly. Just in case.

And then he heard it once more: other footsteps in the soggy underbrush. But they were soft and stealthy. Were they human? Or did they belong to the lion?

Jonah stood still again. If nothing else, he had learned patience in prison. Not that he had liked it.

243

But for the moment it made sense simply to wait. To see who—or what—emerged from the thick stand of trees surrounding him.

Suddenly there was a flash of bright orange beside him. *The hunters! Good.* Now he could tag along with them, make their lives miserable up here on the mountain, until they'd wish they could shoot him instead of the cougar. He would—

His thoughts were interrupted by a familiar, husky, beautiful female voice. "Jonah!" exclaimed Dawn Perry. "What are you doing here?"

Chapter Fifteen

Dawn was thrilled and relieved. She had been sure the footsteps she had heard belonged to Ray Koslowski—although she'd realized there seemed to be only one person, and Ray probably had brought an entire troop of hunters to back him up.

Unless, to make sure he himself scored the kill, he had come alone to shoot the mountain lion.

The thought made Dawn ill.

She'd had no success that morning when she tried to find the cougar where it had first appeared to her. Nor was it where Jonah and she together had spotted it.

When she heard the footsteps to her left, she'd been on her way, through thick woods, to where Jonah had seen the lion when they'd sought Amos. She had not been sure what she could do to thwart Ray, but she'd intended to try.

Ray had guns and anger and blood lust. She had

Linda O. Johnston

only herself and her wits. And a few medical supplies.

What was she going to do?

She was glad now that she didn't have to find out. Not immediately, anyway.

The footsteps were Jonah's. Despite all that had passed between them—perhaps because of all that had passed between them—she was incredibly happy to see him.

She hitched up her large backpack to try to make it more comfortable. She fell in beside him as he continued up the trail, barely glancing at her. A deep twinge of hurt sliced at her at his obvious intent to ignore her. His strides stretched his long, denim-clad legs so she had to take several paces to his one. His strong chin was raised, and though his mouth was slightly open, he did not seem out of breath despite his rugged pace.

"What brings you here?" she asked softly, needing to make conversation but not wanting to be too loud, in case Ray and his gang were close by.

"Probably the same as you: our good friend, the mountain lion." The bitter sarcasm in his tone was nearly as hurtful as his ignoring her. "Have you figured out where you're going to keep it? Maybe you can train it to leap on command—right against the bars of its cage."

"Jonah, please." Dawn nearly choked on the lump in her throat.

"Please what?" he snapped back. "Please help you catch it? Turn it into a pet? Break its spirit?"

He put on a spurt of speed that left her behind. She watched his tall form for a moment. He wore a blue denim jacket she'd seen before. But this time it did not emphasize the breadth of his wide shoulders. No, his posture was slumped. Defeated. Even his head hung forward, though his tawny hair was long enough to ruffle in the mountain breeze.

Her heart went out to him. But how could she understand his agony? How could she even begin to comprehend?

She couldn't. But there was a place near here she could share with him. A place she had discovered years ago, where she still went when troubles bore down too hard on her. A peaceful, majestic place where nature provided unfathomable solace.

She had spent a lot of time there after Billy's murder.

This time it took her several minutes to catch up with Jonah, since, though he must have heard her coming, he did not slow even a little.

Perhaps he even sped up.

When she got to his side, she took his arm. "I want to show you something. Will you come with me?"

He finally decreased his pace, though not by much. He looked down at her. The green in his eyes seemed nearly washed away with gray pain, and his frown was like acid that etched deep, horizontal lines into his tanned flesh. "Where?"

The syllable seemed fraught with suspicion, but there was also a hint of curiosity.

"You'll see," Dawn said.

It was her favorite spot on Eskaway, maybe anywhere: the natural rock quarry through which a wide, bubbling stream galloped and gurgled downhill.

Trees surrounded the clearing. Some stretched into the cloudless blue sky. Others had been warped and displaced in earlier days of spring when the stream turned into a torrent from melting snow; they now leaned over the water, branches extended as though greeting fellows equally bowed and disfigured on the other side.

Dawn looked around, then smiled. She had not been certain that this was the right time of year—but there it was, a carpet of spring flowers in the flat patch off to the east.

Bluebells and jack-in-the-pulpits grew in riotous display along with the beautiful blush pink blossoms of mountain laurel. Their aroma permeated the clearing, along with the moist freshness cast into the air by the rapid stream.

She still held Jonah's arm. It remained rigid, but he had not pulled away. "That," she said, "is what I wanted you to see."

He said nothing for a long while. He did not seem to move. Maybe he was too angry inside to appreciate this offering of some of the most beautiful sights nature had to offer.

But then he said, nearly too softly for her to hear, "It's beautiful, Dawn. Thank you."

"You're welcome," she replied. That darned lump was back in her throat, for she'd heard the deep emotion in his voice. She took his arm and used it to lead him to one of the mounds of boulders.

She removed her backpack and set it on the ground. The rubber soles of her athletic shoes made it easier for her to climb, and she scrambled up the rocks, then scooted her behind around to find as comfortable a position as possible up an unyielding rock. *There*. She looked around. From there, she had a marvelous view of the stream, the surrounding woods and the field of flowers.

A panorama of beauty that symbolized the spirit of Eskaway.

"Come join me," she called. "It's incredible up here."

To her surprise, he obeyed, settling his substantial

body unnervingly close to her on the rock. Their shoulders touched.

She closed her eyes, bathed suddenly in the memory, not so long ago, of when more than their shoulders had touched. When he had touched her all over, had made such extraordinarily tender and passionate love—

"We can't stay long," she said hurriedly, opening her eyes again. "We need to be out there to save the mountain lion."

His smile was wry. "Both of us in our own ways."

She nodded, filled suddenly with a sense of frustration that had nothing to do with the nearness of him. How could she get through to him? "I'm sorry they can't be the same, Jonah," she said. "I really am."

"Me, too," he said simply.

That wasn't enough. Maybe if she knew fully what he meant, if he could explain to her . . . "Then tell me," she blurted. "I know you don't want the cougar captured, but how could it be that bad? It would stay alive, and—"

"You can't possibly understand." His voice was a growl of anguish that made her heart pause. He barely moved on the rock, but she felt as if he had dashed a mile away.

"Tell me, then," she repeated. Despite her eagerness to push him, she made herself speak softly this time, for she knew he wasn't talking only about the mountain lion. "What is it that I'm trying to do to the cougar? What was it like for *you?* In prison, I mean. What was it like to lose your freedom?"

She heard his sharp intake of breath. It sounded almost like the gasp of pain uttered at the stab of knife. Or maybe as it was being twisted in one's guts.

"I'm sorry," she said quickly. "I shouldn't have asked. Shall we go on and look for the cougar?"

Linda O. Johnston

She attempted to stand, but her own emotion made her unsteady, and she had to reach out to stabilize herself. Instead of touching the granite of the boulder, however, it was Jonah's hand that she felt. He pulled her gently back to the rock, then let go. His hip was against hers, but otherwise they did not touch. "No," he said, his voice a ragged whisper. "You shouldn't have asked. But since you did, I'm going to tell you."

As she waited for him to begin, she could feel him start to shake against her, until he quelled it. She wondered what she could say, what she could do to make it easier for him. It took several long minutes before he began.

"You can't imagine," he finally said. His voice was so husky that he sounded as though he had swallowed pebbles from the streambed. "The anger at being accused of something you didn't do. Knowing you couldn't defend yourself, not completely, since to do so would be to hurt someone else. Someone innocent and needy. And then the arrest. Being put into handcuffs, as though I were the vilest of criminals."

Dawn noticed he had switched from *you* to *I*. Perhaps he had started off thinking he could relate his emotions impersonally, but it hadn't worked.

"It must have been horrible."

He nodded. His gaze seemed riveted on a spot in the sparkling stream. Maybe he saw his past reflected in its shallow water. Dawn rested her hand lightly on his knee.

"I was so sure," he continued, "that things would work out. But that first time they put me in a cell . . ." He closed his eyes, and the grimace of pain that shot over his face made her wince in sympathy. "I tried to tell myself it didn't matter. I almost didn't make bail, but my brother-in-law posted it for me. He said he did it for my sister. She, on the other hand, seemed reluctant to risk their hard-earned money. They had children at home, after all, and if I did something wrong, well, maybe I should pay." The bitterness in his laugh was terrible to hear. Dawn saw his right hand curl into a fist. "I wanted so badly to tell her the truth, but what good would it have done? But my bail was paid, and I was free to defend myself—for a while."

"Did you hire a good lawyer?" Dawn was sure what the answer would be.

"With what? I had no money, nothing. I had to use a public defender. Some are great, I know. My guy—well, to give him some credit, he'd have done better if I'd told him all I knew. And it didn't help that the prosecutor had all those wonderful political ambitions that sent him from his little office in Philadelphia to a much grander position in the state capital in Harrisburg. He was tough on crime, even white-collar stuff. And that's how your damned legal system works." His voice rose. "I was innocent but was convicted anyway."

"The system seeks culpability, Jonah," Dawn said gently. "For you to have been released, your brother-in-law or some other innocent person would have been convicted."

"Damn it, I know that! On some level, at least. But all I asked was justice for me."

"And protection for your sister. That was really special, Jonah, even if she doesn't know or appreciate it. And you succeeded in helping her. You could have appealed. Told the whole story. And—"

"And I was convicted. End of story."

"But it wasn't really the end of the story, Jonah," Dawn contradicted softly. "There was a lot more, wasn't there?"

"I can't—" He practically shouted the words at her as he began to rise on the rock. His eyes were wide and glazed, and she could see his chest heave as he breathed rapidly.

"It's all right," she said. "You've told me enough."

He shook his head abruptly. "No," he snapped. "I started; I'll finish it." He stood, staring into the distance as he continued. "I won't tell you about strip searches or the idiotic rules in prison meant to break a man. But . . . the worst was the loss of autonomy. I wasn't Jonah Campion anymore. I was prisoner number . . . whatever. I've chosen to forget. I had no ability to choose *anything* there: when to wake up, when to go to sleep, when and what to eat, what to do even when to do the most private of bodily functions. It was all regulated and regimented. And I had to show respect to the most brutal of guards, who didn't give a damn about whether I was innocent or guilty; I was there, wasn't I? Then there were the other inmates." His laugh was a bark of agony. "That's another thing I won't tell you about. You've seen my scar." He looked at her for the first time since she had sat down again. She huddled as small as she could make herself, shaking with the emotion he shared with her. "And that, my dear Dawn, was what it was like to lose my freedom." As though exhausted, he lowered himself beside her.

She put her arm about him, holding him as he shuddered.

He'd lost it. Damn it, Campion! Jonah shouted repeatedly inside himself.

He had never wanted to think of that hell again, let alone speak of it. But all Dawn had had to do was to ask, and he'd opened up like sand gushing through a hole in a canvas bag.

He made himself breathe deeply as he got hold of himself. He felt Dawn's arm around him, and the comfort of it made him want to bat it away, to yell at her.

To thank her.

It took all the effort he could muster, but eventually he calmed. He lifted his head and looked down at the rushing stream.

The last thing he wanted to do was to meet Dawn's eyes, for his own were damp. And men did not cry.

"Okay," he finally said, trying to sound cheerful despite the throatiness of his voice. "So let's go find our mountain lion. Maybe something will come to us when we see it—a compromise to make all three of us happy."

"Okay, Jonah." Dawn sounded small beside him. He looked over at her.

She certainly had no compunction about crying. Her face was wet, her lovely dark eyes rimmed in red. Even her small nose was pink, and though she had sucked in her lush lips, he could see them tremble.

"I'm sorry, Dawn. You didn't really want to hear all that."

"I did," she protested softly. "I . . . I want to know all about you, Jonah." He felt the arm about his shoulders tighten. Her lips were no longer trembling as they drew closer to his.

She was going to kiss him. Out of pity.

Abruptly he pulled away and stood. "Well, you've heard all you're going to for now. I'm ready to continue searching." He held out his hand to help her down from the rocks.

She stared at him for a moment. She looked as though she were going to cry again. And then she squared her shoulders. "All right," she said. "Let's go." But she did not take his hand. Instead she scrambled down the boulders by herself, resettled her backpack on her back, and handed him his.

He realized then how the emotional drain of talking

about his ordeal had sapped him of energy. He wished he could hold Dawn's hand for strength.

He wished he could simply touch her as they hiked, for comfort.

But he didn't. This time he let her set the pace as they walked through the forest. Not that he could have kept up the grueling rate he had started before, when his unconscious goal had been to leave her behind.

Now he wanted her with him. He wanted to talk with her some more. He did not want silence between them. Not now.

But he couldn't begin to think of how to start a casual conversation with her.

Except . . . "Do you have any idea now where to look?" he asked. "Our mountain lion could be anywhere."

"Yes," she said. "It could. But I think we need to follow our instincts, don't you?"

She sounded surprised by her own words. He glanced at her sidelong and found her frowning and shaking her head.

"Yes," he said. "We'll follow our instincts."

"But—"

To his amazement, he laughed aloud. It was a rusty sound even to him, but he liked it. "You don't like that, do you? Depending on something other than your mind."

She laughed, too. "You're getting to know me a little. No, I don't like it at all."

The ice was broken again. For a while, he chatted aimlessly with her about the forest, childhood memories—good ones only, as though they had tacitly agreed not to bring up the bad again for now—and characters in Eskmont whom they both knew.

"I'm so sorry for Amos now," Dawn said when the conversation turned inevitably to Lettie. "He seems really broken up about her going back to Ray."

Would it be disloyal to Lettie to repeat some of what she had said to him yesterday? Or had she spoken with him because she knew he might talk with Dawn?

Lettie had not known about his last angry conversation with Dawn before they had met on this mountain.

"I think my boss is confused," he finally said. "She's perturbed that the two men she cares about are at each other's throats over an animal." He paused. "Plus, she only partly recognizes the other issue between them."

"What's that?" Dawn asked.

"Lettie herself." He laughed fondly. "Who would have thought that grumpy old lady would be such a femme fatale?"

Dawn's laughter joined his. He liked that. He liked being with her.

He also felt as though someone had reached deep inside him and begun dislodging the ice pick that had sat in his vital organs for years, stabbing at him whenever he began thinking he might be okay. He recalled that Dawn had offered to listen to him before, just after they had met. That night when Amos and Lettie had set up what had appeared to be a double date.

Then, he had wanted no part of spilling his guts. Now he was glad he had. And not just once. Little by little, she was drawing the whole, sordid story from him.

He'd come to trust her with it. With a little piece of him.

They reached a fork in the path. "Which way do your instincts say now, boss?" he asked her.

She grimaced at him, but even scrunched for a moment her face was beautiful. *She* was beautiful.

It was all he could do to keep his hands off her.

"My instincts are resting at this moment. Let's follow yours."

He pulled a quarter from his pocket and flipped it. "Thataway," he said, pointing off to the right.

But as they walked in the direction he designated, he had a fleeting thought of concern. Maybe it was his instincts. Maybe it was his imagination. But he suddenly worried what they would run into along this path.

He did not have long to wonder. In a few minutes, he heard voices.

Beside him, Dawn was describing a hike she'd taken as a child with Amos, before he had created the Haven. It had been her grandfather's impetus for starting the animal sanctuary, for on that magical walk through the woods they had found an injured raccoon. "The poor thing was obviously suffering," Dawn was saying, her own voice reflecting the animal's pain.

"Sssh." He put his index finger up to his mouth in a gesture of silence. She obeyed immediately.

They listened. The voices were male, muted though boisterous, laughing. Dawn whispered toward his ear, "Ray." He nodded.

She pointed in the direction of the men, then shrugged her slender shoulders beneath her backpack and vest, as though asking Jonah if the two of them should confront the hunters.

He shook his head in the negative, then put his arm around her to lead her back in the direction from which they had come.

Too late. "Hey! What's that?" shouted one voice.

"Looks like we ain't the only hunters on the mountain," said another. "Someone's got on one of them safety jackets. Come on over here!" he called.

It was Jonah's turn to shrug. "Maybe we can talk some sense into them."

Dawn's expression was incredulous. "Right. And they'll just toddle back on down Eskaway and leave the mountain lion alone. Tell me another fairy tale, Campion."

Before he could retort, three men appeared on the path in front of them: Ray, Syd, and Larry. All three wore many-pocketed hunting jackets, and all carried nasty-looking rifles. "It's not hunters." Ray guffawed. "It's a couple of bleeding hearts out to save the damned cougar that attacked me."

"Look, Ray," Dawn said. She reached out in a placating gesture. "Maybe we can figure out a compromise. I'd just like to get the cougar off the mountain. That way it won't bother Syd's cattle, and it won't be able to attack anyone."

Jonah bit his tongue despite his irritation with Dawn. This was no time to voice his own opinion on keeping the animal free. He was sure she was a damned good lawyer, but her likelihood of succeeding in negotiating with these bloodthirsty hunters was virtually nil.

His assumption was proven correct when Ray quickly closed the distance between Dawn and him. Though she was tall, the older man's thick, beefy body dwarfed hers, and he drew himself up to tower over her. To intimidate her.

She stood her ground as Jonah stepped forward to intercede. Her chin was raised in defiance.

But her eyes widened as Ray brought his rifle in front of him, clutching it with his pudgy fingers. "These two bleeding hearts are likely to get bloody themselves," he said in a furious tone, "if they don't just hie their little butts back down off Eskaway and let us take care of our business."

Jonah planted himself in front of Dawn. With icy control, he said, "Your business is our business if it concerns the cougar. And I'd suggest you put those guns away before you hurt yourselves with them. Or do you need to hide behind them?"

Ray's fat face reddened, but before he could say anything, Dawn moved around Jonah despite his attempt to keep her back. "You'd better remember that a lot of people know we're up here looking for the mountain lion," she spat. "If anything happens to us, they'll know who to question."

"Yeah," Ray said, "but if they find your poor, mauled corpses . . ." He let the words trail off.

Jonah recalled Ray's threat that, if the mountain lion could be taken legally only if killed while attacking someone, then that was exactly what would happen. He had already planned to stage that scenario to suit his own purposes.

Who was to say that he couldn't stage another? Suddenly, despite his anger, Jonah was afraid. Not for himself; he didn't much care what happened to him. But Dawn—would they really make it appear as though the mountain lion had gotten her? That seemed a little extreme, but Ray did look angry enough to do something stupid. Would the others participate?

Could he take the chance?

He whispered an order into her ears. "Let's go."

"But the cougar—" she protested. And then stopped. Her lovely dark brown eyes widened, and she tilted her head as though she were listening to something.

"What is it?" he asked.

She waved her hand remotely, as though she had hardly heard him. And then, her full lips parted, she looked up into his face. There was a glow about her, an excitement he could not understand. She smiled, then wiped it off her face as she turned back to Ray and the others.

"All right," she said. "We'll leave you alone. But remember that we saw you here. And I have a cell phone. I'll report to Clemson that we ran into you, and where. If anything happens to us, he'll know why." Her expression turned defiant once more. "And don't count on killing yourselves a cougar, boys. I'm going to save it. I *am* going to save it."

With that, she turned on her heel and headed back down the path from which they had come.

Jonah was not eager to turn his back on these angry men. He had learned in prison to watch behind him. But he could not let Dawn go on without him. He tossed a threatening look at them—knowing it was almost worthless—and followed her, listening for footsteps behind him. He heard none.

He caught up with her in less than a minute. "What's going on?" he asked.

She looked up at him. Her expression was bewildered yet ecstatic. "I don't know exactly," she said, "but we decided to follow our instincts. And mine are telling me just where to go."

Chapter Sixteen

What was happening to her? Dawn didn't know. But something inside was pulling at her, urging her to follow a path atop Eskaway that she had never been on before.

"What's going on, Dawn?" Jonah's long legs clearly had no problem keeping up with her brisk pace. "Was that just a ploy to get away from those fools?"

She shook her head forcefully. "I wish it were that simple." She turned to him without slackening her speed. His eyes regarded her quizzically. "Jonah, what did it feel like when you saw the mountain lion, then had an urge to follow?"

He laughed uncomfortably. "It's not something I can explain. It just . . . was."

"Well, I'm feeling it now."

He was silent for a while as they continued on, crunching leaves and skirting fallen branches on the path. And then she felt him take her hand.

She smiled at him, and he smiled back with so much warmth in his eyes that she felt as though she were melting beneath them. "Go to it, kid," he said softly. "Follow those instincts."

Dawn wished she could stop, could throw herself into Jonah's arms. They might not agree on much. On anything. But he understood.

In a short while, they burst from the trees into a clearing. A thin, effervescent waterfall poured from far above them into a narrow stream that continued down the mountain. The crags about it were weathered. "How lovely!" Dawn exclaimed. And then she drew in her breath. "Oh, Jonah—look!"

Jonah's gaze followed hers, up the waterfall and onto the cliff beside it.

There, standing still, was the mountain lion. It was watching them, poised on the rocks, its expression wary—and yet Dawn felt a connection with it.

"You beautiful creature," Dawn whispered. "You have to survive all this. You—"

The animal began to move. Slowly and gracefully, it leaped from one rock to the next, coming toward them.

Jonah stretched his arm in front of her, moving as though to thrust her behind him. To defend her with his body. His life.

She felt cherished at that moment. Protected. And she loved Jonah for it, even though it was unnecessary.

"It's all right," she said softly. "Let's just wait."

The cougar kept on its downhill path for a few more moments. Then, with a final glance at them, it turned its back and seemed to disappear.

Dawn blinked. "Where did it go?"

"I'm not sure," Jonah said, "but I suspect there's a hole in those rocks. A cave, maybe."

"We need to find out." Jonah glanced at her, apparently surprised by the firmness in her voice, but she didn't care. It was critical to learn where the lion had gone. She knew it, without knowing why.

"Sure," he said. He grasped her hand tightly once more and headed toward the boulders. Dawn was glad of the support his strong grip suggested. She was glad of his presence, for she sensed that something momentous was about to happen, and she wanted to share it with Jonah.

Her muscles ached as she climbed slowly up the tall, rounded rocks, her backpack growing heavier by the moment. Jonah preceded her, helping her up. She glanced frequently at the spot where she had last seen the mountain lion. It looked like just another mound of stones, shadowed in the late-morning sun. A *solid* mound.

"You don't think the cougar just disappeared, do you?" Her voice was ragged, as she was out of breath from exertion.

Jonah's laugh sounded hollow. "You're really giving supernatural qualities to your grandfather's legend now."

Shrugging off thoughts of the strange impulse that had driven her to this spot, she said, "I don't mean to, but how *did* this mountain lion come back here? I've found only one person who even suggested that there had been a recent escape of a cougar from his menagerie." And he was lying, Dawn thought. She didn't want to tell that to Jonah . . . yet. Not until she decided whether she was going to make use of Bertram's willingness to bend the truth to save the animal.

"Really? This mountain lion may have broken out of captivity? Good for him!" Jonah sounded pleased, and Dawn laughed.

In a short while, they stood on the ledge where they

had last seen the mountain lion. They looked around. There were other boulders perched on it, and behind them rose what appeared to be a sheer cliff face.

"Where is he?" Dawn asked, frustrated.

"Use your instincts," Jonah replied.

For the moment, she had none; nothing inside told her where to go. Until . . .

She heard a noise. It was like nothing else she had ever heard before: a purr, followed by several chirps, and then—a chuckle. "What is that?" she whispered, feeling spooked.

"I don't know. The other question is where it's coming from."

They looked around. And then, as they rounded the side of a pile of rocks that looked pressed against the mountainside, Dawn saw a large, dark opening that was nearly obscured. "A cave?"

She looked at Jonah. He nodded. "I'll bet that's where our cougar lives."

They'd done it! Dawn thought. Here would be the place to have the state game commission lay a trap. But she was not about to mention that to Jonah. Not now, while they seemed to be acting together, for once.

"We need to go inside," she said.

Jonah was silent for a moment. "That's why we're here," he finally agreed, "but let me go first, in case there's danger."

"All right, Mr. Macho." But Dawn wasn't really scoffing at him. Even though everything inside her told her she had to enter that cave, she was nervous about it. No matter what affinity she felt for it, that mountain lion was a wild animal. It had attacked Ray Koslowski. And maybe her odd sense that it had led Jonah and her here, that it wanted them to follow, was just her overactive imagination.

Right. As though she'd have found this location without help. Still, she appreciated Jonah's offer. She loved that he wanted to protect her. But she was worried that something would happen to him.

"I'll be right behind you," she told him. She squeezed his hand hard, then let it go as he headed for the opening.

He stooped to get his tall body inside, maneuvering his backpack on his shoulders. Then Dawn couldn't see him. The strange noises sounded again.

"Jonah? Are you all right? Can you see anything?" She didn't hesitate, but followed him inside.

The cave was surprisingly well lit. All Dawn could figure was that there were more openings to the outside than the one they had found. The cave appeared to be a large, irregular chamber, complete with thick stalagmites sticking up from the floor and sturdy stalactites hanging from the roof. There was an opening off to one side, perhaps to a second chamber. The cave smelled of damp rocks and dust and bat guano, and of something resembling wet animal fur. Plus, there was a metallic aroma—like that of blood.

In a moment, Dawn stood beside Jonah near a craggy wall. On one side, her back against the wall, lay the mountain lion. For the first time, Dawn was sure it *was* a "her"; she lay there nursing two babies, a month or two old but still young enough to have their spots. The noises they heard were the mother mountain lion, talking to her little ones.

But not only the ones that were nursing. As the cougar lay there, with two kittens suckling greedily at her, a third spotted baby lay listlessly by her head. The mother merely looked at Dawn as she drew closer, her green eyes wary but neither afraid nor angry. It was as though she, too, felt an affinity toward Dawn. She clearly felt no threat from the humans, for she made no attempt to protect her babies from them.

But something was clearly wrong with the third kitten. And as Dawn drew closer, its problem was obvious. There was a large, bloody spot on one shoulder. It had been injured. And if Dawn was any judge, it appeared that the baby had been nicked by a bullet.

"Ray!" Dawn exclaimed aloud. "He shot that kitten. That must be why the mother attacked him."

"Damn him!" Jonah knelt down by the small cougar. Dawn could see the mother shift uneasily, but still she made no threatening move as Jonah began probing the little one's wound. It made a small screaming noise, and the mother sat up, knocking the others away from their nursing.

"It's okay, mama," Jonah said in a soothing voice. "Dawn, do you have anything in your backpack that might help here?"

"Yes!" Dawn whipped it off her back. "I have a first-aid kit right here." As she opened it, she noticed the hypodermic on top that she had planned to use to sedate the mountain lion if the opportunity arose. She glanced guiltily at Jonah, but he just dug it out, put it on the floor, then pulled gauze, antibiotics and other items from the bag.

"How about some water?"

Dawn pulled from her pack a plastic bottle of drinking water that was still nearly full and handed it to him.

Jonah got busy at once, spraying on the topical anesthetic that smelled like bananas, cleaning the blood off, then using a pocketknife to scrape some fur away from around the wound. He used alcohol from the first-aid kit to sterilize the long, deep path of the bullet. Despite the anesthetic, the young mountain lion shrieked in pain, then bared its little teeth and emitted a feral growl. "I'm sorry, little one," Jonah crooned, obviously not scared off by the animal's threats—though he did manage to keep his hands away from its mouth. "We'll stop the bleeding. You'll be fine soon. We'll take care of you." He turned to Dawn. "Any sugar water in your kit? I've got a thin blanket in my pack to keep him warm. He's in shock."

Getting the items Jonah requested, Dawn kept one eye on the mother, who had shaken off her other babies and now crouched in the corner of the cave, protecting the two well kittens and looking prepared to spring at Jonah. She reacted each time her baby made angry, hurt noises. But despite being poised to leap, she did not move toward Jonah. It was as if, somehow, she understood that he was helping.

After a while, Jonah put a piece of gauze over the wound. Dawn helped by snipping off small pieces of tape to hold it down.

"How is it?" Dawn asked softly.

"It's a he," Jonah answered. "And he's lost a lot of blood. He's very weak."

Dawn caught the sorrow in Jonah's voice.

"Will he make it?" Dawn braced herself for a negative answer.

Jonah shrugged. "If I'd gone all the way through medical school and spent some time in an emergency room as I'd planned, I'd probably have a better idea." He smiled grimly at her. "Or maybe not. I don't imagine I'd have run into many mountain lion kittens in an ER."

Dawn managed to smile back at him. Please get well, little one, she prayed inside. She could tell by his attempt at a joke how much it meant to Jonah.

It meant no less to her.

"We'll hang around for a while," Jonah said. "See how he gets along."

* * *

She had thought of everything, and Jonah was glad of it. The magical backpack Dawn carried with her contained not only the animal first-aid kit, but food and drink for them as well.

Which was good, since by the time he was done tending to the little cougar, it was late afternoon. Jonah was prepared to spend the night to ensure the animal's survival. Sitting with his back against the stone wall of the cave, the now sleeping kitten on his lap, he told Dawn, "You'd better head back down the mountain soon."

"Why?" Kneeling nearby, she stopped unpacking more stuff from her backpack and looked at him.

"You'll want to get back before dark. I'm going to stay till I'm sure this baby is going to be all right." He stroked the kitten's soft fur.

"I am, too." Her tone brooked no debate, but that didn't matter to him.

"I'll be here for a long time, Dawn. All night, at least."

"And you'd rather spend the night alone than have me around?" Sounding hurt, she returned to her unpacking. There were a couple of cans of tuna on the rocky floor beside her, some granola bars and fruit rolls. And a cellular phone.

"I'd love to have you around, Dawn. But camping out in a cave with a nervous mountain lion isn't the most delightful way to spend an evening. You could be at home in front of the television, or having a nice dinner with your grandfather—"

"In other words, home acting like a lawyer who's never gotten her hands dirty. Do you really think that's me?" She was standing now, hands on her hips. Her long, black hair flowed down her back, and she looked more like the Native American side of her heritage here, in this cave in her hiking clothes, than she ever did as a prim, sophisticated attorney.

"No," he said quietly. "That's not you." He wanted to stand up. To take her into his arms. She looked hurt, standing in the dimness of the cave and glaring at him as though she could wound him with her piercing stare.

And she could, damn it. He cared about the argumentative woman. Too much.

"Do you want to stay up here with us?" he asked, knowing her answer would be affirmative—and that it would be a mistake to let her remain. Up here, on the mountain, their differences seemed so often to disappear. But eventually they would have to return to civilization. To reality.

To all their misunderstandings and disagreements.

"Do you want me to?" Though her posture remained defiant, her tone was small, fragile.

Damn. What did tomorrow matter? For now, yes, he wanted her to stay. He held out his arm toward her and beckoned. "Come here," he ordered. And when she joined him on the hard cave floor, he hugged her close.

The light in the cave faded as evening drew near. Dawn watched the mother mountain lion grow restless, pacing near the mouth of the cave.

"They like to hunt best at twilight," she told Jonah, snuggling up to him. Her backside was sore from sitting on the hard floor of the cave, but she hadn't wanted to move. It felt wonderful, leaning up against Jonah, feeling his warm, solid body against hers. "I wish there were a way to tell her to stay here tonight. Ray and his cronies are probably still out there."

"She's feeding babies. I'll bet that means she has to hunt even more than usual."

Dawn nodded. "I'd go with her if she'd let me. If I'd thought about it, I could have gone down to a grocery store and brought back some steaks."

Jonah smiled and hugged her tighter. "I could have built a fire, and we could have had a barbecue, Mama Lion, you and me."

"Don't laugh at me. I'm worried."

His face grew serious. "So am I."

"Do you suppose there are two adult mountain lions here?" Dawn asked. "Mama must have had help conceiving those babies."

"I don't know," Jonah replied. "What did your grandfather's legend say about more than one cougar? Or babies?"

She elbowed him lightly. "This isn't a joking matter."

"Who's joking?"

The cougar slipped out of the cave at that moment.

"I'm going to follow her," Dawn said, struggling back into the orange vest she had discarded earlier. "Maybe I can distract the hunters."

"I'll come, too." Jonah placed the small fellow that had been on his lap beside the other two kittens, who were sleeping.

But when they got outside the cave, daylight had faded to shadowy dusk, and there was no sign of the mountain lion. The rocks of the ledge loomed about them.

"Maybe we can find Ray and the others," Dawn said to Jonah. "We could send them off in some other direction."

"It'd be dangerous for us to try to leave this ledge until daylight," he said. "Even with a light, we'd have a hard time maintaining our footing."

Dawn sighed. "I don't suppose you know how long is normal for a cougar's hunting expedition?"

Jonah shook his head. "But I'm sure you'll be worrying every moment of it. So will I." He took her into his arms and pulled her against the hard planes of his chest. She looked up, barely making out his familiar facial features in the deepening gloom. But she saw enough to know just when his lips began to descend. Hers rose to meet them.

His kiss was sweet and comforting at first. And then it turned heated. She felt her entire body respond in ways that made her want to feel more of him. Everywhere.

But here, on a ledge outside a cave? She felt exposed. Inside, though, away from possible prying eyes of people . . . *People!*

"Wait, Jonah," she said, regretfully pulling away. "I forgot to tell my grandfather I wouldn't be home tonight."

She ducked back into the cave and returned outside to the ledge with the cellular phone.

"I'll check on the kitten while you talk." Jonah went inside.

Dawn considered a moment before placing her call. Was she doing the right thing?

After feeling such a deep affinity for the mother, after seeing the babies, after helping Jonah save that poor injured kitten . . . yes! There was no other answer.

Ignoring the niggling at her conscience for not explaining first to Jonah, she pressed in her grandfather's number.

Amos sounded excited but more than a little concerned. "The poor little one was shot? Ray, of course."

Dawn agreed, cursing the plumber deep inside. Then she told Amos what she had in mind.

He grasped it quickly and agreed. "I'll start things rolling here, make a few calls in the morning. You be careful up there tonight, Granddaughter. You hear?"

She smiled. "I hear, Grandpa." She said good-bye just as Jonah returned outside.

"He's fine," Jonah said, smiling at her.

He looked so handsome, even in the dimness. And so relaxed. Nearly happy. And that made Dawn happy, too—almost.

It brought out her guilt as well. Yes, she had done what was best, but Jonah . . . Now is the time, she thought. She should tell Jonah what she'd done, and why. He would understand. He had to.

But she knew he wouldn't agree, at least not right away. And they were committed now to staying in the cave all night. She didn't want to argue with him again. Not here. Not now.

She would tell him first thing in the morning. That would give her time to think of how to present it, so Jonah would buy into the plan.

She hoped.

They remained on the ledge for a while longer while it grew even darker. Dawn had brought out flashlights from their backpacks, but they turned them on only to duck inside now and then to check on the wounded baby. Stars sprinkled the clear sky everywhere, and the cool night air would have made Dawn shiver, except that she remained tucked close against Jonah's side.

The mountain lion had not yet returned.

"We'd hear a shot, if they'd found her," Dawn said eventually. "Sounds carry a long way up on the mountain."

"Probably." Jonah's qualified agreement gave her little comfort.

And then—there she was! The mountain lion suddenly appeared, her pale hide visible as she bounded up the rocks toward the cave.

271

Linda O. Johnston

She was fine. There was no way to tell whether she was sated, but Dawn imagined she was, or she would not have returned.

As the cougar dashed past them into the dark opening, Jonah took Dawn's hand. "I think it's time for us to settle down for the night, too. I suspect we'll have a big day tomorrow."

They checked on the wounded kitten. He was nursing along with his siblings. "That's a good sign," Dawn said happily.

"I'll wake up and look at him from time to time," Jonah promised.

The mother mountain lion's eyes glimmered in the dim light. She regarded the humans benignly as she lay on her side, letting her little ones feed.

"That's such a wonderful sight," Dawn said, filled with awe.

Jonah stood beside her for a minute, watching alongside her. She felt his fingertips glide up her back. "I've seen only one thing more beautiful," he whispered into her hair. "You."

She turned toward him, and they kissed once more. His thumbs stroked her jaw. "Dawn," he whispered against her lips.

She melted against him, though inside she knew she should stop—at least until he knew, and accepted, what she had set in motion by calling Amos.

But his kiss was sweeping away all her good sense. She tried one more time. "Jonah, we're not really alone here. . . ."

"Our friend the mountain lion won't care what we do." His tone sounded light, but there was an unmistakable huskiness to his voice.

Her backpack included a thin sleeping bag. So did Jonah's. He took them through the opening in the cave into the second, smaller chamber. In the light of the

272

flashlights, he zipped the two sleeping bags together, laid them on the floor at the far end of a broad stalagmite, then handed Dawn inside. She snuggled in, then smiled as he slipped in beside her.

The floor of the cave was sandy here, though it was still hard beneath them. The backpacks softened the harshness. Once the flashlights were turned off, Dawn could see nothing.

She knew mountain lions had excellent night vision, but even if the mama cougar prowled within their chamber, Jonah and she would be hidden by the sleeping bags and the stalagmite. And she knew they were in no danger from this particular wild animal.

Dawn was unable to see, but in the dark her sense of touch felt magnified, as though it were her most highly honed sense. There was little to hear, too; the night sounds of the mountain had mostly been left outside. She heard the deep breathing of the mountain lions, and their occasional stirring. She heard the staccato breaths from Jonah and herself as they prepared for bed.

Inside the goose-down sleeping bags with her, Jonah's body was as warm as a soothing bath. She reached out to pull him close—and touched bare skin. He had already removed his shirt. Sighing, she let her hands rove, in the cramped confines of their nest, over the taut planes of his back, feeling his shoulder blades and the valleys between, allowing her fingertips to experience every inch of his smooth, heated skin.

His hands dropped between them, unbuttoning her work shirt. She shivered as the backs of his hands brushed her breasts. And then, after a little maneuvering, her shirt was gone. Her bra, too. His fingers cupped first one breast, then the other. His thumb slid over her nipples, teasing them until they stood like small, sensitive peaks.

Linda O. Johnston

She moaned, feeling heat pulse through her. She wondered momentarily if Eskaway had ever been a volcano, for she felt lava surge through her, molten heat and desire flowing until she could hardly stand it. "Please, Jonah." She did not quite know what she was asking of him, but he must have understood anyway, for in moments he had managed to remove the jeans from both of them.

His lips replaced his fingers on her breasts, and she writhed as he gently sucked and teased. She heard his breathing become as ragged as hers.

His hard, probing flesh pushed against her, and she reached down to hold him. It was his turn to groan, and she softened her grip while commencing a slow, easy rhythm with her hand. When he touched her in her most private places she gasped. "Please," she said again. Whatever she had intended, he must have interpreted her plea as a request to explore her further, and soon she was breathing in small, needy gasps.

Confined by the sleeping bags, they had little room to maneuver, but Jonah managed nevertheless to roll on top of her. In moments, she felt him inside her, and he took up the rhythm she had begun, slowly at first, then faster and faster until she could barely breathe. All she could think about was Jonah, with her, on her, in her—until, finally, she cried out in a sound of primitive pleasure that he echoed.

Long after his breathing had returned to normal, Jonah hugged Dawn tightly to him. "Are you okay?" he asked. "This wasn't the most comfortable place, and you were on the bottom for a long time. You made a great cushion, but did I hurt you?"

She laughed, a soft, throaty, suggestive laugh, and he reveled in it. "No, Jonah, you didn't hurt me. You made me feel wonderful."

"Good." He felt proud, as though he had completed some major accomplishment. And he felt sated. Very sated. Although with her wonderful body still pressed against him, he wondered hopefully how long it might be before they could begin again.

"Jonah?" Her voice sounded small and frightened all of a sudden.

"What?" he answered immediately, pulling her close. "You're sure you're all right?"

"Yes, in the way you mean," she said. "But Jonah . . ." Her voice drifted off, as though she were searching for words that wouldn't come.

"Dawn, please tell me." He was becoming scared now. What if he had hurt her? What if—

"I love you," she whispered. Her voice sounded full of both wonder now—and fright. As though she were braced for him to strike her.

It would be like a slap if he were to hurt her now. He didn't want to. And so he told her the simple truth.

"I love you, too, Dawn."

Chapter Seventeen

Dawn did not sleep well.

It had a lot to do with the hard surface beneath her sleeping bag, but discomfort wasn't the only reason.

She was not used to sleeping so close to a warm, breathing man—a man she loved—and she wanted to enjoy every moment.

She did love him. She had been afraid to admit it, but she'd also wanted to. Here, in the cave, with the mountain lion present.

For, like it or not, she now believed in her grandfather's legend. The mountain lion had come back to Eskaway.

And she had found true love.

For Jonah had admitted he loved her, too.

Each time she'd stirred that night, so had Jonah. "Are you all right, Dawn?" he'd asked.

"Yes," she'd told him. He was so sweet to worry that

he'd hurt her. The only way he could have hurt her was to reject her.

She hadn't really expected him to admit his love—but she was thrilled that he had.

"Go back to sleep, Jonah, dear," she'd told him each time. And she would snuggle closer, reveling in the sweet smell of his soft, tawny hair that she still could not see in the dark.

She couldn't see much until the soft sunlight of morning began to trickle in. And then with it came cold reality, the realization that today she would have to tell Jonah what she had done.

And then? Surely, if they were truly in love, they could reach a mutually acceptable truce. Couldn't they?

She drifted off now and then despite her fears, even when day began to dawn.

And then she was awakened abruptly. By a gunshot.

She stood, slipped into her shoes, and clutched her shirt around her. Jonah was beside her as she hurried to the other chamber. They looked around. The mountain lion kittens were still there, in their corner. But their mother was gone.

"Oh, no!" Dawn whispered. "She's out again. Jonah . . ." She looked at him pleadingly. "She's all right, isn't she?"

"Yeah." But his expression was stone-hard again, and far from reassuring.

Dawn's heart was racing. She knew she had to say something now, but she had wanted more time to explain. "Jonah, I intended to tell you before. I'm sorry. I'm really, really sorry." Sorry for holding it back from him, she thought, not for what she had done. "I've set in motion something I thought would protect her—but now it may do no good."

"What are you talking about?" he demanded.

"There's no time. I'll tell you later." She gave him a hard, swift kiss. "Please, Jonah," she said. "Trust me."

But he didn't. She realized that from the blank, rigid expression that had returned to his face.

There was no time to feel the hurt, though. Dawn finished dressing faster than she could ever remember in her life. Jonah was even faster.

They stood on the ledge, looking down at the scenic rocks and trees below. "What direction did the shot come from?" Dawn asked. She had her bright orange vest on and wished he had one, too. No matter. She'd make sure they stayed together, so no one could mistake Jonah's movements in the woods for a wild animal's.

Jonah shrugged. "I can't tell where it came from. Let's go. We'll figure it out."

He helped her over the boulders, down toward the forest.

Another shot rang out.

"Oh, no!" Dawn cried, and began to run.

Following Dawn down the mountain, through the forest, Jonah felt ready to kill. If those damned hunters had hurt the cougar . . . had slaughtered it—

He thought of the helpless kittens still asleep in the cave, waiting for their mother, of the one that had been wounded. He had saved it, he believed. But for what? Could they keep the babies alive and free if they had no mother to care for them?

Before him, Dawn's bright orange vest bobbed with each quick step she took. He didn't know why she chose the directions she did; perhaps it was because of those finely honed instincts again.

This time his own were dormant, but he believed in them. In Dawn's as well as his own.

But he did not believe, at this moment, in *her*. What had she hidden from him? What had she done?

Had their lovemaking last night been to keep him from asking questions? He didn't even know right now what questions he'd have asked, if he had been alert, undistracted by her lovely body, her incredible sensuality—

Their footsteps resounded among the trees, stopping the twittering of birds. The hum of an airplane above sounded incongruous in this natural setting. The air smelled of the sweetness of some unseen flower.

Dawn finally slowed. He took his place walking beside her. Her breathing was raspy as she said, "There. In front of us." She pointed—and there were Ray and the others, stalking through the forest. They appeared still to be hunting, not finishing off a kill, but Jonah refused to feel relieved. Not till he was certain the cougar had escaped.

Dawn called out, "Hey, Ray! It's us. Don't shoot."

Jonah remembered the plumber's thinly veiled threats before and wondered if he would shoot anyway. It was unlikely, he knew. He hoped.

He knew they valued the lives of people, even if they had no compunction about slaughtering wild animals.

"Dawn, is that you?"

She stepped from behind the trees into the area where the three men stood. Though taller than the slight farmer, Syd, she appeared dwarfed by Ray's beefy presence and even Larry's. But she appeared fearless as she faced them, which made Jonah crazy inside. He was upset that she had hidden something from him, but he would continue to protect her with his life. Still, there was only one of him. If these men presented any danger—

Linda O. Johnston

"Yes, it's me, Ray. I heard your shots. Did you see the mountain lion?"

"Yeah, we saw it. And we shot at it." Ray's beady little eyes sparkled in defiance, and Jonah suppressed the urge to attack the miserable old punk. He appeared as though he had slept in his overalls and wrinkled cotton shirt, and he held himself stiffly—although that could have been from a guilty conscience as much as an uncomfortable night.

The recollection of how Jonah had spent his own night flashed through his mind, heating him despite the cool spring day. He planted himself even closer to Dawn—the woman he'd thought he loved. And now?

"Did the mountain lion attack you first?" Dawn demanded of Ray. "You said you'd only shoot in self-defense."

"Well . . ." Syd spoke hesitantly. "We were—"

"Yeah, it was ready to attack us," Ray proclaimed. "Wasn't it, Larry?"

The other man glanced at Ray, then nodded. "Sure, it was."

"Syd?" Ray looked toward the farmer for support.

"Yes," said Syd. His tone was certain, though his eyes shifted uneasily.

"I don't believe you." Dawn crossed her arms and faced the three men belligerently.

"Neither do I," Jonah said, placing himself decisively in front of her. If they were angry at being called liars, better that they direct it toward him than toward Dawn.

"Yeah, well, it don't matter what you believe," Ray said. "We missed the devil cat—this time. But we'll get it."

"Her," Dawn said.

Ray looked at her blankly.

"The mountain lion is a her, not an it—as you well

know. You shot at one of her kittens, didn't you? Isn't that why she attacked you?"

Ray didn't meet her eye. "So what if I did? Last thing we need around here is a whole bunch of cougars killing off deer and livestock. Ain't that right, Syd?"

But Syd looked ashamed. "It's right," he said quietly, "but I don't agree with killing the young one for sport, Ray."

"Well, you won't have the opportunity to kill the mother or babies for sport now." Dawn's chin was lifted in defiance, and her smile lit her entire face. But Jonah did not understand her certainty. Not until she continued. And then he knew what she had hidden from him. "There's a surprise waiting for you down the mountain. No, I won't tell you what it is." She held up her hands as though erasing Ray's question before he could get it out of his mouth. "But it's sufficient for you to know that, as we stand here, Amos is coming up Eskaway with people from the Pennsylvania Game Commission. We know where the cougar sleeps, and she and her babies are about to be captured for their protection. They'll be taken to the Haven."

Pain as strong as any he had felt when he had heard his sentence, when he had first gone to prison, washed through Jonah.

It was a betrayal, and one more hurtful than his brother-in-law's, his sister's, the legal system's. It pained him even more than the loss of his onetime girlfriend, who'd chosen not to believe in him.

He loved Dawn. He'd thought she finally understood and accepted his need to keep the mountain lion from captivity. He had believed that seeing the animal with her little ones had convinced Dawn that the cougar had to remain on the mountain. Not captured, not waiting, at best, for a possibly nonexistent place to set it free—at worst, captured forever. Dawn had to realize, he'd thought, that the babies had to grow up wild.

He hadn't had any idea how they would do it, but he had let himself begin to believe that, together, Dawn and he would find a way to keep the animal safe up here, in its habitat on Eskaway.

But he had made too many assumptions without asking the right questions. And Dawn had simply gone behind his back. Set in motion the cougar's capture.

The mountain lion would be caught. Caged. Defeated.

But not him, Jonah thought. And certainly not by caring for a scheming, lying woman.

She should have felt wonderful, Dawn thought, as she watched from the rocks near the cave. Amos, Clemson and the others were starting down Eskaway with the mountain lion and her kittens.

The mother and two of the babies, sedated, rode in special cages built to protect people in case the animals awoke.

The small, injured one was in Jonah's arms.

Dawn nearly cried as she saw the way Jonah cradled the spotted baby mountain lion against him. His face was an unemotional mask, his large shoulders squared, his strides long and proud. But she knew how defeated he felt. And he had refused to give her an opportunity to explain.

Stubborn man, she thought. *Lovable man.*

But no longer hers to love. She was sure of that, for he would never forgive her.

As he passed her going downhill, he glanced at her. No look of recognition showed in his eyes at all.

Jonah! His name resounded in her head. She wanted to cry out, to beg his forgiveness. She felt inside as though her heart had been wrung from her, tossed on the ground and trampled by him. Or perhaps fed to the mountain lions.

His reaction had been partly her own fault—but what if she *had* explained to him last night? Would it have made any difference?

At least this way, she had been able to pretend, for one night, that Amos's legend was real. That she had found true and lasting love.

But didn't trust come with that kind of love? And understanding? And compassion? She felt all those for Jonah. Still, she had gone ahead and done something she knew he would hate. She had killed his love of her to save the mountain lions.

Maybe her plan had been wrong. But at least the animals—mother and babies—would live. And the likes of Ray would be forbidden access to the Haven. The kittens would grow to maturity in safety.

She had watched, midmorning, as the people from the game commission, roused by Amos for this emergency situation, had set up the culvert trap with the sliding door, and placed the bait inside. It had not taken long. The adult cougar, undoubtedly hungry after being chased back to her cave this morning by the hunters, had probably been eager to eat, to feed the babies. The trap had been set close to her lair. She'd been quickly captured.

It had been easy. Perhaps too easy. Had she wanted to be taken?

Dawn laughed at herself. Thanks to Amos and his legend, to her affinity for the mountain lion, to the way her instincts had told her not to fear the mother cougar—Dawn had somehow come to give the animal, in her own mind, human qualities.

But the cougar was still an animal. She had paced and screamed inside the cage until sedated.

How would she react to her new home at the Haven?

Dawn would find out in a short while.

Sighing, she followed the successful entourage down the mountain.

Dawn was not surprised, when they reached the parking lot, to see all the equipment. There were huge white trucks, wires and lights strung all over the place, and large cameras everywhere. It appeared as though everyone in the town of Eskmont stood on the pavement, waiting and gawking and chattering. Even Dawn's partner, Marnie, who usually avoided town meetings and other local extravaganzas, was there, dressed in a green business suit.

In the midst of all the chaos stood Bertram Alexander.

The television talk-show host was as good-looking as most of his movie-star guests. He was tall, dark and so handsome that he almost looked too pretty. He had a British accent, and his female viewers were said to be crazy about him.

Someone in the crowd must have pointed her out, for he rushed over to her, microphone in hand. "Ah, there you are, Dawn. Where are your hunters? Are they here?"

"No, but my grandfather called me with his new cellular phone on our way down the mountain. His friend Lettie said she would try to get Ray and the others back here."

"All right." He looked around. "Okay, fellows," he said, addressing the cameramen near him. "Time to roll." He raised his voice and projected into the microphone. "Ah, there she is!" Everyone in the parking lot looked at him. "My little mama mountain lion." He rushed over to where the sleeping cougar lay in a cage in the back of a pickup truck. "How are you, my pet?" he crooned. "Are you ready to go to your new home?"

He gathered the crowd around him. "Ladies and gentlemen, I just want to explain a few things. You may know that I have a private zoo outside Philadelphia, where I keep all sorts of treasured, sometimes endangered animals. This mountain lion escaped from there a few months ago. I knew she was pregnant, and I was frantic at first, but there was no sign of her. Now she has been found, and I'm glad to say she has a new home. I'm not set up to keep a mother and babies, but I am certain this fine man"—he put an arm around Amos's shoulders—"Amos Wilton, who has a wonderful animal sanctuary near here called Double Lock Haven, will take great care of mama and babies. Right, Amos?"

"Right, Bertram."

Dawn smiled as her grandfather got into the act, explaining to the camera—and the widespread audience that would view the segment—all about the Haven, and how he took in wild animals that were injured or otherwise in need of a home. "We get a lot of our funding from private sources," Amos concluded, "and if anyone watching would like to contribute to the welfare of these wonderful mountain lions, their help would be greatly appreciated."

"And now, I'd especially like to thank this special young lady, who tracked me down—Dawn Perry." Bertram stuck the microphone into Dawn's face. "She called me. Dawn, would you please explain to everyone what happened?"

Dawn met Marnie's eye in the crowd. Her partner was smiling smugly, knowingly, as Dawn prepared to lie for the camera. "Well, I was trying to find out if the mother mountain lion had escaped from any local zoo. I had a list of all local menageries and you were on it." She took a deep breath, then plunged ahead. "I was very pleased when you and I spoke to learn that you had lost a mountain lion. That meant I had found this one's owner."

She wasn't struck either dumb or dead. In fact, afterwards, she felt very much alive as Bertram continued his interviews. Thanks to her call, to her fibbing, the mountain lions, too, would remain very much alive.

"What's that all about, Dawn?"

She flinched at the coldness in the voice that, last night, had held such warmth. She turned to find Jonah standing behind her. He no longer held the mountain lion cub. He looked down at her. At that moment she would have preferred that he wear his typical unreadable expression on his face. Instead, he looked angry. Disgusted. Unforgiving. The shadow of a beard on his face reminded her poignantly that they had spent the night together. Had made love.

Her elation at the interview, at her success, vanished. Hot tears puddled in her eyes, but she refused to let them fall. What good would they do?

But she could not stop the pain that pooled inside. It tore her apart. *Please understand, Jonah,* her heart cried out—knowing full well that, even if he could hear, he would never understand.

Never love her again.

She couldn't meet Jonah's eye. She loved him, of course. Completely. Unreservedly. It no longer mattered to her that he was an ex-con.

The only reason Jonah had gone to prison was that he hadn't told the whole truth that would have cleared him. The only way Dawn was able to save the cougar was not to tell the whole truth about the animal's origin.

She understood now that things were not always

black or white, but sometimes came in shades of gray.

She swallowed hard and looked toward Bertram, as though he were the most fascinating person on earth.

Jonah continued. "Why hold a media circus on top of everything else?"

She forced her emotions under control. "It's like this," she said brightly. "We were very lucky. There might have been a lot of government red tape if the mountain lion had been something other than an escapee from a local zoo. We might have had to prove she wasn't a member of an endangered species, and all. The wait for the government to find a hospitable place to release her and the kittens could have taken months. Years, even. By then, they could be dead. But when I contacted Bertram, he said she had run away from his own menagerie. That meant that she could be taken back into captivity right away, with as little fuss as possible—for the safety of the public, you know." She smiled at Jonah, trying to look as though she had done something utterly wonderful.

She *had*, she told herself. Despite what Jonah thought, she had done what was right. She had saved the mountain lion.

"That's baloney, Dawn, and you know it." She flinched at the scorn in Jonah's voice. "That animal was wild; it never belonged to Bertram Alexander. And I thought you were the one lawyer who never lied."

"Jonah," she cried out despite herself, wanting to beg for his forgiveness, his understanding. But he turned his back.

Just then, Lettie's car drove up. In it were Ray, Syd and Larry. Bertram ran over to Dawn, microphone in hand. He covered it, then asked, "Are those the hunters?"

"Yes," she said, then watched as Bertram walked

toward the car and began interviewing them.

The talk-show host skewered Ray, embarrassing him for having shot Bertram's "dear little kitten."

"It was an accident," Ray protested. "I was aiming for the mother. She attacked me, you know."

Bertram nodded. "I see. And I don't suppose you shot her baby before she attacked, did you?"

Ray looked flustered. "This accusation isn't going on national television, is it?" he said in a squeak.

"Not exactly." Bertram smiled snidely. "My program isn't just shown nationally; it's aired all over the world."

Ray's head sagged; then he looked up into the camera. "I'm sorry," he said. "I didn't mean to shoot the baby cougar. Really. And I'll never aim at one again. In fact, I'm going to make a big contribution to my friend Amos's sanctuary to help with his wonderful work to protect wild animals." He looked beseechingly toward Amos, who stood quietly off to one side talking to Lettie.

Lettie and Amos, together again, Dawn thought with bittersweet happiness. Now that the mountain lion and her kittens were out of danger, the family legend seemed to have worked for her grandfather. He deserved it.

At Bertram's request, Amos got back before the camera. "Yes, I heard Mr. Koslowski's generous offer," he said. "And I'm most appreciative. There is certainly a place in this world for people who like to hunt, since overpopulation in some species can lead to starvation and painful death. And Mr. Koslowski is one of this area's best sportsmen in this respect." He held out his hand to Ray, who took it and pumped it as though he were Amos's best friend, smiling from Bertram to the camera and back again.

As Bertram made a final statement, Dawn heard

Ray say to Amos in a low, bitter tone, "You'll get your check, Wilton. But stay away from Lettie."

"That's up to her, isn't it?" Dawn loved the roguish grin that drew more happy wrinkles onto her grandfather's face.

Lettie joined the two men then. "Good show, Ray," she said. "Couldn't have said it any better myself—though I expect to see several zeros at the end of the check you give to Amos after all that poor little kitten and its mother went through. Right?" She scowled at him.

Ray sighed. "A couple, maybe. Lettie, you up for dinner tonight?"

"Well, if you really want, you can join Amos and me." She took Amos's hand.

Ray's face reddened as though he were about to explode. Dawn wondered if he was about to punch her grandfather.

But just then Bertram Alexander came over again. "Thank you all," he said in his suave British accent. "This should air on my show in the next week. I want to thank you especially, Ray. You were a good sport." As he regarded Ray, he pursed his lips speculatively, raising one arched eyebrow. "And of course I'd hate to hear if that changes. There are always follow-up shows, you know. My public eats them up."

"I'm sure they do," Ray said in a growl. "See you around sometime, Lettie. Amos. Dawn. Mr. Alexander." He turned, and Dawn watched his bulky form lumber toward his car.

Amos laughed and hugged Lettie.

"Now enough of that," she scolded. She looked at Bertram. "You're not filming now, are you, Mr. Alexander?"

He pivoted, pointing toward the parking lot, where

his crews were packing up equipment. "Not now," he said.

"Good." Lettie gave Amos a big, smacking kiss right on the mouth. "Congratulations, Amos," she said. The two of them walked off arm in arm.

Dawn stood there for a moment with Bertram before Clemson and Isabelle Moravian, from the Pennsylvania Game Commission, joined them. Isabelle had driven up to supervise the moving of the mountain lion from Eskaway to the Haven.

"Thank you all," Dawn said sincerely. "That mountain lion means a lot to Amos." More than she could explain, for her grandfather did, indeed, appear to have found true love. "He'll take good care of all of them, the babies, too. We couldn't have done it without any one of you."

She looked particularly at Bertram, who winked. "I'm sure *my* cougar will have a fine home now," he said.

The truck with the cougars was about to leave, and Amos and Lettie prepared to follow it. So did Clemson and Isabelle. Bertram told Dawn he was headed back to Philadelphia.

"I will do a follow-up one of these days," he told Dawn. "That'll help generate more funds for your grandfather's Haven. And it makes me feel proud to have helped to save these wonderful animals."

On impulse, Dawn hugged him and watched him walk away.

The parking lot was nearly empty now. Dawn thought about Bertram's words. Did she feel proud she had helped to save the mountain lions? Absolutely! Did she feel proud she'd had to lie, to say the mother had belonged to Bertram, to do it?

No. She hated lies. She never lied.

But she would do it again if she had to.

She looked around. Jonah was nowhere to be seen.

She was alone. She felt as though someone had scraped out her insides, leaving them raw, exposed, painful. Her heart especially.

For such a short while, she had dared to believe that the legend could come true for her, too. "Oh, Jonah," she said aloud. "If only you'd let me explain." As if it would have mattered; the cougars were no longer free. And that was what was most important to Jonah.

"I just hope you live long, wonderful lives now," Dawn whispered toward the road where the truck bearing the animals had disappeared.

Saving them had been important. Worth the cost.

She walked toward her car. Only when she was inside, by herself, did she put her head down on the steering wheel and cry.

Chapter Eighteen

Dawn stood in the big-animal barn at the Haven. She looked into the cage holding the mountain lions, though, at the moment, neither the mother cougar nor her kittens were visible.

Amos had done an excellent job, she thought, of forming the enclosure into a habitat. Beneath a wide expanse of high, barred windows that let in plenty of light were low rock ledges along the walls, earthen floors strewn with bushes and small trees—and even a compact concrete cave off to one side.

But it was still a cage. There was a double-rowed iron fence between the area where the animals were kept and the rest of the barn. Even if a human reached in, the cougars could not touch him. Dawn peered in through bars set close together. She touched the metal: cold. Confining.

She thought of Jonah, and how he had been confined, also through no fault of his own. His experience had been unbelievably horrifying.

No wonder he hated her now.

Oh, how she wished she had been able to keep the cougars free! Jonah had been right about that. It had been so wonderful to see the mother ranging all over Eskaway Mountain, leaping lightly from rock to rock.

But how terrible it had been to find the baby injured by a hunter. No, better that they be here, safe.

The barn now smelled of warm, living cougars; the deer had been taken to a separate shelter outside. The building resounded with odd encouraging sounds like chirps and chuckles, purrs and groans, which emanated from the artificial cave: the mother speaking with her babies that Dawn had heard before.

"Hello," Dawn called to the animals. "I don't want to bother you, but I wanted to let you know that I came today."

As she had yesterday and the day before—every day since the animals had been brought to the Haven nearly a week earlier.

Sometimes Amos came to the barn with her. Other times, like today, he was busy with another of the minor crises that happened constantly at the animal shelter. One of the red-tailed hawks had injured its wing again this morning, and Amos was busy doctoring it.

Dawn heard a stirring noise from the enclosure. Out came the mother cougar, tawny and proud, stalking gracefully along the dirt floor of the cage. She was followed by all three of her spotted, playful babies, growling and roughhousing and tumbling over one another. Even the injured one moved well now.

Jonah, the man who had wanted to be a doctor and

now doctored only automobile engines, had saved its life.

Dawn swallowed hard. Why was it that everything now reminded her of Jonah?

Maybe because he had insinuated himself into every part of her life. And she had let him in. Foolish woman.

Enough of that. "Hi," she called to the mountain lions. "How are you doing? Are you all getting enough to eat?"

Her only answer was from the mother, who stared at Dawn. What was she thinking? Dawn felt none of the inexplicable connection she'd once before had with this wild animal, and she missed it. Now all there was from the cougar was disquietude and impatience and even anger. Or was Dawn simply assuming the mountain lion was mad at her?

She made herself smile. Did cougars understand human facial expressions? "I hope you're getting used to this place. It won't be forever, you know. I've already sent some of your hair and nail clippings along for testing. What I'm hoping is that you're an eastern cougar. If you're a member of an endangered species and we can convince the federal government that you can be the beginnings of repopulating the area—"

She stopped, realizing she was getting carried away. She'd had the same conversation with Amos and with Marnie, and even with Isabelle Moravian. It was probably a long shot—but it had become Dawn's goal to free the cougars, all four of them, once the babies were grown and could take care of themselves. Back on Eskaway Mountain, of course, if possible, though she was certain there would be opposition. Having them declared endangered would be an additional means of protecting them.

The kittens had exhausted themselves and now lay

in a small heap together near the mouth of the artificial cave. The mother cougar stretched and yawned, revealing a long pink tongue. And then she turned her back on Dawn and lay down behind a bush.

For a reason she did not understand—a guilty conscience, perhaps—Dawn took the animal's gesture personally. Whatever connection she had felt with the cougar now had turned into stark, hurtful rejection.

"I did what I thought best," she whispered huskily, clutching the cave bars with her fingers. "I even—I even lied about where you had come from. And I got the result I wanted—sort of. But please don't hate me. Jonah hates me now because of what I did, and I couldn't stand it if you hated me, too."

"I don't hate you, Dawn."

Startled, Dawn pivoted toward the sound of the wonderfully familiar deep voice.

Jonah stood a few feet behind her in the barn. Why hadn't she heard him come in? Tall and still, his arms at his sides, he was dressed in a beige cotton shirt and khaki trousers. The usual unruly wave of his light brown hair had slipped appealingly onto his forehead. He watched her with his gray-green eyes, and although she could not read his expression, it was not his typical, hurtful blank and emotionless stare.

She felt her pulse accelerate as she made herself stand motionless as well, when every impulse within her shrieked for her to throw herself into his arms.

He'd said he didn't hate her. She was thrilled to hear it. But it was a far cry from having forgiven her.

From loving her still.

"Hello, Jonah," she said softly. "Come see how they're getting along."

He did as she asked, drawing closer to the cage. He sidestepped, though, so he was still several feet from Dawn.

She felt such sorrow well within her that she thought she would dissolve into a puddle on the cold barn floor.

Instead, she said, "They seem to be doing fine. The mother—I've tried to sense how she feels. To use my instincts. The best I can tell is that she's glad she and the little ones are still alive, but I know she doesn't like it here. She paces a lot. She glares at me and sometimes turns her back, but—" Dawn's voice broke, and she stopped, closing her eyes to try to get her breathing under control.

Jonah remained silent, watching the animals, who all slept. The mother had joined her babies, and was now curled up against them. To Dawn, they appeared peaceful. Perhaps even content.

They would survive this, and then—

"I hope to free them again, Jonah," Dawn said. "That was my intent before, too. I'm not sure we'll be able to. And I'm truly sorry I didn't tell you earlier what I'd set in motion. I should have, but I was hoping for that one last night with you before we . . . before we argued again. It was selfish, and I apologize for everything. I just did what I thought was right." She hesitated and then said, "Well, not right, but—"

"But lawyerly," Jonah said. She listened for bitterness, but his tone was matter-of-fact. For now, at least. "You withheld information from me; you lied to the government and to the public; and you got the results you wanted."

She wanted to lash out at him for his hurtful words but couldn't, for they were true. Instead, she simply watched him, pretending no awareness of the unwelcome moistness that rushed to her eyes. He was still the most gorgeous man she had ever seen. She still loved him deeply.

And that was to be her punishment for having used

all the ugly means she had to get to this end, for she had lost him—not the way she had lost Billy, but had lost him nonetheless. She would love alone.

"Yes," she said simply. "I did. I'll leave you with them for now."

She turned slowly, waiting one last time for the sense of awareness she had felt in the forest when the mountain lion had been around. The sense of connection. Of rightness.

It wasn't there.

"Good-bye, Jonah," she whispered.

She wanted to run out of the barn, through the woods and away from the Haven.

She wanted to scream and cry—but there would be plenty of time for tears to fall later.

For now, she had to maintain her dignity.

Before she had taken two steps, though, Jonah said, "Come here, Dawn, will you? I need to try something."

She turned slowly. "What?"

"Something is missing," he said. "I think you can help me find it."

Having no idea what he was talking about, she nevertheless began walking back toward him, toward the large cage. "If you mean there's anything wrong with the habitat," she said with a resigned sigh, "I believe Amos thought of everything, but I know he's open to suggestions."

"No, it's not that. Come right over here."

She approached slowly. As she drew close he put out his arm and pulled her nearer yet. "Here," he repeated. When they got right up to the cage, he did not let her go but looked inside.

The mother mountain lion was standing now. She stared out at them, and Dawn suddenly felt it once more: the connection between them—whatever it was. It was back!

"That's it!" Jonah exclaimed. "It's that damned legend of your grandfather's. I only have this odd feeling with the cougar when we're working toward making it come true. I mean, you and I on the mountain together, and now here." He turned to look at her. "What about you?"

Dawn nodded slowly, afraid to put too much hope into what she felt, what he was saying. "She doesn't seem upset to be here, but she still didn't seem particularly interested in me—until now. But Jonah, it is still a silly fairy tale. We don't have to make it come true."

"It's not us who are making it come true." Jonah's contradiction was said against her hair, for he had pulled her close. "It's coming true because the mountain lion came back. Right? Isn't that the way it's supposed to go? That your family can't find true love until the mountain lion returns to Eskaway?"

"But the mountain lion isn't on Eskaway now, so the legend can't be fulfilled." Dawn did not let herself move, for she was reveling in the feel of Jonah's hard body against hers, his chin nuzzling her head . . . as though he still cared.

For just that moment, she could pretend—

"She came back here, to the mountain," Jonah contradicted. "And she'll go back, with her kittens, once it's safe. I heard you tell her that."

Dawn closed her eyes. It couldn't be this easy, could it? Was Jonah forgiving her for the sake of making Amos's story come true?

"What if we can't ever let them go back?" she protested. "I couldn't promise her." She bit her bottom lip, then said, "And I certainly can't promise you. I took away her freedom, Jonah, to try to save her and her kittens. Maybe we didn't feel the connection, the magic, because she's mad. And now we're just imagining it."

Jonah loosened his hold on her a little. It was over, Dawn thought. At least she'd had another moment in his arms. But then he turned her to face the cage. "Does she look angry to you?"

The babies had awakened, and the mother cougar now lay on her side so they could nurse. She regarded her kittens benignly, then looked straight at Dawn. There was no anger in her pale green eyes, just curiosity. And interest. And connection.

"No," Dawn said softly. "She doesn't look angry at all." She drew in her breath, then turned to face Jonah. She took his hand to try to soften the blow she knew she would be dealt, then asked, "And you? Are you still angry with me, Jonah?"

His fingertips closed tightly over hers. "No, Dawn," he said, looking down at her. Although he did not let go of her, they were separated by more than a foot, and he did not seem inclined to draw her any closer. "I was at first. If you had told me what you were up to—well, I'm not sure it would have made a difference. I doubt I could have stopped you. But I'd have tried. By God, I'd have tried."

"I know," she said. There was a catch in her voice, and she watched his shoes rather than his face. He was wearing moccasins again. She liked the way they looked on his large, sturdy feet.

In fact, there wasn't much she didn't like about him. And who he was.

It was a horrible, horrible shame she had lost him.

She swallowed hard, trying to rid her throat of the deep lump of sorrow that had settled there. "Well," she said brightly, "I'd better go. I told Amos I'd be in to help with—"

"You didn't let me finish, Dawn." His fingers lifted

Linda O. Johnston

her chin, and she found herself looking into his gray-green eyes. There was an intensity in them that made her feel like turning and running, but she didn't.

"I'm not angry with you. You did what you should have. I hated to admit it to myself, but that was my conclusion over these last few days. That's why I came. I didn't want them to die, our friends over there." He motioned toward the cage and the nursing mother and babies. "If I had done things my way, I couldn't have protected them. They'd have been free, but as you had warned, they would probably have died free, not lived."

Dawn bit her bottom lip and let her fingernails press into the flesh of her palms, for she wanted again to throw herself into this man's arms, to caress the slight afternoon stubble on his cheeks. But she had no right, for even if he weren't angry any longer, he was not hers.

"There's more I learned this week, Dawn."

"What's that?" Her voice was so low that she was not sure he could hear it.

"I learned that freedom without love is meaningless. Our mountain lion friend has the love of her kittens to sustain her. And though I'm free now . . ." She saw his Adam's apple work along his throat, as though he, too, were full of emotion. This time she was unable to suppress the tears that filled her eyes, but she did stop them from spilling over. "Though I'm free now, I have nothing unless I have you. Dawn, I love you. Will you forgive me for being so hardheaded and foolish?"

This time she did not have to keep herself from moving. In an instant she had pressed herself against him, felt his strong arms close around her. "Oh, yes, Jonah, but only if you'll forgive me."

"Marry me," he whispered huskily into her ear.

And as she said, "Yes," she felt his lips close over hers. Somewhere in the recesses of her mind, she thought she sensed the mountain lion's approval.

Chapter Nineteen

It was a lovely, late-summer day. The trees that sheltered the Haven blew in a slight breeze, and the sun shone down on the clearing outside the large animal barn, where Dawn stood, warming her. Beneath her was a long red carpet, rented for the occasion.

"Aren't you the pretty one," said Lettie Green, straightening Dawn's exquisite train, which fanned out behind her.

"Thanks, Lettie," Dawn said. "For everything." The older woman was dressed in an ankle-length dress with lacy sleeves. Its purple shade went well with the red-orange curls that framed her smiling, powdered face. "You didn't have to postpone your wedding till we had ours, you know."

"Amos and I weren't about to upstage your big event. You youngsters count more than us old folks—at least in the romance department."

"But—"

"Such a wonderful idea," Lettie interrupted. "Having your wedding here at the Haven."

"There was no place else we wanted it," Dawn replied simply. When the time came, she would do everything she could to make Amos and Lettie's wedding as wonderful as hers.

"Dawn! Honey!" The spirited shout came from just up the hill toward Amos's house. Dawn cringed.

It was her mother, wobbling down the driveway on four-inch spike heels. She was accompanied by a man. Was this husband number six, or someone else?

In moments, Dawn was engulfed in a small but enthusiastic hug. Then her mother stepped back.

She looked great, Dawn had to admit. Patty Karlotti—was that still her name—had shining black hair like Dawn's own, but hers was clipped short in a becoming style that curled softly about her oval face. There was hardly a wrinkle on her lovely, smooth complexion. She smelled of Chanel, and she wore a slim, understated dress in peach that had to be designer.

"Congratulations, dear," she said, looking Dawn over critically. Dawn began to cringe, then caught herself. This was her wedding day. She was happy, and nothing her mother said or did could spoil it for her.

"Thanks, Mother," she said. She looked questioningly at her mother's companion, a good-looking man in a tuxedo. His thick hair was silver, his eyes were blue, and he beamed indulgently at her mother. Love was in his eyes. Dawn sighed inside. Was this the bloom of yet another new relationship?

"Dawn, dear, I'm not sure Carl and you have ever met. Carl Karlotti, this is your stepdaughter, Dawn."

He gave her a quick hug. "So glad to meet you at last, Dawn. I've heard a lot about you over the four years your mother and I have been married."

Linda O. Johnston

Four years? Was this a record?

Patty put one arm around Dawn and pulled her to one side of the red carpet outside the barn. "I should give you some motherly advice," she said, "but till recently I wasn't exactly the best adviser on having a long, happy marriage." Her voice was self-mocking, and Dawn stared at her.

Patty put one hand up. "Oh, I know how much you hated to see me flit from— Well, never mind. It's over now. Do you know that Carl and I were nearly ready to split three months ago? But I started thinking about how exciting life was with him, and how much I'd miss him. We both decided to give it another chance and—yes, that's the best advice I can give you. Always be ready to kiss and make up and give it another chance." She hugged Dawn. "I've never been happier. And that's what I wish for you. Now, we'd better find our seats and let the bride get ready."

Dawn felt a little overwhelmed watching her mother and stepfather—the latest, and perhaps the last—disappear into the barn. And then she smiled.

They had decided to kiss and make up about three months ago. That had been when the mountain lion had first appeared on Eskaway.

The family legend.

"Ah, there you are." Her grandfather came hurrying down the path from the house. He looked smashing in a tuxedo with a purple cummerbund that matched Lettie's dress, and a large bow tie tucked under his sagging chin. He gave Lettie a big, smacking kiss right on the lips, then turned to Dawn. His eyes misted. "You look great, Granddaughter."

"She certainly does."

Dawn turned at the sound of the deep, husky voice. "You're not supposed to be out here," she scolded Jonah. "It's bad luck for the groom to see the bride before the wedding."

"Not this groom, or this bride," he said, taking both her hands in his. "We're going to make our own luck from now on. Together." He bent down and met her mouth, ever so softly, with his—but he gently insinuated his tongue between her lips, a kiss hinting of the passion yet to come.

As the kiss ended, Dawn looked at the man who, in just a few minutes, would become her husband. He looked utterly gorgeous in his coat and tails—perhaps even more handsome, if that were possible, than he always was to her in his auto-mechanic work clothes, his hiking gear, the sport clothes he now wore to school. His eyes were more green than gray as they stared deeply into hers. Gone was the unemotional, stony look that had irritated her so when she had first met him. It had been replaced with love.

Warmth flooded through her, from adoration of the man she was about to marry, not to mention anticipation of all that was to come. She felt so happy that she wanted to cry—except that it would have ruined her makeup.

"Is everyone here?" Lettie asked, nodding toward the barn.

"Judging by all the cars in the lot near the house," Amos said, "the entire town's inside."

Jonah nodded. "The seats look full. Did you meet my sister?" he asked Dawn. He looked bemused.

"Yes, and your nieces and nephew. They're adorable."

"Louise has a job now. She's a teacher's aide, and she's in a special program that allows her to take classes toward her own degree and teaching certificate." He leaned toward Dawn. "She had to do something. Her damned fool of a husband is on his way to prison.

This time he got caught with his hand in the till and without a scapegoat."

"Oh, Jonah!" Dawn exclaimed. "Does this mean you'll be cleared?"

"We'll see." But the big grin on his face told her that he believed his nightmare would soon be far behind him. He glanced at his watch. "I think it's time to begin." He took Dawn's hand in his and squeezed it gently. "No second thoughts?" he asked quietly.

"None whatsoever," she said, smiling at him. "You?"

In response, he kissed her again, this time fiercely and quickly. When he broke away he repeated her words: "None whatsoever."

"Hey, will you two stop smooching and come in and get married? The crowd is getting restless."

Dawn looked away from her fiancé to see Marnie hurrying from the barn. As Dawn's maid of honor, she looked little like the brash, risk-taking lawyer she was; her gown was a soft yellow that went well with her blond hair.

"We're just about ready," Dawn assured her, though she was reluctant to let go of Jonah's warm, comforting hands.

He smiled at her again, then looked toward Lettie and Amos. "I'll go take my place up front now. Okay?"

"Sure," said Lettie. "I'll alert the organist." She gave Amos a quick hug, then accompanied Jonah inside the barn.

"So, kid, you ready?" Marnie asked. "You're sure you want to go through with your wedding to this grease-monkey hunk?"

Dawn laughed. "Grease-monkey hunk who's about to become both a veterinarian and a wildlife and fishery scientist."

"Yeah, guess he's got some ambition after all," Marnie said "A dual degree, yet."

"It's more than ambition; it's caring about living things—their well-being and their freedom," Dawn said, refusing to rise to the bait. Marnie and she had had this discussion before, and Dawn knew her law partner was just teasing—this time.

"Jonah got that latest bunch of money, didn't he?" Amos asked. "From the Jonah Campion Scholarship Fund?"

"Yes. Oh, Grandpa, that was just the most wonderful thing anyone could have done for him." Dawn hugged Amos.

"I only started the idea," her grandfather said with a smile. "It was all the townsfolk who funded it, when they heard that the guy was too stubborn to marry you until he had enough money saved to put himself through school and support you, too. You could have been engaged for years!"

"He's proud," Dawn said—and though she would have gladly supported Jonah through school, she admired the strength of his convictions. "And what means even more to him than the money is that people in this town accepted him enough to contribute. I can't tell you how thrilled he is."

"His fund wasn't hurt by your friend Bertram Alexander's mentioning it on his show," Marnie said dryly.

Dawn just laughed. "It took attention away from the questions raised about how a mountain lion that turned out to be a member of an endangered species wound up in his private menagerie. He was able to focus on how, by the time Jonah got his degree and was out practicing wildlife management, our baby cougars would be out there with the others of similar DNA makeup that the U.S. Fish and Wildlife Service were going to import from Texas. They'll repopulate the mountains of central Pennsylvania that are most remote from human civilization, or someplace else Jonah will find that'll be safe for them."

"Let's hope it'll be around here," Amos said. "That'll help keep the deer population controlled. Though Ray will never forgive any of us for limiting his hunting. No sign yet of the male that fathered those babies, is there?"

Dawn shook her head. "Who knows where your magical cougars came from, Grandpa. And who can explain their magic?"

Amos grinned. "That's—" He was interrupted by several loud, euphonic chords from the organ, which had been moved inside the barn for the occasion. "It's time, Granddaughter," he said, offering his arm to Dawn.

"Me first," Marnie said. She picked up her bouquet from a table set up beside the barn door and handed Dawn hers—filled with pink roses and daisies and baby's breath. "You ready to get married, partner?"

"Ready," Dawn said.

Amos threw open both doors to the barn. Dawn watched as her maid of honor started down the makeshift aisle.

And then it was her turn. To the triumphant strains of "Here Comes the Bride," she walked along the red runner, between the rows of folding chairs filled with familiar people: a grinning Bertram Alexander, directing a video cameraman at the side; Dawn's mother and stepfather, sitting surprisingly with Jonah's sister and her kids; Ray Koslowski, sitting with his hunter friends; Susie Frost, sitting with Tom Carter and the others who helped with the Haven; Carleen from the diner who'd finally come out of mourning—and her in-laws, who would cater the reception later; and all the other townsfolk whom Dawn adored.

The odors of the barn were tempered by the scents

of the marvelous cascades of flowers hung around the windows and in a bower at the end of the aisle . . . where Jonah stood with the minister.

Behind him was the large enclosure that contained the family of mountain lions—the reason the wedding was held at the Haven, in this particular barn. As Dawn walked slowly down the aisle with her grandfather, smiling nervously at the seated people they passed, she watched the exhilarated smile on the face of the man she loved—and the interested expression on the face of the mother mountain lion as she paced inside her cage.

The connection was there that day; Dawn felt it. The mountain lion was part of the celebration, nearly part of the family—for she had caused Amos's family legend to come true.

Dawn reached Jonah. The music stopped. She felt her husband-to-be take her hands, and she looked up into his wide gray-green eyes, so filled with emotion that her heart leaped. He mouthed the words, "I love you," and together they turned to face the future.

The mountain lion paced, uneasy with the presence of so many members of the species that hunted her. They stared. They made noise.

She herded her kittens away from the bars separating them from the other creatures. The beings that had come to her, that had injured her kitten, were present. She would be wary.

Yet none came close. She sensed no danger.

Still, she remained on guard.

This enclosure was small. She was no longer free to roam the mountains. It disturbed her.

And yet there was peace, too.

Food was brought to her—enough to let her feed her young.

The beings with which she felt the bond were around often. They stood in front of her now. For now, she was safe. Her kittens were safe.

Someday she would find her chance. She would be free once more. She and her kittens.

For now, she settled down, content as her babies played.

It was time for patience. There was serenity on the mountain she had chosen as her home.

She was a stranger to the mountain no longer.

Something Wild

Kimberly Raye

Dependent only upon twentieth-century conveniences, Tara Martin seeks to make a name for herself as a top-notch photojournalist. But when a plea from her best friend sends her off into the Smoky Mountains to snap a sasquatch, a twisted ankle leaves her in a precarious position—and when she looks up, she sees the biggest foot she's ever seen. Tara learns that the big foot belongs to an even bigger man—with a colossal heart and a body to die for. And that man, who was raised alone in the wilds of Appalachia, will teach Tara that what she needs is something wild.

___52272-1 $5.50 US/$6.50 CAN

Dorchester Publishing Co., Inc.
P.O. Box 6640
Wayne, PA 19087-8640

Please add $1.75 for shipping and handling for the first book and $.50 for each book thereafter. NY, NYC, and PA residents, please add appropriate sales tax. No cash, stamps, or C.O.D.s. All orders shipped within 6 weeks via postal service book rate. Canadian orders require $2.00 extra postage and must be paid in U.S. dollars through a U.S. banking facility.

Name_____
Address_____
City_____State_____Zip_____
I have enclosed $_____ in payment for the checked book(s).
Payment <u>must</u> accompany all orders. ❑ Please send a free catalog.
      CHECK OUT OUR WEBSITE! www.dorchesterpub.com

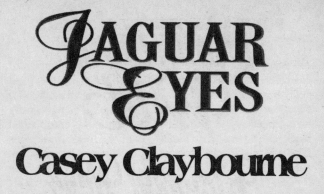

JAGUAR EYES

Casey Claybourne

Daniel Heywood ventures into the wilds of the Amazon, determined to leave his mark on science. Wounded by Indians shortly into his journey, he is rescued by a beautiful woman with the longest legs he's ever seen. As she nurses him back to health, Daniel realizes he has stumbled upon an undiscovered civilization. But he cannot explain the way his heart skips a beat when he looks into the captivating beauty's gold-green eyes. When she returns with him to England, she wonders if she is really the object of his affections—or a subject in his experiment. The answer lies in Daniel's willingness to leave convention behind for a love as lush as the Amazon jungle.

___52284-5 $5.50 US/$6.50 CAN

Dorchester Publishing Co., Inc.
P.O. Box 6640
Wayne, PA 19087-8640

Please add $1.75 for shipping and handling for the first book and $.50 for each book thereafter. NY, NYC, and PA residents, please add appropriate sales tax. No cash, stamps, or C.O.D.s. All orders shipped within 6 weeks via postal service book rate. Canadian orders require $2.00 extra postage and must be paid in U.S. dollars through a U.S. banking facility.

Name_____
Address_____
City_____State_____Zip_____
I have enclosed $_____ in payment for the checked book(s).
Payment <u>must</u> accompany all orders. ❏ Please send a free catalog.

DON'T MISS OTHER *LOVE SPELL* PARANORMAL ROMANCES!

HOUSE OF FOUR SEASONS

Abigail McDaniels

Subject of myth and legend, the wisteria-shrouded mansion stands derelict, crumbling into the Louisiana bayou until architect Lauren Hamilton rescues it from the encroaching swamps.

Then things begin to appear and disappear...lights flicker on and off...and a deep phantom voice that Lauren knows can't be real seems to call to her from the secret shadows and dark recesses of the wood-paneled rooms.

Lauren knows she should be frightened, but there is something soothing in the voice, something familiar that promises a long-forgotten joy that she knew in another time, another place.

__52061-3 $4.99 US/$6.99 CAN

MADELINE BAKER

Beneath A Midnight Moon

Winner Of The *Romantic Times* Reviewers Choice Award!

He comes to her in visions—the hard-muscled stranger who promises to save her from certain death. She never dares hope that her fantasy love will hold her in his arms until the virile and magnificent dream appears in the flesh.

A warrior valiant and true, he can overcome any obstacle, yet his yearning for the virginal beauty he's rescued overwhelms him. But no matter how his fevered body aches for her, he is betrothed to another.

Bound together by destiny, yet kept apart by circumstances, they brave untold perils and ruthless enemies—and find a passion that can never be rent asunder.

_3649-5 $4.99 US/$5.99 CAN

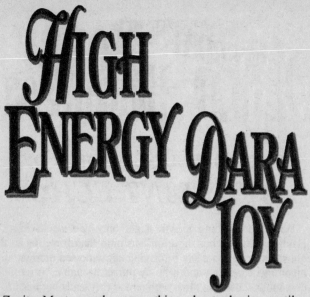

HIGH ENERGY DARA JOY

Zanita Masterson knows nothing about physics, until a reporting job leads her to Tyberius Evans. The rogue scientist is six feet of piercing blue eyes, rock-hard muscles and maverick ideas—with his own masterful equation for sizzling ecstasy and high energy.

___4438-2 $4.99 US/$5.99 CAN

Dorchester Publishing Co., Inc.
P.O. Box 6640
Wayne, PA 19087-8640

BESTSELLING AUTHOR OF
A DISTANT ECHO

With her wedding to Mr. Right only two weeks away, Hannah Gilmore has more on her mind than traveling to a ghost town. Yet here she is, driving her widowed mother, an incontinent poodle, and a bossy nurse through a torrential downpour. Then she turns onto a road that leads her back to the days of Canada's gold rush—and into the heated embrace of Mr. Wrong.

Logan McGraw has every fault that Hannah hates in a man. But after one scorching kiss, Hannah swears that nothing will stop her from sharing with Logan a passion that is far more precious than yesterday's gold.

___4311-4 $5.50 US/$6.50 CAN

Love Me Tender

Sandra Hill

Once upon a time, in the magic kingdom of Manhattan, there lived a handsome designer-shoe magnate named Prince Charming, and a beautiful stockbroker named Cinderella. And as the story goes, these two are destined to live happily ever after, at least according to a rhinestone-studded fairy godfather named Elmer Presley.

__4457-9 $5.99 US/$6.99 CAN

Dorchester Publishing Co., Inc.
P.O. Box 6640
Wayne, PA 19087-8640

Please add $1.75 for shipping and handling for the first book and $.50 for each book thereafter. NY, NYC, and PA residents, please add appropriate sales tax. No cash, stamps, or C.O.D.s. All orders shipped within 6 weeks via postal service book rate. Canadian orders require $2.00 extra postage and must be paid in U.S. dollars through a U.S. banking facility.

Name_____
Address_____
City_____ State_____ Zip_____
I have enclosed $_____ in payment for the checked book(s).
Payment <u>must</u> accompany all orders. ☐ Please send a free catalog.

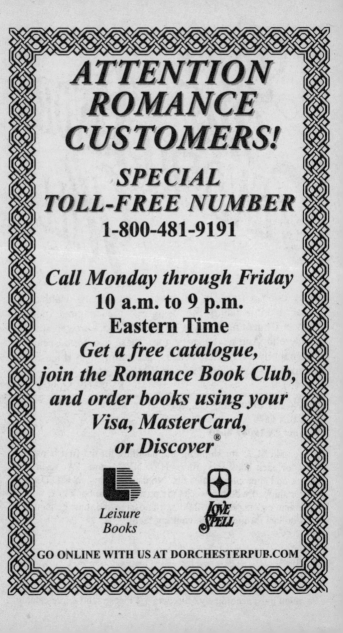